Anna Jameson

Memoirs of the Early Italian Painters

Ninth Edition

Anna Jameson

Memoirs of the Early Italian Painters
Ninth Edition

ISBN/EAN: 9783337234843

Printed in Europe, USA, Canada, Australia, Japan

Cover: Foto ©Andreas Hilbeck / pixelio.de

More available books at **www.hansebooks.com**

MEMOIRS

OF THE

EARLY ITALIAN PAINTERS.

BY

MRS. JAMESON.

FROM THE LAST LONDON EDITION.

NINTH EDITION.

BOSTON:

HOUGHTON, MIFFLIN AND COMPANY.

The Riverside Press, Cambridge.

CONTENTS.

		PAGE
GIOVANNI CIMABUE		7
GIOTTO		25
LORENZO GHIBERTI		64
MASACCIO		75
FILIPPO LIPPI AND ANGELICO DA FIESOLE		84
BENOZZO GOZZOLI		95
ANDREA CASTAGNO AND LUCA SIGNORELLI		102
DOMENICO DAL GHIRLANDAJO		106
ANDREA MANTEGNA		113
THE BELLINI		134
PIETRO PERUGINO		141
FRANCESCO RAIBOLINI, CALLED IL FRANCIA		149
FRA BARTOLOMEO, CALLED ALSO BACCIO DELLA PORTA AND IL FRATE		159
LIONARDO DA VINCI		170
MICHAEL ANGELO		191
ANDREA DEL SARTO		223
RAPHAEL SANZIO D'URBINO		228

(5)

VI   CONTENTS.

THE SCHOLARS OF RAPHAEL 280

CORREGGIO AND GIORGIONE, AND THEIR SCHOLARS . 290

PARMIGIANO 302

GIORGIONE 310

TITIAN 319

TINTORETTO 339

PAUL VERONESE 347

JACOPO BASSANO 350

MEMOIRS

OF THE

EARLY ITALIAN PAINTERS.

GIOVANNI CIMABUE,

Born at Florence, 1240 ; died about 1302.

To Cimabue for three centuries had been awarded
the lofty title of " Father of Modern Painting ; "
and to him, on the authority of Vasari, had been
ascribed the merit, or rather the *miracle*, of having
revived the art of painting when utterly lost, dead
and buried ;—of having by his single genius brought
light out of darkness, form and beauty out of chaos.
The error or gross exaggeration of Vasari in making
these claims for his countryman has been pointed
out by later authors.   Some have even denied to
Cimabue any share whatever in the regeneration
of art; and, at all events, it seems clear that his
claims have been much over-stated; that, so far
from painting being a lost art in the thirteenth
century, and the race of artists annihilated, as Va-

(7)

sari would lead us to believe, several contemporary painters were living and working in the cities and churches of Italy previous to 1240; and it is possible to trace back an uninterrupted series of pictorial remains and names of painters even to the fourth century. But, in depriving Cimabue of his false glories, enough remains to interest and fix attention on the period at which he lived. IIis name has stood too long, too conspicuously, too justly, as a landmark in the history of art, to be now thrust back under the waves of oblivion. A rapid glance over the progress of painting before his time will enable us to judge of his true claims, and place him in his true position relative to those who preceded and those who followed him.

The early Christians had confounded, in their horror of heathen idolatry, all imitative art and all artists. They regarded with decided hostility all images, and those who wrought them as bound to the service of Satan and heathenism; and we find all visible representations of sacred personages and actions confined to mystic emblems. Thus, the Cross signified Redemption ; the Fish, Baptism ; the Ship represented the Church ; the Serpent, Sin, or the Spirit of Evil. When, in the fourth century, the struggle between paganism and Christianity ended in the triumph and recognition of the latter, and art revived, it was, if not in a new form, in a new spirit, by which the old forms were to be gradually moulded and modified. The Christians found the shell of ancient art remaining ; the traditionary handicraft still existed ; certain models of figure and drapery, &c., handed down from antiquity, though degenerated - and distorted, remained in use, and were applied to illustrate, by direct or symbolical representations, the tenets of a purer faith. From the beginning, the figures selected to typify our redemption were those of the Saviour and the Blessed Virgin, first separately, and then conjointly as the Mother and Infant. The earliest monuments of Christian art remaining are to be found, nearly effaced, on the walls and ceilings of the catacombs at Rome, to which the persecuted martyrs of the faith had fled for refuge. The first recorded representation of the Saviour is in the character of the Good Shepherd, and the attributes of Orpheus and Apollo were borrowed to express the character of him who " redeemed souls from hell," and " gathered his people like sheep." In the cemetery of St. Calixtus, at Rome, a head of Christ was discovered, the most ancient of which any copy has come down to us. The figure is colossal ; the face a long oval ; the countenance mild, grave, melancholy ; the long hair parted on the brow, falling in two masses on either shoulder ; the beard not thick, but short and divided. Here, then, obviously imitated from some traditional description (probably the letter of Lentulus to the Roman Senate, supposed to be a fabrication of the third century), we have the type, the conventional character, since adhered to in the representations of the Redeemer. In the same manner traditional heads of St. Peter and St. Paul, rudely sketched, became, in after-times, the groundwork of the highest dignity and beauty, still retaining that peculiarity of form and character which time and long custom had consecrated in the eyes of the devout.

A controversy arose afterwards in the early Christian church, which had a most important influence on art, as subsequently developed. One party, with St. Cyril at their head, maintained that the form of the Saviour having been described by the prophet as without any outward comeliness, he ought to be represented in painting as utterly hideous and repulsive. Happily the most eloquent and influential among the fathers of the church, St. Jerome, St. Augustin, St. Ambrose, and St. Bernard, took up the other side of the question. The pope, Adrian I., threw his infallibility into the scale; and from the eighth century we find it irrevocably decided, and confirmed by a papal bull, that the Redeemer should be represented with all the attributes of divine beauty which art, in its then rude state, could lend him.

The most ancient representations of the Virgin Mary now remaining are the old mosaics, which are referred to the latter half of the fifth century.*

* In the churches of Rome, Pisa, and Venice.

In these she is represented as a colossal figure, majestically draped, standing, one hand on her breast, and her eyes raised to heaven; then succeeded her image in her maternal character, seated on a throne, with the infant Saviour in her arms. We must bear in mind, once for all, that from the earliest ages of Christianity the Virgin Mother has been selected as the allegorical type of RELIGION, in the abstract sense; and to this, her symbolical character, must be referred those representations of later times, in which she appears as trampling on the Dragon; as folding her votaries within the skirts of her ample robe; as interceding for sinners; as crowned between heaven and earth by the Father and the Son.

Besides the representations of Christ and the Virgin, some of the characters and incidents of the Old Testament were selected as pictures, generally with reference to corresponding characters and incidents in the Gospel; thus, St. Augustin, in the latter half of the fourth century, speaks of the sacrifice of Isaac as a common subject, typical, of course, of the Great Sacrifice. The elevation of the brazen serpent signified the Crucifixion; Jonah and the whale, the Resurrection, &c This system of corresponding subjects, of type and anti-type, was afterwards, as we shall see, carried much further.

In the seventh century, painting, as it existed in Europe, may be divided into two great schools or

styles : the Western, or Roman, of which the central point was Rome, and which was distinguished,
amid great rudeness of execution, by a certain dignity of expression and solemnity of feeling ; and
the Eastern, or Byzantine school, of which Constantinople was the head-quarters, and which was
distinguished by greater mechanical skill, by ad-
herence to the old classical forms, by the use of
gilding, and by the mean, vapid, spiritless conception of motive and character.

From the seventh to the ninth century the most
important and interesting remains of pictorial art
are the mosaics in the churches,* and the miniature
paintings with which the MS. Bibles and Gospels
were decorated.

But during the tenth and eleventh centuries Italy
fell into a state of complete barbarism and confusion, which almost extinguished the practice of
art in any shape. Of this period only a few works
of extreme rudeness remain. In the Eastern empire painting still survived. It became, indeed,
more and more conventional, insipid, and incorrect,
but the technical methods were kept up ; and thus
it happened that when, in 1204, Constantinople
was taken by the Crusaders, and that the intercourse between the east and west of Europe was
resumed, several Byzantine painters passed into
Italy and Germany, where they were employed to

* Particularly those in the church of Santa Maria Maggiore, at
Rome, and in the church of St. Mark, at Venice.

decorate the churches; and taught the practice of their art, their manner of pencilling, mixing and using colors, and gilding ornaments, to such as chose to learn of them. They brought over the Byzantine types of form and color, the long, lean limbs of the saints, the dark-visaged Madonnas, the blood-streaming crucifixes; and these patterns were followed more or less servilely by the native Italian painters who studied under them. Specimens of this early art remain, and in these later times have been diligently sought and collected into museums as curiosities, illustrating the history and progress of art. As such they are, in the highest degree, interesting; but it must be confessed that, otherwise, they are not attractive. In the Berlin Gallery, and in that of the fine arts at Florence, the best specimens have been brought together, and there are a few in the Louvre.* The subject is generally the Madonna and Child, throned; sometimes alone, sometimes with angels or saints ranged on each side. The characteristics are, in all cases, the same. The figures are stiff, the extremities long and meagre, the features hard and expressionless, the eyes long and narrow. The head of the Virgin is generally declined to the left; the infant Saviour is generally clothed, and sometimes crowned. Two fingers of his right hand are extended in act to bless; the left hand holding a globe, a scroll, or a book. With regard to the ex-

* Nos. 980, 981, 982.

ecution, the ornaments of the throne and borders of the draperies, and frequently the background, are elaborately gilded ; the local colors are generally vivid; there is little or no relief: the handling is streaky ; the flesh-tints are blackish or greenish. At this time, and for two hundred years afterwards (before the invention of oil painting), pictures were painted either in fresco, — an art never wholly lost, — or on seasoned board, and the colors mixed with water, thickened with white of egg or the juice of the young shoots of the fig-tree. This last method was styled by the Italians *a colla* or *a tempera*, by the French *en détrempe*, and in English *distemper;* and in this manner all movable pictures were executed previous to 1440.

It is clear that, before the birth of Cimabue, that is, from 1200 to 1240, there existed schools of painting in the Byzantine style, and under Greek teachers, at Sienna and at Pisa. The former city produced Guido da Sienna, whose Madonna and Child, with figures the size of life, signed and dated 1221, is preserved in the church of San Domenico, at Sienna. It is engraved in Rossini's " Storia della Pittura," on the same page with a Madonna by Cimabue, to which it appears superior in drawing, attitude, expression, and drapery. Pisa produced, about the same time, Giunta de Pisa, of whom there remain works with the date 1236. One of these is a Crucifixion, engraved in Ottley's " Italian School of Design," and, on a smaller scale, in Rossini's " Storia della Pittura," in which the expression of grief in the hovering angels, who are wringing their hands and weeping, is very earnest and striking. But undoubtedly the greatest man of that time, he who gave the grand impulse to mod ern art, was the sculptor Nicola Pisano, whose works date from about 1220 to 1270. Further, it appears that even at Florence a native painter, a certain Maestro Bartolomeo, lived and was employed in 1236. Thus Cimabue can scarcely claim to be the " father of modern painting," even in his own city of Florence. We shall now proceed to the facts on which his traditional celebrity has been founded.

Giovanni of Florence, of the noble family of the Cimabue, called otherwise Gualtieri, was born in 1240. He was early sent by his parents to study grammar in the school of the convent of Santa Maria Novella, where (as is also related of other inborn painters), instead of conning his task, he distracted his teachers by drawing men, horses, buildings, on his school-books. Before printing was invented, this spoiling of school-books must have been rather a costly fancy, and no doubt alarmed the professors of Greek and Latin. His parents, wisely yielding to the natural bent of his mind, allowed him to study painting under some Greek artists who had come to Florence to decorate the church of the convent in which he was a scholar. It seems doubtful whether Cimabue *did* study under the identical painters alluded to by Vasari, but that his masters and models were the Byzantine painters of the time seems to admit of no doubt whatever. The earliest of his works mentioned by Vasari still exists, — a St. Cecilia, painted for the altar of that saint, but now preserved in the church of San Stefano. He was soon afterwards employed by the monks of Vallombrosa, for whom he painted a Madonna with Angels on a gold ground, now preserved in the Academy of the Fine Arts, at Florence. He also painted a Crucifixion for the church of the Santa Croce, still to be seen there, and several pictures for the churches of Pisa, to the great contentment of the Pisans ; and by these and other works his fame being spread far and near, he was called in the year 1265, when he was only twenty-five, to finish the frescoes in the church of St. Francis at Assisi, which had been begun by Greek painters, and continued by Giunta Pisano.

The decoration of this celebrated church is memorable in the history of painting. It is known that many of the best artists of the thirteenth and fourteenth centuries were employed there ; but only fragments of the earliest pictures exist, and the authenticity of those ascribed to Cimabue has been disputed by a great authority.* Lanzi, however, and Dr. Kugler agree in attributing to him the paintings on the roof of the nave, representing. in medallions, the figures of Christ, the Madonna, St

---

* Rumohr, " Italienische Forschungen."

John tho Baptist, St. Francis, and the four Evangelists. " Tho ornaments which surround these medallions are, however, more interesting than the medallions themselves. In the lower corners of tho triangles are represented naked Genii, bearing tasteful vases on their heads; out of these grow rich foliage and flowers, on which hang other Genii, who pluck the fruit, or lurk in tho cups of the flowers." * If these are really by the hand of Cimabue, we must allow that here is a great step in advance of the formal monotony of his Greek models. He executed many other pictures in this famous church, " *con diligenza infinita,*" from the Old and New Testament, in which, judging from the fragments which remain, he showed a decided improvement in drawing, in dignity of attitude, and in the expression of life, but still the figures have only just so much of animation and significance as are absolutely necessary to render the story or action intelligible. There is no variety, no express imitation of nature. Being recalled by his affairs to Florence, about 1270, he painted there the most celebrated of all his works, tho Madonna and Infant Christ, for the church of Santa Maria Novella. This Madonna, of a larger size than any which had been previously executed, had excited in its progress great curiosity and interest among his fellow-citizens; for Cimabue refused to uncover it to public view. But it happened

* Kugler, " Hand book "

2

about that time that Charles of Anjou, brother of
Louis IX., being on his way to take possession of
the kingdom of Naples, passed through Florence,
and was received and feasted by the nobles of that
city; and, among other entertainments, they conducted him to visit the atelier of Cimabue, which
was in a garden near the Porta San Piero. On
this festive occasion the Madonna was uncovered,
and the people in joyous crowds hurried thither to
look upon it, rending the air with exclamations of
delight and astonishment, whence this quarter of
the city obtained and has kept ever since the name
of the Borgo Allegri. The Madonna, when finished, was carried in great pomp from the atelier
of the painter to the church for which it was destined, accompanied by the magistrates of the city,
by music, and by crowds of people, in solemn and
festive procession. This well-known anecdote has
lent a venerable charm to the picture, which is yet
to be seen in the church of Santa Maria Novella,
but it is difficult in this advanced state of art to
sympathize in the *naïve* enthusiasm it excited in
the minds of a whole people six hundred years ago.
Though not without a certain grandeur, the form
is very stiff, with long, lean fingers and formal
drapery, little varying from the Byzantine models;
but the Infant Christ is better; the angels on either
side have a certain elegance and dignity, and the
coloring in its first freshness and delicacy had a
charm hitherto unknown. After this, Cimabue

became famous in all Italy. He had a school of painting at Florence, and many pupils; among them one who was destined to take the sceptre from his hand, and fill all Italy with his fame, — and who, but for him, would have kept sheep in the Tuscan valleys all his life, — the glorious Giotto, of whom we are to speak presently. Cimabue, besides being a painter, was a worker in mosaic and an architect. He was employed, in conjunction with Arnolfo Lapi, in the building of the church of Santa Maria del Fiore, at Florence. Finally, having lived for more than sixty years in great honor and renown, he died at Florence about the year 1302, while employed on the mosaics of the Duomo of Pisa, and was carried from his house, in the Via del Cocomero, to the church of Santa Maria del Fiore, where he was buried. The following epitaph was inscribed above his tomb :

"CREDIDIT UT CIMABOS PICTURÆ CASTRA TENERE ;
    SIC TENUIT VIVENS — NUNC TENET ASTRA POLI." *

Besides the undoubted works of Cimabue preserved in the churches of San Domenico, la Trinità, and Santa Maria Novella, at Florence, and in the Academy of Arts in the same city, there are two Madonnas in the Gallery of the Louvre (Nos. 950, 951), recently brought there ; one as large as life,

* Cimabue thought himself master of the field of painting ;
    While living he was so — now he holds his place among the
    stars of heaven.

with angels, originally painted for the convent of
St. Francis, at Pisa, the other of a smaller size.
From these productions we may judge of the real
merit of Cimabue. In his figures of the Virgin he
adhered almost servilely to the Byzantine models.
The faces are ugly and vapid, the features elon-
gated, the extremities meagre, the general effect
flat. But to his heads of prophets, patriarchs, and
apostles, whether introduced into his great pictures
of the Madonna, or in other sacred subjects, he
gave a certain grandeur of expression and largeness
of form, or, as Lanzi expresses it, "un non so che
di forte e sublime," in which he has not been
greatly surpassed by succeeding painters; and this
energy of expression — his chief and distinguishing
excellence, and which gave him the superiority
over Guido of Sienna and others who painted only
Madonnas — was in harmony with his personal
character. He is described to us as exceedingly
haughty and disdainful, of a fiery temperament,
proud of his high lineage, his skill in his art, and
his various acquirements, for he was well studied
in all the literature of his age. If a critic found
fault with one of his works when in progress, or if
he were himself dissatisfied with it, he would at
once destroy it, whatever pains it might have cost
him. From these traits of character, and the bent
of his genius, which leaned to the grand and terrible rather than the gentle and graceful, he has
subsequently been styled the Michael Angelo of his

time. It is recorded of him by Vasari that he painted a head of St. Francis *after nature*, a thing, he says, till then unknown. It could not have been a portrait from life, because St. Francis died in 1225 : and the earliest head after nature which remains to us was painted by Giunta Pisano, about 1235. It was the portrait of Frate Elia, a monk of Assisi. Perhaps Vasari means that the San Francesco was the first representation of a sacred personage for which nature had been taken as a model.

There is a portrait of Cimabue copied from a tracing of the original head, painted on the walls of the Chapel degli Spagnuoli, in the church of Santa Maria Novella, by Simone Memmi of Sienna, who was at Florence during the lifetime of Cimabue, and must have known him personally. This painting, though executed after the death of Cimabue, has always been considered authentic as a portrait. It is the same alluded to by Vasari, and copied for the first edition of his book.

Cimabue had several remarkable contemporaries. The greatest of these, and certainly the greatest artist of his time, was the sculptor Nicola Pisano. The works of this extraordinary genius, which have been preserved to our time, are so far beyond all contemporary art in knowledge of form, grace, expression, and intention, that, if indisputable proofs of their authenticity did not exist, it would be pronounced incredible. On a comparison of the

works of Cimabue and Nicola Pisano, it is difficult
to conceive that Nicola executed the bas-reliefs of
the pulpit in the Cathedral of Pisa while Cimabue
was painting the frescoes in the church of Assisi
He was the first to *ave the stiff monotony of the
traditional forms for the study of nature and the
antique. The story says that his emulative fancy
was early excited by the beautiful antique sarcoph
agus on which is seen sculptured the Chase of
Hipolytus.* In this sarcophagus had been laid, a
hundred years before, the body of Beatrice. the
mother of the famous Countess Matilda. In the
time of Nicola it was placed, as an ornament, in
the Duomo of Pisa ; and as a youth he had looked
upon it from day to day, until the grace, the life
and movement of the figures struck him, in comparison with the barbarous art of his contempora-
rics, as nothing less than divine. Many before him
had looked on this marble wonder, but to none had
it spoken as it spoke to him. He was the first,
says Lanzi, to see the light and to follow it.† There
is an engraving after one of his bas-reliefs — a
Deposition from the Cross, in Ottley's " School of
Design," which should be referred to by the reader,
who may not have seen his works at Pisa, Florence,

* Now preserved in the Campo Santo, at Pisa.

† Rosini, in his " Storia della Pittura," has rectified some errors
into which Vasari and Lanzi have fallen with regard to the dates
of Nicola Pisano's works. It appears that he lived ar d worked si
late as 1290.

Sienna, and Orvieto. There are also several of his works engraved in Cicognara's "Storia della Scultura."

Another contemporary of Cimabue, and his friend, was Andrea Tafi, the greatest worker in mosaic of his time. The assertion of Vasari, that he learned his art from the Byzantines, is now discredited; for it appears certain that the mosaic-workers of Italy (the forerunners of painting) excelled the Greek artists then, and for a century or two before. Andrea Tafi died, very old, in 1294; and his principal works remain in the Duomo of St. Mark, at Venice, and in the church of San Giovanni, at Florence. Another famous mosaic-worker, also an intimate friend of Cimabue, was Gaddo Gaddi, remarkable for being the first of a family illustrious in several departments of art and literature. It must be remembered that the mosaic-workers of those times prepared and colored their own designs, and may, therefore, take rank with the painters.

Further, there remain pictures by painters of the Sienna school which date before the death of Cimabue, and particularly a picture by a certain Maestro Mino, dated 1289, which is spoken of as wonderful for the invention and greatness of style. Another painter, who sprung from the Byzantine school, and surpassed it, was Duccio of Sienna, who painted from 1282 (twenty years before the death of Cimabue) to about 1339, and "whose influence on the progress of art was unquestionably great."

A large picture by him, representing in many compartments the whole history of the Passion of Christ, is preserved at Sienna. It excited, like Cimabue's Madonna, the pride and enthusiasm of his fellow-citizens, and is still regarded as wonderful for the age in which it was produced.

All these men (Nicola Pisano excepted) still worked on in the trammels of Byzantine art. The first painter of his age who threw them wholly off, and left them far behind him, was Giotto.

GIOTTO.

Born 1276, died 1336.

" **Credette Cimabue nella Pittura**
    Tener lo campo, ed ora ha Giotto il grido ;—
    Sicchè la fama di colui oscura."

    " ———— Cimabue thought
    To lord it over painting's field ; and now
    The cry is Giotto's, and his name eclipsed."

Carey's I ın.e.

THESE often-quoted lines, from Dante's " Purgatorio," must needs be once more quoted here ; for
it is a curious circumstance that, applicable in his
own day, five hundred years ago, they should still
be so applicable in ours. Open any common history, not intended for the very profound, and there
we still find Cimabue " lording it over painting's
field," and placed at the head of a revolution in art,
with which, as an artist, he had little or nothing to
do, — but much as a man ; for to him, to his quick
perception and generous protection of talent in the
lowly shepherd-boy, we owe GIOTTO, than whom no
single human being of whom we read has exercised,
in any particular department of science or art, a
more immediate, wide, and lasting influence. The

(25)

total change in the direction and character of art must, in all human probability, have taken place sooner or later, since all the influences of that wonderful period of regeneration were tending towards it.   Then did architecture struggle as it were from the Byzantine into the Gothic forms, like a mighty plant putting forth its rich foliage and shooting up towards heaven ; then did the speech of the people — the *vulgar tongues*, as they were called — begin to assume their present structure, and become the medium through which beauty and love and action and feeling and thought were to be uttered and immortalized ; and then arose GIOTTO, the destined instrument through which his own beautiful art was to become, not a mere fashioner of idols, but one of the great interpreters of the human soul with all its " infinite " of feelings and faculties, and of human life in all its multifarious aspects.   Giotto was the first painter who " held as it were the mirror up to nature."   Cimabue's strongest claim to the gratitude of succeeding ages is, that he bequeathed such a man to his native country and to the world.

About the year 1289, when Cimabue was already old and at the height of his fame, as he was riding in the valley of Vespignano, about fourteen miles from Florence, his attention was attracted by a boy who was herding sheep, and who, while his flocks were feeding around, seemed intently drawing on a smooth fragment of slate, with a bit of pointed stone, the figure of one of his sheep as it was quietly grazing before him. Cimabue rode up to him, and, looking with astonishment at the performance of the untutored boy, asked him if he would go with him and learn ; to which the boy replied, that he was right willing, if his father were content. The father, a herdsman of the valley, by name Bondone, being consulted, gladly consented to the wish of the noble stranger, and Giotto henceforth became the inmate and pupil of Cimabue.

This pretty story, which was first related by Lorenzo Ghiberti, the sculptor (born 1378), and since by Vasari and a thousand others, luckily rests on evidence as satisfactory as can be given for any events of a rude and distant age, and may well obtain our belief, as well as gratify our fancy ; it has been the subject of many pictures, and is introduced in Rogers' " Italy : "

> " —— Let us wander through the fields
> Where Cimabue found the shepherd-boy
> Tracing his idle fancies on the ground."

Giotto was about twelve or fourteen years old when taken into the house of Cimabue. For his instruction in those branches of polite learning necessary to an artist, his protector placed him under the tuition of Brunetto Latini, who was also the preceptor of Dante. When, at the age of twenty-six, Giotto lost his friend and master, he was already an accomplished man as well as a celebrated painter, and the influence of his large origi-

nal mind upon the later works of Cimabue is dis
tinctly to be traced.

The first recorded performance of Giotto was a
painting on the wall of the Palazzo dell' Podestà,
or council-chamber of Florence, in which were
introduced the portraits of Dante, Brunetto Latini,
Corso Donati, and others. Vasari speaks of these
works as the first successful attempts at portraiture
in the history of modern art. They were soon afterwards plastered or whitewashed over, during the
triumph of the enemies of Dante; and for ages,
though known to exist, they were lost and buried
from sight. The hope of recovering these most
interesting portraits had long been entertained, and
various attempts had been made at different times
without success, till at length, as late as 1840, they
were brought to light by the perseverance and enthusiasm of Mr. Bezzi, an Italian gentleman, now
residing in England. On comparing the head of
Dante, painted when he was about thirty, prosperous and distinguished in his native city, with the
later portraits of him when an exile, worn, wasted,
embittered by misfortune and disappointment and
wounded pride, the difference of expression is as
touching as the identity in feature is indubitable.

The attention which in his childhood Giotto seems
to have given to all natural forms and appearances
showed itself in his earlier pictures; he was the
first to whom it occurred to group his personages
into something like a situation, and to give to their

attitudes and features the expression adapted to it
Thus, in a very early picture of the Annunciation
he gave to the Virgin a look of fear ; and in another,
painted some time afterwards, of the Presentation
in the Temple, he made the Infant Christ shrink
from the priest, and, turning. extend his little arms
to his mother — the first attempt at that species of
grace and naïveté of expression afterwards carried
to perfection by Raffaelle. These and other works
painted in his native city so astonished his fellow-
citizens, and all who beheld them, by their beauty
and novelty, that they seem to have wanted ade-
quate words in which to express the excess of their
delight and admiration, and insisted that the figures
of Giotto so completely beguiled the sense that they
were mistaken for realities ; a commonplace eulo-
gium, never merited but by the most commonplace
and mechanical of painters.

In the church of Santa Croce, Giotto painted a
Coronation of the Virgin, still to be seen, with
choirs of angels on either side. In the refectory
he painted the Last Supper, also still remaining ;
a grand, solemn, simple composition, which, as a
first endeavor to give variety of expression and attitude to a number of persons, — all seated, and all
but two actuated by a similar feeling, — must still
be regarded as extraordinary. In a chapel of the
church of the Carmine, at Florence, he painted a
series of pictures from the life of John the Baptist.
These were destroyed by fire in 1771 ; but, happily,

an English engraver, then studying at Florence, named Patch, had previously made accurate drawings from them, which he engraved and published. A fragment of the old fresco, containing the heads of two of the Apostles, who are bending in grief and devotion over the body of St. John, is now in the collection of Mr. Rogers, the poet. It certainly justifies all that has been said of Giotto's power of expression, and, when compared with the remains of earlier art, more than excuses the wonder and enthusiasm of his contemporaries.

The pope, Boniface VIII., hearing of his marvellous skill, invited him to Rome; and the story says, that the messenger of his holiness, wishing to have some proof that Giotto was indeed the man he was in search of, desired to see a specimen of his excellence in his art; hereupon Giotto, taking up a sheet of paper, traced on it, with a single flourish of his hand, a circle so perfect that "it was a miracle to see;" and (though we know not how or why) seems to have at once converted the pope to a belief of his superiority over all other painters. This story gave rise to the well-known Italian proverb, "*Più tondo che l'O di Giotto*" (rounder than the O of Giotto), and is something like a story told of one of the Grecian painters. But to return.—Giotto went to Rome, and there executed many things which raised his fame higher and higher; and among them, for the ancient Basilica of St. Peter's the famous mosaic of the *Navicella*, or the *Barca*

us it is sometimes called It represents a ship,
with the Disciples, on a tempestuous sea; the
winds, personified as demons, rage around it.
Above are the Fathers of the Old Testament; on
the right stands Christ, raising Peter from the
waves. The subject has an allegorical significance,
denoting the troubles and triumphs of the Church.
This mosaic has often changed its situation, and
has been restored again and again, till nothing of
Giotto's work remains but the original composition
It is now in the vestibule of St. Peter's, at Rome.

For the same Pope Boniface, Giotto painted the
Institution of the Jubilee of 1300, which still exists in the Lateran, at Rome.

In Padua Giotto painted the chapel of the Arena
with frescoes, from the life of Christ and the Virgin, in fifty square compartments. Of this chapel
the late Lady Callcott published an interesting account. There is exceeding grace and simplicity in
some of the outline groups with which her work is
illustrated, particularly the Marriage of the Virgin
and St. Joseph. At Padua Giotto met his friend
Dante; and the influence of one great genius on
another is strongly exemplified in some of his succeeding works, and particularly in his next grand
performance, the frescoes in the church of Assisi.
In the under church, and immediately over the
tomb of St. Francis, the painter represented the
three vows of the Order — Poverty, Chastity, and
Obedience: and in the fourth compartment, the

Saint enthroned and glorified amidst the host of heaven. The invention of the allegories under which Giotto has represented the vows of the Saint, his Marriage with Poverty, — Chastity seated in her rocky fortress, — and Obedience with the curb and yoke, are ascribed by a tradition to Dante. Giotto also painted, in the Campo Santo, at Pisa, the whole history of Job, of which only some fragments remain.

By the time Giotto had attained his thirtieth year, he had reached such hitherto unknown excellence in art, and his celebrity was so universal, that every city and every petty sovereign in Italy contended for the honor of his presence and his pencil, and tempted him with the promise of rich rewards. For the lords of Arezzo, of Rimini, and Ravenna, and for the Duke of Milan, he executed many works, now almost wholly perished. Castruccio Castricani, the warlike tyrant of Lucca, also employed him; but how Giotto was induced to listen to the offers of this enemy of his country is not explained. Perhaps Castruccio, as the head of the Ghibelline party, in which Giotto had ap parently enrolled himself, appeared in the light of a friend rather than an enemy. However this may be, a picture which Giotto painted for Castruccio, and in which he introduced the portrait of the tyrant, with a falcon on his fist, is still preserved in the Lyceum at Lucca. For Guido da Polento, the father of that hapless Francesca di Rimini, whose story is so beautifully told by Dante, he painted the interior of a church ; and for Malatesta di Rimini (who was father of Francesca's husband) he painted the portrait of that prince in a bark, with his companions and a company of mariners ; and among them, Vasari tells us, was the figure of a sailor, who, turning round with his hand before his face, is in the act of spitting in the sea, so life-like as to strike the beholders with amazement. This has perished. But the figure of the thirsty man stooping to drink, in one of the frescoes at Assisi, still remains, to show the kind of excellence through which Giotto excited such admiration in his contemporaries, — a power of imitation, a truth in the expression of natural actions and feelings, to which painting had never yet ascended or descended. This leaning to the *actual* and the *real* has been made a subject of reproach, to which we shall hereafter refer.

It is said — but this does not rest on very satis-factory evidence — that Giotto also visited Avig-non, in the train of Pope Clement V., and painted there the portraits of Petrarch and Laura.

About the year 1327, King Robert of Naples, the father of Queen Joanna, wrote to his son, the Duke of Calabria, then at Florence, to send to him, on any terms, the famous painter Giotto ; who accord-ingly travelled to the court of Naples, stopping on his way in several cities, where he left specimens of his skill. He also visited Orvieto for the purpose of viewing the sculpture with which the brothers Agostino and Agnolo were decorating the cathedral ; and not only bestowed on it high commendation, but obtained for the artists the praise and patronage they merited. There is at Gaeta a Crucifixion painted by Giotto, either on his way to Naples or on his return, in which he introduced himself kneeling in an attitude of deep devotion and contrition at the foot of the cross. This introduction of portraiture into a subject so awful was another innovation, not so praiseworthy as some of his alterations. Giotto's feeling for truth and propriety of expression is particularly remarkable and commendable in the alteration of the dreadful but popular subject of the crucifix. In the Byzantine school, the sole aim seems to have been to represent physical agony, and to render it, by every species of distortion and exaggeration, as terrible and repulsive as possible. Giotto was the first to soften this awful and painful figure by an expression of divine resignation, and by greater attention to beauty of form. A Crucifixion painted by him became the model for his scholars, and was multiplied by imitation through all Italy; so that a famous painter of crucifixes after the Greek fashion, Margaritone, who had been a friend and contemporary of Cimabue, confounded by the introduction of this new method of art, which he partly disdained and partly despaired to imitate, and old enough to hate innovations of all kinds, took to his bed "*infastidito*" (through vexation), and so died.

But to return to Giotto, whom we left on the road to Naples. King Robert received him with great honor and rejoicing, and, being a monarch of singular accomplishments, and fond of the society of learned and distinguished men, he soon found that Giotto was not merely a painter, but a man of the world, a man of various acquirements, whose general reputation for wit and vivacity was not unmerited. He would sometimes visit the painter at his work, and, while watching the rapid progress of his pencil, amused himself with the quaint good sense of his discourse. "If I were you, Giotto," said the king to him, one very hot day, "I would leave off work, and rest myself." — "And so would I, sire," replied the painter, "if I were *you!*" The king, in a playful mood, desired him to paint his kingdom ; on which Giotto immediately sketched the figure of an ass, with a heavy pack-saddle on his back, smelling with an eager air at another pack-saddle lying on the ground, on which were a crown and sceptre. By this emblem the satirical painter expressed the servility and the fickleness of the Neapolitans, and the king at once understood the allusion.

While at Naples Giotto painted in the church of the Incoronati a series of frescoes representing the Seven Sacraments according to the Roman ritual. These still exist, and are among the most authentic

and best preserved of his works. The Sacrament
of Marriage contains many female figures, beautifully designed and grouped, with graceful heads
and flowing draperies. This picture is traditionally said to represent the marriage of Joanna of
Naples and Louis of Taranto; but Giotto died in
1336, and these famous espousals took place in
1347. A dry date will sometimes confound a very
pretty theory. In the Sacrament of Ordination
there is a group of chanting-boys, in which the
various expressions of the act of singing are given
with that truth of imitation which made Giotto the
wonder of his day. His paintings from the Apoc-
alypse, in the church of Santa Chiara, were whitewashed over, about two centuries age, by a certain
prior of the convent, because, in the opinion of this
barbarian, *they made the church look dark!*

Giotto quitted Naples about the year 1328, and
returned to his native city with great increase of
riches and fame. He continued his works with un-
abated application, assisted by his pupils; for his
school was now the most famous in Italy. Like
most of the early Italian artists, he was an architect and sculptor, as well as a painter; and his last
public work was the famous Campanile, or Bell-
tower, at Florence, founded in 1334, for which he
made all the designs, and even executed with his
own hand the models for the sculpture on the three
lower divisions. According to Kugler, they form
a regular series of subjects, illustrating the develop

ment of human culture, through religion and laws,
" conceived," says the same authority, " with profound wisdom." When the Emperor Charles V.
saw this elegant structure, he exclaimed that it
ought to be " kept under glass." In the same
allegorical taste Giotto painted many pictures cf
the Virtues and Vices, ingeniously invented, and
rendered with great attention to natural and appropriate expression. In these and similar representations we trace distinctly the influence of the
genius of Dante. A short time before his death he
was invited to Milan by Azzo Visconti. He executed some admirable frescoes in the ancient palace
of the Dukes of Milan ; but these have perished.
Finally, having returned to Florence, he soon afterwards died, " yielding up his soul to God in the
year 1336 ; and having been," adds Vasari, " no
less a good Christian than an excellent painter."
He was honorably interred in the church of Santa
Maria del Fiore, where his master Cimabue had
been laid with similar honors, thirty-five years
before. Lorenzo de' Medici afterwards placed
above his tomb his effigy in marble. Giotto left
four sons and four daughters but we do not hear
that any of his descendants became distinguished
in art or otherwise.*

* In the foregoing sketch some disputed points in the life of
Giotto are, for obvious reasons, left at rest ; and the order of events
has been somewhat changed, in accordance with more exact chron
iclers than Vasari

Before we proceed to give some account of the personal character and influence of Giotto, both as a man and an artist, of which many amusing and interesting traits have been handed down to us, we must turn for a moment to reconsider that revolution in art, which originated with him,—which seized at once on all imaginations, all sympathies; which Dante, Boccaccio, and Petrarch, have all commemorated in immortal verse or as immortal prose; which, during a whole century, filled Italy and Sicily with disciples formed in the same school, and penetrated with the same ideas. All that had been done in painting, before Giotto, resolved itself into the imitation of certain existing models, and their improvement to a certain point in style of execution. There was no new method. The Greekish types were everywhere seen, more or less modified,—a Madonna in the middle, with a couple of lank saints or angels stuck on each side; or saints bearing symbols, or with their names written over their heads, and texts of Scripture proceeding from their mouths; or, at the most, a few figures, placed in such a position relatively to each other as sufficed to make a story intelligible, the arrangement being generally traditional and arbitrary. Such seems to have been the limit to which painting had advanced previous to 1280.

Giotto appeared; and almost from the beginning of his career he not only deviated from the practice of the older painters, but stood opposed to them.

He not only improved — he changed; he placed himself on wholly new ground. He took up those principles which Nicola Pisano had applied to sculpture, and went to the same sources,— to nature, and to those remains of pure antique art which showed him how to look at nature. His residence at Rome while yet young, and in all the first glowing development of his creative powers, must have had an incalculable influence on his after-works. Deficient to the end of his life in the knowledge of form, he was deficient in that kind of beauty which depends on form, but his feeling for grace and harmony in the airs of his heads and the arrangement of his groups was exquisite; and the longer he practised his art, the more free and flowing became his lines. But, beyond grace and beyond beauty, he aimed at the expression of natural character and emotion, in order to render intelligible his newly-invented scenes of action and his religious allegories. A writer near his time speaks of it as something new and wonderful that in Giotto's pictures " the personages who are in grief look melancholy, and those who are joyous look gay." For his heads he introduced a new type, exactly reversing the Greek pattern : long-shaped, half-shut eyes; a long, straight nose ; and a very short chin. The hands are rather delicately drawn, but he could not design the feet well, for which reason we generally find those of his men clothed in shoes or sandals wherever it is possible, and those of his women covered with flowing drapery. The management of his draperies is, indeed, particularly characteristic; distinguished by a certain lengthiness and narrowness in the folds, in which, however, there is much taste and simplicity, though, in point of style, as far from the antique as from the complicated meanness of the Byzantine models; and it is curious that this peculiar treatment of the drapery, these long perpendicular folds, correspond in character with the principles of Gothic architecture, and with it rose and declined. For the stiff, wooden limbs, and motionless figures, of the Byzantine school, he substituted life, movement, and the *look*, at least, of flexibility. His notions of grouping and arrangement he seems to have taken from the ancient bassorelievos; there is a statuesque grace and simplicity in his compositions which reminds us of them. His style of coloring and execution was, like all the rest, an innovation on received methods; his colors were lighter and more roseate than had ever been known, the fluid by which they were tempered more thin and easily managed, and his frescoes must have been skilfully executed to have stood so well as they have done. Their duration is, indeed, nothing compared to the Egyptian remains; but the latter have been for ages covered up from light and air, in a dry, sandy climate. Those of Giotto have been exposed to all the vicissitudes of weather and of underground damp, have been whitewashed and every way ill-treated, yet the fragments which remain have still a surprising freshness, and his distemper pictures are still wonderful. It is to be regretted that the reader cannot be referred to any collection in England for an example of the characteristics here enumerated. We have not in the National Gallery a single example of Giotto or his scholars; the earliest picture we have is dated nearly two hundred years after his death. The only one in the Louvre (a St. Francis, as large as life) is dubious and unworthy of him. In the Florentine Gallery are three pictures : Christ on the Mount of Olives, one of his best works ; and two Madonnas, with graceful angels. In the gallery of the Academy of Arts, in the same city, are more than twenty small pictures (the best works of Giotto are on a small scale — these measure about a foot in height). Two of the same series are at Berlin, all representing subjects from the life and acts of Christ, of the Virgin, or St. Francis. Those who are curious may consult the engravings after Giotto, in the plates to the "Storia della Pittura," of Rosini ; those in D'Agincourt's "Histoire de l'Art par les Monumens ; " and in Ottley's " Early Italian School," a copy of which is in the British Museum.

Giotto's personal character and disposition had no small part in the revolution he effected. In the union of endowments which seldom meet together in the same individual — extraordinary inventive and poetical genius, with sound, practical, energetic sense, and untiring activity and energy —

Giotto resembled Rubens; and only this rare combination could have enabled him to fling off so completely all the fetters of the old style, and to have executed the amazing number of works which are with reason attributed to him. His character was as independent in other matters as in his own art. He seems to have had little reverence for received opinions about anything, and was singularly free from the superstitious enthusiasm of the times in which he lived, although he lent his powers to embodying that very superstition. Perhaps the very circumstance of his being employed in painting the interiors of churches and monasteries opened to his acute, discerning, and independent mind reflections which took away some of the respect for the mysteries they concealed. There is extant a poem of Giotto's, entitled " A Song against Poverty," which becomes still more *piquante* in itself, and expressive of the peculiar turn of Giotto's mind, when we remember that he had painted the Glorification of Poverty as the Bride of St. Francis, and that in those days songs in *praise* of poverty were as fashionable as devotion to St. Francis, the " Patriarch of Poverty." Giotto was celebrated, too, for his joyous temper, for his witty and satirical repartees, and seems to have been as careful of his worldly goods as he was diligent in acquiring them. Boccaccio relates an anecdote of him, not very important, but, as it contains several traits which are divertingly characteristic, we will give it here:

"Fair and dear ladies!" (Thus the novelist is
wont to address his auditory.) ' It is a wondrous
thing to see how oftentimes nature hath been
pleased to hide within the most misshapen forms
the most wondrous treasures of soul, which is evident in the persons of two of our fellow-citizens, of
whom I shall now briefly discourse to you. Messer
Forese da Rabatta, the advocate, being a personage
of the most extraordinary wisdom, and learned in
the law above all others, yet was in body mean
and deformed, with, thereunto, a flat, currish
(*ricagnato*) physiognomy ; and Messer Giotto, who
was not in face or person one whit better favored
than the said Messer Forese, had a genius of that
excellence, that there was nothing which nature
(who is the mother of all things) could bring forth,
but he with his ready pencil would so wondrously
imitate it, that it seemed not only *similar*, but *the
same ;* thus deluding the visual sense of men, so
that they deemed that what was only pictured
before them did in reality exist. And seeing that
through Giotto that art was restored to light which
had been for many centuries buried (through fault
of those who, in painting, addressed themselves to
please the eye of the vulgar, and not to content the
understanding of the wise), I esteem him worthy to
be placed among those who have made famous and
glorious this our city of Florence. Nevertheless,
though so great a man in his art, he was but little
in person, and, as I have said, ill-favored enough

Now, it happened that Messer Forese and Giotto
had possessions in land in Mugello, which is on the
road leading from Florence to Bologna, and thither
they rode one day on their respective affairs, Messer
Forese being mounted on a sorry hired jade, and
the other in no better case. It was summer, and
the rain came on suddenly and furiously, and they
hastened to take shelter in the house of a peasant
thereabouts, who was known to them ; but, the
storm still prevailing, they, considering that they
must of necessity return to Florence the same day,
borrowed from the peasant two old, worn-out pil-
grim-cloaks, and two rusty old hats, and so they
set forth. They had not proceeded very far, when
they found themselves wet through with the rain,
and all bespattered with the mud ; but, after a
while, the weather clearing in some small degree,
they took heart, and from being silent they began
to discourse of various matters. Messer Forese
having listened a while to Giotto, who was in truth
a man most eloquent and lively in speech, could not
help casting on him a glance as he rode alongside ;
and, considering him from head to foot thus wet,
ragged, and splashed all over, and thus mounted
and accoutred, and not taking his own appearance
into account, he laughed aloud. ' O, Giotto,' said
he, jeeringly, ' if a stranger were now to meet us,
could he, looking on you, believe it possible that
you were the greatest painter in the whole world ?
— ' Certainly,' quoth Giotto, with a side glance at

his companion, ' certainly, if, looking upon your worship, he could believe it possible that you knew your A B C!' Whereupon Messer Forese could not but confess that he had been paid in his own coin."

This is one of many humorous repartees which tradition has preserved, and an instance of that readiness of wit — that *prontezza* — for which Giotto was admired; in fact, he seems to have presented in himself, in the union of depth and liveliness, of poetical fancy and worldly sense, of independent spirit and polished suavity, an epitome of the national character of the Florentines, such as Sismondi has drawn it. We learn, from the hyperboles used by Boccaccio, the sort of rapturous surprise which Giotto's imitation of life caused in his imaginative contemporaries, and which assuredly they would be far from exciting now; and the unceremonious description of his person becomes more amusing when we recollect that Boccaccio must have lived in personal intercourse with the painter, as did Petrarch and Dante. When Giotto died, in 1336, his friend Dante had been dead fifteen years ; Petrarch was thirty-two, and Boccaccio twenty-three years of age. When Petrarch died, in 1374, he left to his friend Francesco da Carrara, Lord of Padua, a Madonna, painted by Giotto, as a most precious legacy, " a wonderful piece of work, of which the ignorant might overlook the beauties, but which the learned must regard with amazement." All writers who treat of the ancient glories of Florence, — Florence the beautiful, Florence the free, — from Villani down to Sismondi, count Giotto in the roll of her greatest men. Antiquaries and connoisseurs in art search out and study the relics which remain to us, and recognize in them the dawn of that splendor which reached its zenith in the beginning of the sixteenth century; while to the philosophic observer Giotto appears as one of those few heaven-endowed beings whose development springs from a source within, — one of those unconscious instruments in the hand of Providence, who, in seeking their own profit and delight through the expansion of their own faculties, make unawares a step forward in human culture, lend a new impulse to human aspirations, and, like the " bright morning star, day's harbinger," may be merged in the succeeding radiance, but never forgotten.

Before we pass on to the scholars and imitators of Giotto, who during the next century filled all Italy with schools of art, we may here make mention of one or two of his contemporaries, not so much for any performances left behind them, but because they have been commemorated by men more celebrated than themselves, and survive embalmed in their works as " flies in amber." Dante has mentioned, in his " Purgatorio," two painters of the time, famous for their miniature illustrations of Missals and MSS. Before the invention of printing, and indeed for some time after, this was an important branch of art. It flourished from the days of Charlemagne to those of Charles V., and was a source of honor as well as riches to the laymen who practised it. Many, however, of the most beautiful specimens of illuminated manuscripts are the work of the nameless Benedictine monks, who labored in the silence and seclusion of their convents, and who yielded to their community most of the honor and all the profit. This was not the case with Oderigi, whom Dante has represented as expiating in purgatory his excessive vanity as a painter, and humbly giving the palm to another, Franco Bolognese, of whom there remains no relic but a Madonna, engraved in Rosini's " Storia della Pittura." He retains, however, a name as the founder of the early Bolognese school. The fame of Buffalmacco as a jovial companion, and the tales told in Boccaccio of his many inventions and the tricks he played on his brother-painter, the simple Calandrino, have survived almost every relic of his pencil. Yet he appears to have been a good painter of that time, and to have imitated, in his later works, the graceful simplicity of Giotto.* He had also much honor and sufficient employment, but,

* An elegant little figure of St. Catherine, attributed to Buffal ma co, is engraved in Rosini, p. 52. A picture of St. Ursula, an early work of the same painter, is quite Byzantine in style. The Frescoes in the Campo Santo, at Pisa, so long attributed to him, are by another hand. (See Kugler and Rumohr.)

having been more intent on spending than earning, he died miserably poor in 1340.

Cavallini studied under Giotto, at Rome, but seems never to have wholly laid aside the Greekish style in which he had been first educated. He was a man of extreme simplicity and sanctity of mind and manners, and felt some scruples in condemning as an artist the Madonnas before which he had knelt in prayer. This feeling of earnest piety he communicated to all his works. There is by him a picture of the Annunciation preserved in the church of St. Mark, at Florence, in which the expression of piety and modesty in the Virgin, and of reverence in the kneeling angel, is perfectly beautiful. The same devout feeling enabled him to rise to the sublime in a grand picture of the Crucifixion which he painted in the church of Assisi, and which is reckoned one of the most important monuments of the Giotto school. The resignation of the divine sufferer, the lamenting angels, the fainting Virgin, the groups of Roman soldiers, are all painted with a truth and feeling quite wonderful for the time. Engravings after Cavallini may be found in Ottley's " Early Italian School," and in Rosini (p. 21). He became the pupil of Giotto when nearly forty years old, and survived him only a short time, dying in 1340. With Cavallini begins the list of painters of the Roman school, afterwards so illustrious. Among the contemporaries of Giotto we must refer once more to Duccio of Sienna.

Though an established painter in his native city when Giotto was a child, his later works show that the influence of that young and daring spirit had given a new impulse to his mind. His best picture, still preserved, and described with enthusiasm in Kugler's "Handbook," was painted in 1311. Duccio died very old, about 1339.

The scholars and imitators of Giotto, who adopted the new method (*il nuovo metodo*), as it was then called, and who collectively are distinguished as the *Scuola Giottesca*, may be divided into two classes: 1. Those who were merely his assistants and imitators, who confined themselves to the reproduction of the models left by their master. 2. Those who, gifted with original genius, followed his example rather than his instructions, pursued the path he had opened to them, introduced better methods of study, more correct design, and carried on in various departments the advance of art into the succeeding century.

Of the first it is not necessary to speak. Among the men of great and original genius who immediately succeeded Giotto, THREE must be especially mentioned for the importance of the works they have left, and for the influence they exercised on those who came after them. These were Andrea Orcagna, Simone Memmi, and Taddeo Gaddi.

The first of these, Andrea Cioni, commonly called ANDREA ORCAGNA, did not study under Giotto, but owed much indirectly to that vivifying influence which he breathed through art. Andrea was the son of a goldsmith at Florence. The goldsmiths of the fourteenth and fifteenth centuries were in general excellent designers, and not unfrequently became painters, as in the instances of Francia, Verrochio, Andrea del Sarto, &c. Andrea apparently learned design under the tuition of his father. Rosini places his birth previous to the year 1310. In the year 1332 he had already acquired so much celebrity, that he was called upon tc continue the decoration of the Campo Santo at Pisa.

This seems the proper place to give a more detailed account of one of the most extraordinary and interesting monuments of the middle ages. The Campo Santo of Pisa, like the cathedral at Assisi, was an arena in which the best artists of the time were summoned to try their powers ; but the influence of the frescoes in the Campo Santo on the progress and development of art was yet more direct and important than that of the paintings in the church of Assisi.

The Campo Santo, or the " Holy Field," once a cemetery, though no longer used as such, is an open space of about four hundred feet in length and one hundred and eighteen feet in breadth, enclosed with high walls, and an arcade, something like the cloisters of a monastery, or cathedral, running all round it. On the east side is a large chapel, and on the north two smaller chapels, where prayers and masses are celebrated for the repose of the dead. The open space was filled with earth brought from the Holy Land by the merchant ships of Pisa, which traded to the Levant in the days of its commercial splendor. This open space, once sown with graves, is now covered with green turf. At the four corners are four tall cypress-trees, their dark, monumental, spiral forms contrasting with a little lowly cross in the centre, round which ivy or some other creeping plant has wound a luxuriant bower. The beautiful Gothic arcade was designed and built about 1283 by Giovanni Pisano, the son of the great Nicola Pisano already mentioned. This arcade, on the side next the burial-ground, is pierced by sixty-two windows of elegant tracery, divided from each other by slender pilasters; upwards of six hundred sepulchral monuments of the nobles and citizens of Pisa are ranged along the marble pavements, and mingled with them are some antique remains of great beauty which the Pisans in former times brought from the Greek Isles. Here also is seen the famous sarcophagus which first inspired the genius of Nicola Pisano, and in which had been deposited the body of Beatrix, mother of the famous Countess Matilda. The walls opposite to the windows were painted in the fourteenth and fifteenth centuries with scriptural subjects. Most of these are half ruined by time, neglect, and damp; some only present fragments — here an arm, there a head; and the best preserved are faded, discolored, ghastly in appearance, and solemn in subject. The whole aspect of this singular place, particularly to those who wander through its long arcades at the close of day, when the figures on the pictured walls look dim and spectral through the gloom, and the cypresses assume a blacker hue, and all the associations connected with its sacred purpose and its history rise upon the fancy, has in its silence and solitude and religious destination, something inexpressibly strange, dreamy, solemn, almost awful. Seen in the broad glare of noonday, the place and the pictures lose something of their power over the fancy, and that which last night haunted us as a vision, to-day we examine, study, criticize.

The building of the Campo Santo was scarcely finished when the best painters of the time were summoned to paint the walls all round the interior with appropriate subjects. This was a work of many years. It was indeed continued at intervals through two centuries; and thus we have a series of illustrations of the progress of art during its first development, of the religious influences of the age, and even of the habits and manners of the people, which are faithfully exhibited in some of these most extraordinary compositions.

Those first executed, in the large chapel and on the walls of the cloisters, at the end of the thirteenth and in the very beginning of the fourteenth century, have perished wholly; the earliest in date

which still exist represent the Passion of our
Saviour in a rude but solemn style. We find here
the accompaniments usual in this subject from the
earliest time, and which, from their perpetual repetition down to a late period, appear to be traditional — the lamenting angels, the sorrowing
women, the Virgin fainting at the foot of the cross.
Two angels at the head of the repentant thief prepare to carry his soul into Paradise ; two demons
perched on the cross of the reprobate thief are ready
to seize his spirit the moment it is released, and
bear it to the regions below. This fresco and
another have been traditionally attributed to the
Buffalmacco of facetious memory, already mentioned ; but this is now supposed to be an error.

A series of subjects from the Book of Job was
painted by Giotto. Of these only fragments remain.
Then followed ANDREA ORCAGNA ; and the subjects
selected by him were such as harmonized peculiarly
with the destination of these sacred precincts.
They were to represent in four great compartments
what the Italians call " *I quattro novissimi*,' that
is, the four last or latest things — Death, Judgment, Hell, or Purgatory, and Paradise ; but only
three were completed.

The first is styled the Triumph of Death (*Il Trionfo della Morte*). It is full of poetry, and abounding in ideas then new in pictorial art. On the
right is a festive company of ladies and cavaliers,
who by their falcons and dogs appear to be returned

from the chase. They are seated under orange-trees, and splendidly attired; rich carpets are spread at their feet. A troubadour and singing-girl amuse them with flattering songs; Cupids flutter around them and wave their torches. All tho pleasures of sense and joys of earth are here united. On the left Death approaches with rapid flight,—a fearful-looking woman, with wild stream-ing hair, claws instead of nails, large bats' wings, and indestructible wire-woven drapery. She swings a scythe in her hand, and is on the point of mow-ing down the joys of the company. (This female impersonation of Death is supposed to be borrowed from Petrarch, whose " Trionfo della Morte " was written about this time.) A host of corpses closely pressed together lie at her feet. By their insignia they are almost all to be recognized as the former rulers of the world,—kings, queens, cardinals, bishops, princes, warriors, &c. Their souls rise out of them in the form of new-born infants; angels and demons are ready to receive them; the souls of tho pious fold their hands in prayer; those of the condemned shrink back in horror. The angels are peculiarly yet happily conceived, with bird-like forms and variegated plumage; the devils have the semblance of beasts of prey or of disgust-ing reptiles. They fight with each other. On the right tho angels ascend to heaven with those they have saved, while the demons drag their prey to a fiery mountain, visible on the left, and hurl the

souls down into the flames. Next to these corpses
is a crowd of beggars and cripples, who with outstretched arms call upon Death to end their sor-
rows; but she heeds not their prayer, and has
already passed them in her flight. A rock separates this scene from another, in which is represented a second hunting party descending the mountain by a hollow path; here again are richly-attired
princes and dames on horses splendidly caparisoned,
and a train of hunters with falcons and dogs. The
path has led them to three open sepulchres in the
left corner of the picture; in them lie the bodies
of three princes, in different stages of decay. Close
by, in extreme old age and supported on crutches,
stands the old hermit St. Macarius, who, turning
to the princes, points down to this bitter " Memento
mori." They look on apparently with indifference,
and one of them holds his nose, as if incommoded
by the horrible stench. One queenly lady alone,
deeply moved, rests her head on her hand, her
countenance full of a pensive sorrow. On the
mountain heights are several hermits, who, in contrast to the followers of the joys of the world, have
attained in a life of contemplation and abstinence
to a state of tranquil blessedness. One of them
milks a doe, squirrels are sporting round him; another sits and reads; and a third looks down into
the valley, where the remains of the mighty are
mouldering away. There is a tradition that among

the personages in these pictures are many portraits of the artist's contemporaries.

The second representation is the Last Judgmenc Above, in the centre, Christ and the Virgin are throned in separate glories. He turns to the left. towards the condemned, while he uncovers the wound in his side, and raises his right arm with a menacing gesture, his countenance full of majestic wrath. The Virgin, on the right of her Son, is the picture of heavenly mercy; and, as if terrified at the words of eternal condemnation, she turns away. On either side are ranged the prophets of the Old Testament, the Apostles and other saints—severe, solemn, dignified figures. Angels, holding the instruments of the Passion, hover over Christ and the Virgin; under them is a group of archangels. The archangel Michael stands in the midst, holding a scroll in each hand; immediately before him another archangel, supposed to represent Raphael, the guardian angel of humanity, cowers down, shuddering, while two others sound the awful trumpets of doom. Lower down is the earth, where men are seen rising from their graves; armed angels direct them to the right and left. Here is seen King Solomon, who, whilst he rises, seems doubtful to which side he should turn; here a hypocritical monk, whom an angel draws back by the hair from the host of the blessed; and there a youth in a gay and rich costume, whom another angel leads away to Paradise. There is wonderful and even terrible

power of expression in some of the heads ; and it is
said that among them are many portraits of contemporaries, but unfortunately no circumstantial
traditions as to particular figures have reached us.
The attitudes of Christ and the Virgin were afterwards borrowed by Michael Angelo, in his celebrated Last Judgment; but, notwithstanding the
perfection of his forms, he stands far below the
dignified grandeur of the old master. Later painters have also borrowed from his arrangement of the
patriarchs and apostles — particularly Fra Bartolomeo and Raphael.

The third representation, directly succeeding the
foregoing, is Hell. It is said to have been executed
from a design of Andrea, by his brother Bernardo.
It is altogether inferior to the preceding representations in execution, and even in the composition.
Here, the imagination of the painter, unrestrained
by any just rules of taste, degenerates into the
monstrous and disgusting, and even the grotesque
and ludicrous. Hell is here represented as a great
rocky caldron, divided into four compartments rising one above the other. In the midst sits Satan,
a fearful armed giant — himself a fiery furnace, out
of whose body flames arise in different places, in
which sinners are consumed or crushed. In other
parts, the condemned are seen spitted like fowls,
and roasted and basted by demons, with other such
atrocious fancies, too horrible and sickening for
description. The lower part of the picture was

badly painted over and altered according to the taste of the day, in the sixteenth century ; certainly not for the better.*

ANDREA ORCAGNA is supposed to have painted these frescoes about 1335, and he died about 1370.

Simone Martini, usually called SIMONE MEMMI, was a painter of Sienna, of whom very few works remain ; but the friendship of Petrarch has rendered his name illustrious. Simone Memmi was employed at Avignon, when it was the seat of the popes (about 1340), and there he painted the portrait of Laura, and presented it to Petrarch, who rewarded him with two Sonnets — and immortality. Simone also painted a famous picture on the wall of the Spanish chapel in the church of Santa Maria Novella, which may still be seen there. It represents the church militant and triumphant — with a great number of figures, among which are the portraits of Cimabue, Petrarch, and Laura. He also painted in the Campo Santo, and his pictures there are among the finest in expression and in grouping. He died about 1345. There is a picture in the Louvre, at Paris, No. 1115, attributed to him. It represents the Virgin crowned in Heaven amid a chorus of angels, a subject frequently treated by Giotto and his scholars.

Pietro Lorenzetti painted in the Campo Santo the Hermits in the Wilderness. They are repre-

* The foregoing account of the paintings of Andrea Orcagna is taken, with alterations, from Kugler's "Handbuch."

sented as dwelling in caves and chapels, upon rocks
and mountains; some studying, others meditating,
others tempted by demons in various horrible or
alluring forms, for such were the diseased fancies
which haunted a solitary and unnatural existence.
As the laws of perspective were then unknown, the
various groups of hermits and their dwellings are
represented one above another, and all of the same
size, much like the figures on a china plate.

Antonio Veneziano also painted in the Campo
Santo, about 1387, and showed himself superior
to all who had preceded him in feeling and grace,
though inferior to Andrea Orcagna in sublimity.
A certain Spinello of Arezzo was next employed,
about 1380. He painted the story of St. Ephesus.
Spinello seems to have been a man of genius, but
of most unregulated mind. Vasari tells a story of
him which shows at once the vehemence of his fancy
and his morbid brain. He painted a picture of the
Fallen Angels, in which he had labored to render
the figure of Satan as terrible, as deformed, as re
volting, as possible. The image, as he worked upon
it, became fixed in his fancy, and haunted him in
sleep. He dreamed that the Prince of Hell appeared
before him under the horrible form in which he had
arrayed him, and demanded why he should be thus
treated, and by what authority the painter had
represented him so abominably hideous. Spinello
awoke in terror. Soon afterwards he became dis
tracted, and so died, about the year 1400.

But the great painter of this time, the third alluded to above, was TADDEO GADDI, the favorite pupil of Giotto, and his godson. His pictures are considered the most important works of the fourteenth century. They resemble the manner of Giotto in the feeling for truth, nature, and simplicity; but we find in them improved execution, with even more beauty and largeness and grandeur of style. His pictures are numerous; several are in the Academy at Florence, and the Museum at Berlin; none, that we know of, in England. In Ottley's engravings of the early Italian school are three grand seated figures of the Fathers of the Church, from Taddeo's most famous picture, the fresco in the Spanish chapel at Florence, usually entitled the Arts and Sciences. Between Taddeo Gaddi and Simone Memmi there existed an ardent friendship and a mutual admiration, which did honor to both. All that Taddeo painted in the Campo Santo is destroyed. At Paris, in the Louvre, are four small pictures attributed to him; and at Berlin four others larger, more important, and more authentic. Another of Giotto's most famous followers was Tommaso di Stefano, called Giottino, or " the little Giotto," from the success with which he emulated his master.

Towards the close of this century, the decoration of the Campo Santo was interrupted by the political misfortunes and internal dissensions which distracted the city of Pisa, and were not resumed for nearly a hundred years. Tne paintings in the church of Assisi were carried on by Giottino and by Giovanni di Melano, but were also interrupted towards the close of this century.

We have mentioned here but a few of the most prominent names among the multitude of painters who flourished from 1300 to 1400. Before we enter on a new century, we will take a general view of the progress of the art itself, and the purposes to which it was applied.

The progress made in painting was chiefly by carrying out the principles of Giotto in expression and in imitation. Taddeo Gaddi and Simone excelled in the first; the imitation of form and of natural objects was so improved by Stefano Fiorentino, that he was styled by his contemporaries *Il Scimia della Natura*, "the ape of Nature." Giottino, the son of this Stefano, and others, improved in color, in softness of execution, and in the means and mechanism of the art; but oil-painting was not yet invented, and linear perspective was unknown. Engraving on copper, cutting in wood, and printing, were the inventions of the next century. Portraits were seldom painted, and then only of very distinguished persons, introduced into large compositions. The imitation of natural scenery, that is, *landscape painting*, as a branch of art, now such a familiar source of pleasure, was as yet unthought of. When landscape was introduced into pictures as a background, or accessory, it was merely to indicate the scene of the story. A rock represented a desert; some formal trees, very like brooms set on end, indicated a wood; a bluish space, sometimes with fishes in it, *signified* a river or a sea. Yet in the midst of this ignorance, this imperfect execution, and limited range of power, how exquisitely beautiful are some of the remains of this early time! affording in their simple, genuine grace, and lofty, earnest, and devout feeling, examples of excellence which our modern painters are beginning to feel and to understand, and which the great Raphael himself did not disdain to study, and even to copy.

As yet the purposes to which painting was applied were almost wholly of a religious character. No sooner was a church erected, than the walls were covered with representations of sacred subjects, either from scriptural history or the legends of saints. Devout individuals or families built and consecrated chapels; and then, at great cost, employed painters either to decorate the walls or to paint pictures for the altars; the Madonna and Child, or the Crucifixion, were the favorite subjects — the donor of the picture or founder of the chapel being often represented on his knees in a corner of the picture, and sometimes (as more expressive of humility) of most diminutive size, out of all proportion to the other figures. The doors of the sacristies, and of the presses in which the priests' vestments were kept, were often covered with smal.

pictures of scriptural subjects; as were also the
chests in which were deposited the utensils for the
Holy Sacrament.   Almost all the small movable
pictures of the fourteenth and fifteenth centuries
which have come down to us are either the altar-
pieces of chapels and oratories, or have been cut
from ths panels of doors, from the covers of chests,
or other pieces of ecclesiastical furniture.

LORENZO GHIBERTI.

WE are now to enter on a view of the progress of painting in the fifteenth century — a period perhaps the most remarkable in the whole history of mankind ; distinguished by the most extraordinary mental activity, by rapid improvement in the arts of life, by the first steady advance in philosophical inquiry, by the restoration of classical learning and by two great events, of which the results lie almost beyond the reach of calculation — the invention of the art of printing, and the discovery of America.

The progressive impulse which characterized this memorable period was felt not less in the fine arts. In painting, the adoption of oils in the mixing of colors, instead of the aqueous and glutinous vehicles formerly used for the purpose, led to some most important results. But long before the general adoption of this and other improvements in the *materials* employed, there had been a strong impulse given to the mental development of art, of which we have to say a few words before we come to treat further of the history and efforts of individual minds.

(64)

During the fourteenth century we find all Italy
filled with the scholars and imitators of Giotto. But
in the fifteenth there was a manifest striving after
originality of style ; a branching off into particular
schools, distinguished by the predominance of some
particular characteristic in the mode of treatment :
as expression, form, color, the tendency to the
merely imitative, or the aspiration towards the
spiritual and ideal. At this time we begin to hear
of the Neapolitan, Umbrian, Bolognese, Venetian,
and Paduan schools, as distinctly characterized ;
but from 1400 to 1450 we still find the Tuscan
schools in advance of all the rest in power, invention, fertility, and in the application of knowledge
and mechanical means to a given end ; and, as in
the thirteenth century we traced the new influence
given to modern art by Giotto back to the sculptor
Nicola Pisano, so in the fifteenth century we find
the influence of another sculptor, Lorenzo Ghiberti,
producing an effect on his contemporaries, more
especially his fellow-citizens, which, by developing
and perfecting the principles of imitation on which
Giotto had worked, stamped that peculiar character on Florentine art which distinguished it all
through the century of which we have now to
speak, and the beginning of the next.

For these reasons, the story of Ghiberti, and the
casting of the famous gates of San Giovanni, may
be considered as an epoch in the history of painting. We shall find, as we proceed, almost every

great name, and every important advance in art, connected with it directly or indirectly ; while the competition which is about to take place among our own artists, with a view to the decoration of the houses of Parliament, lends, at the present moment, a particular interest and application to this beautiful anecdote.

Florence, at the period of which we speak, was at the head of all the states of Italy, and at the height of its prosperity. The government was essentially democratic in spirit and form ; every class and interest in the state — the aristocracy, the military, merchants, tradesmen, and mechanics — had each a due share of power, and served to balance each other. The family of the Medici, who a century later seized on the sovereignty, were at this time only among the most distinguished citizens, and members of a great mercantile house, at the head of which was Giovanni, the father of Cosmo de' Medici. The trades were divided into guilds or companies, called ARTI, which were represented in the government by twenty-four CONSOLI, or consuls. It was these consuls of the guild of merchants who, in the year 1401, undertook to erect a second gate or door of bronze to the Baptistery of St. John, which should form a pendant to the first, executed in the preceding century (1330), by Andrea Pisano, from the designs of Giotto, and representing in rich sculpture the various events of

the life of St. John the Baptist.*   To equal or surpass this beautiful gate, which had been for half a
century the admiration of all Italy, was the object
proposed, and no expense was to be spared in its
attainment.

The *Signoria*, or members of the chief government, acting in conjunction with the *Consoli*, made
known their munificent resolve through all Italy,
and, in consequence, not only the best artists of
Florence, but many from other cities, particularly
Siena and Bologna, assembled on this occasion.
From among a great number, seven were selected
by the *Consoli* as worthy to compete for the work,
upon terms not merely just, but munificent.   Each
competitor received, besides his expenses, a fair in-
demnity for his labor for one year.   The subject
proposed was the Sacrifice of Isaac, and at the end
of the year each artist was required to give in a
design, executed in bronze, of the same size as one
of the compartments of the old gate, that is, about
two feet square.

There were thirty-four judges, principally artists,
some natives of Florence, others strangers.   Each
was obliged to give his vote in public, and to state

---

* A Baptistery, as its name imports, is an edifice used for the
purposes of baptism, and always dedicated to St. John the Baptist.
The Baptistery of San Giovanni, at Florence, is a large chapel, of
an octangular form, surmounted by a dome.   On three of the sides
are entrances.   It is an appendage of the cathedral, though separate from it.

at the same time the reasons by which his vote was justified. The names of the seven competitors, as given by Vasari, were Jacopo della Quercia, of Siena; Nicolo d'Arezzo, his pupil; Simon da Colle, celebrated already for his fine workmanship in bronze, from which he was surnamed Simon *dei Bronzi;* Francesco di Valdambrina; Filippo Brunelleschi; Donato, better known as Donatello; and Lorenzo Ghiberti.

Lorenzo was at this time about twenty-three He was the son of a Florentine named Cione, and of a family which had attained to some distinction in Florence. The mother of Lorenzo, left a widow at an early age, married a worthy man named Bartoluccio, known for his skill as a goldsmith. The goldsmiths of those days were not merely *artisans*, but artists in the high sense of the word; they generally wrought their own designs, consisting of figures and subjects from sacred or classical story exquisitely chased in relief, or engraved or enamelled on the shrines or chalices used in the church service; or vases, dishes, sword-hilts, and other implements.

The arts of drawing and modelling, then essential to a goldsmith, as well as practical skill in chiselling, and founding and casting metals, were taught to the young Lorenzo by his father-in-law; and his progress was so rapid, that at the age of nineteen or twenty he had already secured to himself the patronage of the Prince Pandolfo Mala-

testa, Lord of Pesaro, and was employed in the decoration of his palace, when Bartoluccio sent him
notice of the terms of the competition for the execution of the gates of San Giovanni.   Lorenzo immediately hastened to present himself as one of the
competitors, and, on giving evidence of his acquired
skill, he was accepted among the elected seven
They had each their workshop and furnace apart,
and it is related that most of them jealously kept
their designs secret from the rest.   But Lorenzo,
who had all the modest self-assurance of conscious
genius, did not ; on the contrary, he listened grate-
fully to any suggestion or criticism which was
offered, admitting his friends and distinguished
strangers to his *atelier* while his work was going
forward.   To this candor he added a persevering
courage ; for when, after incredible labor, he had
completed his models, and made his preparations
for casting, some flaw or accident in the process
obliged him to begin all over again, he supplied
this loss of time by the most unremitting labor, and
at the end of the year he was not found behind his
competitors.   When the seven pieces were exhibited
together in public, it was adjudged that the work
of Quercia was wanting in delicacy and finish ;
that that of Valdambrina was confused in composition ; that of Simon da Colle well cast, but ill
drawn ; that of Nicolo d'Arezzo heavy and ill-pro-
portioned in the figures, though well composed : in
short, but three among the number united the vari

ous merits of composition, design, and delicacy of workmanship, and were at once preferred before the rest. These three were the work of Brunelleschi, then in his twenty-fifth year; Donatello, then about eighteen; and Lorenzo Ghiberti, not quite twenty-three. The suffrages seemed divided; but after a short pause, and the exchange of a few whispered words, Brunelleschi and Donatello withdrew, generously agreeing and proclaiming aloud that Lorenzo had excelled them all, that to him alone belonged the prize; and this judgment, as honorable to themselves as to their rival, was confirmed amid the acclamations of the assembly.

The citizens of Florence were probably not less desirous than we should be in our day to behold the completion of a work begun with so much solemnity. But the great artist who had undertaken it was not hurried into carelessness by their impatience or his own; nor did he contract to finish it, like a blacksmith's job, in a given time. He set about it with all due gravity and consideration, yet, as he describes his own feelings, in his own words, *con grandissima diligenza e grandissimo amore*, " with infinite diligence and infinite love." He began his designs and models in 1402, and in twenty-two years from that time, that is, in 1424, the gate was finished and erected in its place. As in the first gate Andrea Pisano had chosen for his theme the life of John the Baptist, the precursor of the Saviour, and the patron saint of the Baptistory, Lorenzo continued the history of the Redemption in a series of subjects, from the Annunciation to the Descent of the Holy Ghost. These he represented in twenty panels or compartments, ten on each of the folding-doors; and below these eight others, containing the full-length effigies of the four evangelists and the four doctors of the Latin church — grand, majestic figures; and all around a border of rich ornaments — fruit, and foliage, and heads of the prophets and the sibyls intermingled, wondrous for the beauty of the design and excellence of the workmanship. The whole was cast in bronze, and weighed thirty-four thousand pounds of metal.

Such was the glory which this great work conferred not only on Lorenzo himself, but the whole city of Florence, that he was regarded as a public benefactor, and shortly afterwards the same company confided to him the execution of the third gate of the same edifice. The gate of Andrea Pisano, formerly the principal entrance, was removed to the side, and Lorenzo was desired to construct a central gate which was to surpass the two lateral ones in beauty and richness. He chose this time the history of the Old Testament, the subjects being selected by Leonardo Bruni d'Arezzo, chancellor of the republic, and represented by Ghiberti in ten compartments, each two and a half feet square, beginning with the Creation, and ending with the Meeting of Solomon and the Queen of Sheba; and ho enclosed the whole in an elaborate border or frame, composed of intermingled fruits and foliage, and full-length figures of the heroes and prophets of the Old Testament, standing in niches, to the number of twenty-four, each about fourteen inches high, wonderful for their various and appropriate character, for correct, animated design, and delicacy of workmanship. This gate, of the same material and weight as the former, was commenced in 1428 and finished about 1444.*

It is especially worthy of remark that the only fault of these otherwise *faultless* works was precisely that character of style which rendered them so influential as a school of imitation and emulation for painters. The subjects are in sculpture, in relief and cast in the hardest, severest, darkest, and most inflexible of all manageable materials — in bronze. Yet they are treated throughout much more in accordance with the principles of painting than with those of sculpture. We have here groups of numerous figures, near or receding from the eye in just gradations of size and relief, according to the rules of perspective ; different actions of the same story represented on different planes ; buildings of elaborate architecture ; landscape, trees, and animals ; in short, a dramatic and scenic style of conception

---

* Authorities differ as to dates. Those cited above are from the notes to the last Florence edit. of Vasari (1838). See also Rumohr "Italienische Forschungen," vol. ii. ; and Cicognara, "Storia della Scultura Moderna."

and effect wholly opposed to the severe simplicity
of classical sculpture. Ghiberti's genius, notwithstanding the inflexible material in which he embodied his conceptions, was in its natural bent pictorial rather than sculptural ; and each panel of
his beautiful gates is, in fact, a picture in relief,
and must be considered and judged as such. Re-
garding them in this point of view, and not subject-
ing them to those rules of criticism which apply to
sculpture, we shall be able to appreciate the astonishing fertility of invention exhibited in the various
designs ; the felicity and clearness with which every
story is told ; the grace and naïveté of some of the
figures, the simple grandeur of others ; the luxuriant fancy displayed in the ornaments, and the perfection with which the whole is executed ; — and to
echo the energetic praise of Michael Angelo, who
pronounced these gates " *worthy to be the Gates of
Paradise !* "

Complete sets of casts from these celebrated compositions are not commonly met with, but they are
to be found in most of the collections and acade
mics on the continent. King Louis Philippe has
munificently presented a set to our government
School of Design, and they are now placed at the
upper end of the third room, and cemented together
with the surrounding frieze, so as to give a perfect
idea of the arrangement in the original gates.
Among the casts and models in the School of Design
at Somerset House is an exquisite little basso-rilievo,

representing the Triumph of Ariadne, so perfect, so pure, so classical in taste, that it might easily be mistaken for a fragment of the finest Greek sculpture.*   These are the only specimens of Ghiberti's skill to which the writer can refer as accessible in this country.

Engraved outlines of the subjects on the three gates were published at Florence in 1821, by G. P. Lasinio.†   There is also a large set of engravings from the ten subjects on the principal gate, executed in a good bold style by Thomas Patch, and published by him at Florence in 1771. ‡

Lorenzo Ghiberti died about the year 1455, at the age of seventy-seven.   His former competitors, Brunelleschi and Donatello, remained his friends through life, and have left behind them names not less celebrated, the one as an architect, the other as a sculptor.

This is the history of those famous gates,

" So marvellously wrought,
That they might serve to be the gates of Heaven ! "

---

* This cast (which formed part of the collection in the time of Mr. Tyco, the late director) was not to be found when the writer of this note visited the School of Design in 1845. It was designed to ornament a pedestal for an antique statue of Bacchus.

† " Le tre Porte del Battistero di San Giovanni di Firenze, incise ed illustrate."

‡ The bronze doors of the church De la Madeleine, at Paris, were executed, a few years ago, in imitation of the Gates of Ghiberti, by M. Henri de Triqueti, a young sculptor of singular merit and genius The subjects are the Ten Commandments.

MASACCIO.

It is easily conceivable that, during the **forty** years which Lorenzo Ghiberti devoted to his great work, and others on which he was employed at intervals, the assistance he required in completing his own designs, in drawing, modelling, casting, polishing, should have formed round him a school of young artists who worked and studied under his eye. The kind of work on which they were employed gave these young men great superiority in the knowledge of the human form, and in effects of relief, light and shade, &c. The application of the sciences of anatomy, mathematics, and geometry, to the arts of design, began to be more fully understood. This early school of painters was favorably distinguished above the later schools of Italy by a generous feeling of mutual aid, emulation, and admiration, among the youthful students, far removed from the detestable jealousies, the stabbings, poisonings, and conspiracies, which we read of in the seventeenth century. Among those who frequented the atelier of Lorenzo were Paolo Uccello, the first who applied geometry to the study of perspective; he attached himself to this pursuit with such unwearied assiduity, that it had nearly turned his brain, and it was for his use and that of Brunelleschi that Manetti, one of the earliest Greek scholars and mathematicians in modern Europe, translated the " Elements of Euclid ; " Maso Finiguerra, who invented the art of engraving on copper ; Pollajuolo, the first painter who studied anatomy by dissection, and who became the instructor of Michael Angelo ; and Masolino, who had been educated under Starnina, the best colorist of that time.

There was also a young boy, scarcely in his teens, who learned to draw and model by studying the works of Ghiberti, and who, though not considered as his disciple, after a while left all the regular pupils far behind him. He had come from a little village about eighteen miles from Florence, called San Giovanni, and of his parentage and early years little is recorded, and that little doubtful. His name was properly Tommaso Guido, or, from the place of his birth, Maso di San Giovanni ; but from his abstracted air, his utter indifference to the usual sports and pursuits of boyhood, his negligent dress and manners, his companions called him *Masaccio*, which might be translated *ugly* or *slovenly Tom*, and by this reproachful nickname one of the most illustrious of painters is now known throughout the world and to all succeeding generations. Masaccio was one of those rare and remarkable men whose vocation is determined beyond recall almost from infancy. He made his first essays as a child in his native village ; and in the house in which he was born they long preserved the effigy of an old woman spinning, which he had painted when a mere boy on the wall of his chamber, astonishing for its life-like truth. Coming to Florence when about thirteen, he studied (according to Vasari) under Masolino, who was then employed on the frescoes of the chapel of the Brancacci family, in the church of the Carmelites. Masolino died soon after, leaving his work unfinished ; but Masaccio still continued his studies, acquiring the principles of design under Ghiberti and Donatello, and the art of perspective under Brunelleschi. The passionate energy, and forgetfulness of all the common interests and pleasures of life, with which he pursued his favorite art, obtained him, at an early age, the notice of Cosmo de' Medici. Then intervened the civil troubles of the republic. Cosmo was banished ; and Masaccio left Florence to pursue his studies at Rome with the same ardor, and with all the advantages afforded by the remains of ancient art collected there.

While at Rome, Masaccio painted in the church of San Clemente a Crucifixion, and some scenes from the life of St. Catherine of Alexandria ; but, unhappily, these have been so coarsely painted over, that every vestige of Masaccio's hand has disappeared,—only the composition remains : and from the engravings which exist some idea may be formed of their beauty and simplicity.*

Cosmo de' Medici was recalled from banishment in 1433 ; and soon afterwards, probably through his patronage and influence, the completion of the chapel in the church of the Carmine, left unfinished by Masolino, was intrusted to Masaccio.

This chapel is on the right hand as you enter the church. It is in the form of a parallelogram, and three sides are covered with the frescoes, divided into twelve compartments, of which four are large and oblong, and the rest narrow and upright. All represent scenes from the life of St. Peter, except two, which are immediately on each side as you enter — the Fall, and the Expulsion of Adam and Eve from Paradise. Of the twelve compartments, two had been painted by Masolino previous to 1415 : the Preaching of St. Peter, one of the small compartments, and the St. Peter and St. John healing the Cripple, one of the largest. In this fresco are introduced two beautiful youths, or pages, in the dress of the patricians of Florence. Nothing can be more unaffectedly elegant. They would make us regret that the death of Masolino left another to complete his undertaking, had not that other been MASACCIO.

* In Ottley's " Early Italian School" there is an engraving of St Catherine disputing with the Heathen Philosophers. In Rosini are others. Both these works may be consulted in the British Museum.

Six of the compartments, two large and four small ones, were executed by Masaccio. These represent the Tribute Money; St. Peter raising a Youth to Life; Peter baptizing the Converts; Peter and John healing the Sick and Lame; the same Apostles distributing Alms; and the Expulsion of Adam and Eve from Paradise.

The scene represented in one of the compartments is one of the incidents in the apocryphal History of the Apostles. Simon the Magician challenged Peter and Paul to restore to life a dead youth, who is said to have been a kinsman or nephew of the Roman emperor. The sorcerer fails, of course. The Apostles resuscitate the youth, who kneels before them. The skull and bones near him represent the previous state of death. A crowd of spectators stand around beholding the miracle. All the figures are half the size of life, and quite wonderful for the truth of expression, the variety of character, the simple dignity of the forms and attitudes. Masaccio died while at work on this grand picture, and the central group was painted some years later by Filippino Lippi. The figure of the youth in the centre is traditionally said to be that of the painter Granacci, then a boy. Among the figures standing round are several contemporary portraits: Piero Guicciardini, father of the great historian; Luigi Pulci, the poet, author of the "Morgante Maggiore;" Pollajuolo, the painter, Michael Angelo's master, and others.

The portrait of Masaccio usually given is fr)n the head introduced into the fresco of the two Apostles before Nero — the finest of all, and tho chef-d'œuvre of the painter. It appears that the grand figure of St. Paul standing before the Prison of St. Peter, which Raphael transferred with little alteration into his Cartoon of St. Paul preaching at Athens, is now attributed to Filippino Lippi.* The four remaining compartments were added many years later (about 1470), by the same Filippino Lippi, who seems to have been inspired by the greatness of his predecessors.

But to return to Masaccio. In considering his works, their superiority over all that painting had till then achieved or attempted is such, and so sur- prising, that there seems a kind of break in the progression of the art — as if Masaccio had over leaped suddenly the limits which his predecessors had found impassable ; but Ghiberti and his Gates explain the seeming wonder. The chief excellences of Masaccio were those which he had attained, or at least conceived, in his early studies in modelling. He had learned from Ghiberti not merely the knowl- edge of form, but the effects of light and shade in giving relief and roundness to his figures, which, in

* See Mr. Eastlake's notes to Kugler's "Handbuch." "Some writers on art seem to have attributed all these frescoes indiscrimi- nately to Masaccio ; others have considered only the best portions to be his ; the accuracy of German investigation has perhaps finally settled the distribution as above." (P. 108.)

comparison to those of his predecessors, seemed to start from the canvas. He was the first who successfully foreshortened the extremities. In most of the older pictures the figures appeared to stand on the points of their toes (as in the Angel of Orcagna); the foreshortening of the foot, though often attempted with more or less success, seemed to present insurmountable difficulties. (Masaccio added a precision in the drawing of the naked figure, and a softness and harmony in coloring the flesh, never attained before his time, nor since surpassed till the days of Raphael and Titian. He excelled also in the expression and imitation of natural actions and feelings. In the fresco of St. Peter baptizing the Converts there is a youth who has just thrown off his garment, and stands in the attitude of one shivering with sudden cold. "This figure," says Lanzi, "formed an epoch in art." Add the animation and variety of character in his heads — so that it was said of him that he painted souls as well as bodies — and his free-flowing draperies, quite different from the longitudinal folds of the Giotto school, yet grand and simple, and we can form some idea of the combination of excellence with novelty of style which astonished his contemporaries. The Chapel of the Brancacci was for half a century what the Camere of Raphael in the Vatican have since become — a school for young artists. Vasari enumerates by name twenty painters who were accustomed to study there ; among them, Le-

onardo da Vinci, Michael Angelo, Andrea del Sarto,
Fra Bartolomeo, Perugino, Baccio Bandinelli, and
the divine Raphael himself. Nothing less than first-
rate genius ever yet inspired genius ; and the Chapel
of the Brancacci has been rendered as sacred and
memorable by its association with such spirits, as it
is precious and wondrous as a monument of art :

> " In this Chapel wrought
> One of the Few, Nature's interpreters ;
> The Few, whom Genius gives as lights to shine —
> MASACCIO ; and he slumbers underneath.
> Wouldst thou behold his monument ? Look round,
> And know that where we stand stood oft and long,
> Oft till the day was gone, Raphael himself,
> He and his haughty rival * — patiently,
> Humbly, to learn of those who came before,
> To steal a spark of their authentic fire,
> Theirs who first broke the universal gloom —
> Sons of the morning !" — *Rogers.*

It is strange that so little should be known of
Masaccio's history — that he should have passed
through life so little noted, so little thought of :
scarce any record remaining of him but his works,
and those so few, and yet so magnificent, that one
of his heads alone would have been sufficient to immortalize him, and to justify the enthusiasm of his
compeers in art. We are told that he died suddenly, so suddenly that there were suspicions of
poison ; and that he was buried within the precincts

* Michael Angelo.

of the chapel he had adorned, but without tomb or inscription. There is not a more vexed question in biography than the date of Masaccio's birth and death. According to Rosini, the most accurate of modern writers on art, he was born in 1417, and died in 1443, at the age of twenty-six. Vasari also says expressly that he died before he was twenty-seven; in that case he could not have been, as the same writer represents him, the pupil of Masolino, who died in 1415. According to other authorities, he was born in 1401, and died at the age of forty-two. It seems most probable that, if he had lived to such a mature age, something more would have been known of his life and habits, and he would have left more behind him. His death at the age of twenty-six renders clear and credible many facts and dates otherwise inexplicable; and as to his early attainment of the most wonderful skill in art, we may recollect several other examples of precocious excellence; for instance, Ghiberti, already mentioned, and Raphael, who was called to Rome to paint the Vatican in his twenty-seventh year. The head of Masaccio, painted by himself, in the Chapel of the Brancacci, at most two years before his death, represents him as a young man apparently about four or five and twenty.

FILIPPO LIPPI,

Born 1400, died 1469;

AND

ANGELICO DA FIESOLE,

Born 1387, died 1455.

CONTEMPORARY with Masaccio lived two painters, both gifted with surpassing genius, both of a religious order, being professed monks; in all other respects the very antipodes of each other; and we find the very opposite impulses given by these remarkable men prevailing through the rest of the century at Florence and elsewhere. From this period we date the great schism in modern art, though the seeds of this diversity of feeling and purpose were sown in the preceding century. We now find, on the one side, a race of painters who cultivated with astonishing success all the mental and mechanical aids that could be brought to bear on their profession; profoundly versed in the knowledge of the human form, and intent on studying and imitating the various effects of nature in color and in light and shade, without any other aspiration than the representation of beauty for its own sake and the pleasure and the triumph of difficulties over-

rome : cn the other hand, we find a race of painters
to whom the cultivation of art was a sacred vocation
—the representation of beauty a means, not an end;
by whom Nature in her various aspects was studied
and deeply studied, but only for the purpose of embodying whatever we can conceive or reverence as
highest, holiest, purest in heaven and earth, in such
forms as should best connect them with our intelligence and with our sympathies.

The two classes of painters who devoted their
genius to these very diverse aims have long been
distinguished in German and Italian criticism as the
Naturalists and the *Idealists* or *Mystics*, and these
denominations are now becoming familiarized in our
own language. During the fifteenth century we find
in the various schools of art scattered through Italy
these different aims more or less apparent, sometimes
approximating, sometimes diverging into extremes,
but the distinction always apparent ; and the influence exercised by those who pursued their art with
such very different objects — with such very different feelings — was of course different in its result
Painting, however, during this century was still
almost wholly devoted to ecclesiastical purposes , it
deviated into the classical and secular in only two
places, Florence and Padua.

In the convent of the Carmelites, where Masaccio
has painted his famous frescoes, was a young monk
who, instead of employing himself in the holy offices
passed whole days and hours gazing on those works

and trying to imitate them. He was one whom poverty had driven, as a child, to take refuge there, and who had afterwards taken the habit from necessity rather than from inclination. His name was Filippo Lippi (which may be translated Philip the son of Philip), but he is known in the history of art as Fra Filippo (Friar Philip). In him, as in Masaccio, the bent of the genius was early decided ; nature had made him a painter. He studied from morning to night the models he had before him ; but, restless, ardent, and abandoned to the pursuit of pleasure, he at length broke from the convent and escaped to Ancona. The rest of his life is a romance. On an excursion to sea he was taken by the African pirates, sold as a slave in Barbary, and remained in captivity eighteen months. With a piece of charcoal he drew his master's picture on a wall, and so excited his admiration that he gave him his freedom, and dismissed him with presents. Fra Filippo then returned to Italy, and at Naples and at Rome gained so much celebrity by the beauty of his performances, that his crime as a runaway monk was overlooked, and, under the patronage of the Medici family, he ventured to return to Florence. There he painted a great number of admirable pictures, and was called upon to decorate many convents and churches in the neighborhood. His life during all this time appears to have been most scandalous, even without consideration of his religious habit ; and the sums of money he obtained by the practice of his art were squandered in profligate pleasures. Being called upon to paint a Madonna for the convent of St. Margaret at Prato, he persuaded the sisterhood to allow a beautiful novice, whose name was Lucretia Buti, to sit to him for a model. In the end he seduced this girl, and carried her off from the convent, to the great scandal of the community, and the inexpressible grief and horror of her father and family. Filippo was then an old man, nearly sixty; but for his great fame and the powerful protection of the Medici, he would have paid dearly for this offence against morals and religion. His friends Cosmo and Lorenzo de' Medici obtained from the pope a dispensation from his vows, to enable him to marry Lucretia; but he does not seem to have been in any haste to avail himself of it; the family of the girl, unable to obtain any public reparation for their dishonor, contrived to avenge it secretly, and Fra Filippo died poisoned, at the age of sixty-nine.

This libertine monk was undoubtedly a man of extraordinary genius, but his talent was degraded by his immorality. He adopted and carried on all the improvements of Masaccio, and was the first who invented that particular style of grandeur and breadth in the drawing of his figures, the grouping, and the contrast of light and shade, afterwards carried to such perfection by Andrea del Sarto. He was one of the earliest painters who introduced landscape backgrounds, painted with some feeling for the truth of nature; but the expression he gave to his personages, though always energetic was often inappropriate, and never calm or elevated. In the representation of sacred incidents he was sometimes fantastic and sometimes vulgar ; and he was the first who desecrated such subjects by introducing the portraits of women who happened to be the objects of his preference at the moment. There are many pictures by Fra Filippo in the churches at Florence ; two in the gallery of the Academy there five in the Berlin Museum : in the Louvre there is one undoubtedly genuine, and of great beauty, marked by all his characteristics. It represents the Madonna standing, and holding the Infant Saviour in her arms ; on each side are angels and a kneeling monk. The attitude of the Virgin is grand ; the head commonplace, or worse ; the countenance of the Infant Christ heavy ; the angels, with crisped hair, have the faces of street urchins ; but the adoring monks are wonderful for the natural dignity of their figures and the fine expression in their upturned faces, and the whole picture is most admirably executed. It was painted for the church of the Santo Spirito, at Florence, and is a celebrated production. The writer does not know of any picture by Fra Filippo now in England. He left a son, Flippo Lippi, called Filippino (to distinguish him from his father), who became in after years an excellent painter, and whose frescoes in the Chapel of the Brancacci, which emulated those of Masaccio have been already mentioned.

Contemporary with Fra Filippo, or rather earlier in point of date, lived the other painter-monk, presenting in his life and character the strongest possible contrast to the former. He was, as Vasari tells us, one who might have lived a very agreeable life in the world, had he not, impelled by a sincere and fervent spirit of devotion, retired from it at the age of twenty to bury himself within the walls of a cloister; a man with whom the practice of a beautiful art was thenceforth a hymn of praise, and every creation of his pencil an act of piety and charity, and who, in seeking only the glory of God, earned an immortal glory among men. This was Fra Giovanni Angelico da Fiesole, whose name, before he entered the convent, was Guido Petri de Mugello.* He has since obtained, from the holiness of his life, the title of *Il Beato*, " the Blessed," by which he is often mentioned in Italian histories of art. He was born in 1387, at Fiesole, a beautiful town situated on a hill overlooking Florence and in 1407, being then twenty, and already skilled in the art of painting, particularly miniature illuminations of Missals and choral-books, he entered the Dominican convent of St. Mark, at Florence, and took the habit of the order. It is not known exactly under whom he studied; but he is said to have been taught by Starnina, the best colorist of that time. The rest of his long life of seventy years presents only one unbroken tranquil stream of placid

* Notes to the last Florence edition of Vasari, p. 303.

contentment and pious labors. Except on one oc
casion, when called to Rome by Pope Nicholas V.
to paint in the Vatican, he never left his convent,
and then only yielded to the express command of
the pontiff. While he was at Rome the Arch
bishopric of Florence became vacant, and the pope,
struck by the virtue and learning of Angelico, and
the simplicity and sanctity of his life, offered to
install him in that dignity, one of the greatest in
the power of the papal see to bestow. Angelico
refused it from excess of modesty, pointing out
at the same time to the notice of the pope a brother
of his convent as much more worthy of the honor,
and by his active talents more fitted for the office.
The pope listened to his recommendation ; Frate
Antonio was raised to the see, and became celebrated as the best Archbishop of Florence that had
been known for two centuries. Meantime Angelico
pursued his vocation in the still precincts of his
quiet monastery, and, being as assiduous as he was
devout, he painted a great number of pictures.
some in distemper and on a small scale, to which he
gave all the delicacy and finish of miniature ; and
in the churches of Florence many large frescoes
with numerous figures nearly life-size, as full of
grandeur as of beauty. He painted only sacred
subjects, and never for money. Those who wished
for any work of his hand were obliged to apply to
the prior of the convent, from whom Angelico received with humility the order or the permission to

execute it, and thus the brotherhood was at once
enriched by his talent and edified by his virtue. To
Angelico the art of painting a picture devoted to
religious purposes was an act of religion, for which
he prepared himself by fasting and prayer, implor-
ing on bended knees the benediction of heaven on
his work. He then, under the impression that he
had obtained the blessing he sought, and glowing
with what might truly be called inspiration, took
up his pencil, and, mingling with his earnest and
pious humility a singular species of self-uplifted
enthusiasm, he could never be persuaded to alter
his first draught or composition, believing that
which he had done was according to the will of
God, and could not be changed for the better by
any afterthought of his own or suggestion from
others. All the works left by Angelico are in harmony with this gentle, devout, enthusiastic spirit.
They are not remarkable for the usual merits of the
Florentine school. They are not addressed to the
taste of connoisseurs, but to the faith of worship-
pers. Correct drawing of the human figure could
not be expected from one who regarded the exhibi-
tion of the undraped form as a sin. In the learned
distribution of light and shade, in the careful imitation of nature in the details, and in variety of
expression, many of his contemporaries excelled
him ; but none approached him in that poetical and
religious fervor which he threw into his heads of
saints and Madonnas. Power is not the character

istic of Angelico.   Wherever he has had to express
energy of action, or bad or angry passions, he has
generally failed.   In his pictures of the Crucifixion
and the Stoning of St. Stephen, the executioners
and the rabble are feeble and often ill-drawn, and
his fallen angels and devils are anything but devil-
ish ; while, on the other hand, the pathos of suffering, of pity, of divine resignation — the expression of ecstatic faith and hope, or serene contemplation — have never been placed before us as in his
pictures.   In the heads of his young angels, in the
purity and beatitude of his female saints, he has
never been excelled — not even by Raphael.

The principal works of Angelico are the frescoes
in the church of his own convent of St. Mark, at
Florence, in the church of Santa Maria Novella,
and at Rome in the chapel of Nicholas V., in the
Vatican.   His small easel pictures are numerous,
and to be found in most of the foreign collections,
though unhappily the writer can point out none
that are accessible in England.   There is one in the
Louvre, of surpassing beauty.   The subject is the
Coronation of the Virgin Mary by her Son the Redeemer, in the presence of saints and angels.   It
represents a throne under a rich Gothic canopy, to
which there is an ascent by nine steps.   On the
highest kneels the Virgin, veiled, her hands crossed
on her bosom.   She is clothed in a red tunic, a blue
robe over it, and a royal mantle with a rich border
flowing down behind.   The features are most deli-

cately lovely, and the expression of the face full of humility and adoration. Christ, seated on the throne, bends forward, and is in the act of placing the crown on her head. On each side are twelve angels, who are playing a heavenly concert with guitars, tambourines, trumpets, viols, and other musical instruments. Lower than these, on each side, are forty holy personages of the Old and New Testament; and at the foot of the throne kneel several saints, male and female, among them St. Catherine with her wheel, St. Agnes with her lamb, and St. Cecilia crowned with flowers. Beneath the principal picture there is a row of seven small ones, forming a border, and representing various incidents in the life of St. Dominic. The whole measures about seven and a half feet high by six feet in width. It is painted in distemper; the glories round the heads of the sacred personages are in gold, the colors are the most delicate and vivid imaginable, and the ample draperies have the long folds which recall the school of Giotto; the gayety and harmony of the tints, the expression of the various heads, the divine rapture of the angels, with their air of immortal youth, and the devout reverence of the other personages, the unspeakable serenity and beauty of the whole composition, render this picture worthy of the celebrity it has enjoyed for more than four centuries. It was painted by Frate Angelico for the church of St. Dominic, at Fiesole where it remained till the beginning of the present century. How obtained it does not appear, but it was purchased by the French government in 1812, and exhibited for the first time in the long gallery of the Louvre in 1815. It is now placed in the gallery of drawings at the upper end. A very good set of outlines were engraved and published at Paris, with explanatory notes by A. W. Schlegel; and to those who have no opportunity of seeing the original these would convey some faint idea of the composition, and of the exquisite and benign beauty of the angelic heads.

It is a curious circumstance that the key of the chapel of Pope Nicholas V., in the Vatican, in which Angelico painted some of his most beautiful frescoes, was for two centuries lost, and few persons were aware of their existence, fewer still set any value on them. In 1769 those who wished to see them were obliged to enter by a window.

Fra Giovanni Angelico da Fiesole died at Rome, in 1455, and is buried there in the church of Santa Maria sopra Minerva.

BENOZZO GOZZOLI.

Born 1406, died 1478.

FRA GIOVANNI ANGELICO possessed, among his
other amiable qualities, one true characteristic of
a generous mind, the willingness to impart whatever he knew to others ; and, notwithstanding the
retirement in which he lived, he had several pupils.
But that which formed the principal charm and
merit of his productions, the impress of individual
mind, the profound sentiment of piety, was incom-
municable except to a kindred spirit. Hence it is
that this influence, like the prophetic mantle, fell
on those who had the power to catch it and retain
it, and is more apparent in its general results, as
seen in the schools of Umbria and Venice, than in
any particular painter or any particular work.
Cosimo Roselli, a very distinguished artist of that
time, is supposed to have studied under Angelico,
and certainly began by imitating his manner.
Afterwards he painted like Masaccio. His best
work, a large fresco in the chapel of St. Ambrogio,
at Florence, is engraved in Lasinio's collection
from the old Florentine masters. It was executed
about 1456. A much more celebrated name is that
of BENOZZO GOZZOLI.

(95)

We know very little of the life of this extraordi
nary man ; but that little shows him to have beer
worthy of the particular love of his master, whose
favorite pupil and companion he was, and, during
the last years of Angelico's life, his assistant. According to Vasari, Benozzo was an excellent man,
and a good and pious Christian, but he had no vocation for the cloister. No painter of the time had
such a lively sense of all the beauty and variety of
the external and material world. For him beauty
existed wherever he looked — wherever he moved
He took such delight in the practice of his art, that
he had little time for other pursuits. He succeeded
to the popularity of Angelico as a painter of sacred
subjects, into which he introduced much more ornament, decorating them with landscapes, buildings,
animals, &c. It appears that he did not design the
figure more correctly than Angelico, nor equal him
in the profound feeling and celestial air of his
heads ; but he has shown more invention and
variety in his compositions, and mingled with his
grace a certain gayety of conception, a degree of
movement and dramatic feeling, which are not seen
in the works of Angelico.

Benozzo, before the death of his master, painted
some frescoes in the cathedral at Orvieto, and in
the churches of the little town of Montefalco, near
Foligno, and also at Rome, in the church of the
Ara-celi. The former remain, but those in the
Ara-celi have long since been destroyed. All these

were more or less in the style of his master. After
the death of Angelico, Benozzo was employed to
paint the church at San Geminiano, a little city on
the road from Florence to Sienna ; and here some
of his own peculiar characteristics were first displayed ; here he painted the Death of St. Sebastian, and the history of St. Augustin ; and for
Pietro de' Medici he painted a chapel in the palace
of the Medici (now the Palazzo Ricardi, at Flor·
ence), the subject being the Adoration of the Magi,
which still exists in the Ricardi Palace, but so
built up that it can only be viewed by torch-light.
In all the paintings he executed at this time
(1460) and afterwards, Benozzo introduced many
figures, generally the portraits of distinguished
inhabitants of the place, or those of his friends,
grouped as spectators round the principal incident
or personage represented, having nothing to do
with the action, but so beautifully managed that,
far from appearing intrusive, they rather add to
the solemnity and the poetry of the scene, as if he
would fain represent these sacred events as belonging to all times, and still, as it were, passing before
our eyes. This observation must be borne in mind
as generally applicable to all sacred pictures, in
which the apparent anachronisms are not really
such, if properly considered. Benozzo carried this
and other characteristics of his own original style
still further in his greatest work, the decoration of
the Campo Santo

When the troubles of war, famine, plague, and intestine divisions, which had distracted Pisa during the first half of the fifteenth century, had subsided, the citizens of that rich and active republic resumed those works of peace which had been interrupted for nearly a century, and resolved to complete the painting of their far-famed cemetery, the Campo Santo. One whole side, the north wall, was yet untouched. They intrusted the work to Benozzo Gozzoli, who, though now old (upwards of sixty, and worn with toil and trouble), did not hesitate to undertake a task which, to use Vasari's strong expression, was nothing less than "*terribilissima*," and enough "to frighten a whole legion of painters." In twenty-four compartments he represented the whole history of the Old Testament, from Noah down to King Solomon. The endless fertility of fancy and invention displayed in these compositions; the pastoral beauty of some of the scenes, the scriptural sublimity of others; the hundreds of figures introduced, many of them portraits of his own time; the dignity and beauty of the heads; the exquisite grace of some of the figures, almost equal to Raphael; the ample draperies, the gay, rich colors, the profusion of accessories, as buildings, landscapes, flowers, animals, and the care and exactness with which he has rendered the costume of that time — render this work of Benozzo one of the most extraordinary monuments of the fifteenth century. But it would have been more than extraordinary, it would have been *miraculous*, had it been executed in the space of two years, as Lanzi relates — trusting to a popular tradition, which a moment's reflection would have shown to be incredible. It appears, from authentic records still existing in the city of Pisa, that Benozzo was engaged on this great work not less than sixteen years, from 1458 to 1484.

Those who would form an idea of its immensity, considered as the work of one hand, may consult the large set of engravings from the Campo Santo, published by Lasinio in 1821.

The original frescoes are still in wonderful preservation. Three out of the twenty-four are almost entirely destroyed; the others have peeled off in some parts, but in general the expression of the features and the lucid harmony of the colors have remained. Each compartment contains many incidents and events artlessly grouped together. Thus we have Hagar's presumption, her castigation by Sarah, the visit of the three angels, &c., in one picture. Among the most beautiful subjects may be mentioned the Vineyard of Noah, the first which Benozzo painted, as a trial of his skill. On the left of this composition are two female figures — one who comes tripping along with a basket of grapes on her head, the other holding up her basket for more — which are perfect models of pastoral grace and simplicity. In the Building of the Tower of Babel, a crowd of spectators have assem-

bled to witness the work; among them are introduced the figures of Cosmo de' Medici, the Father
of his country, and his two grandsons, Lorenzo
and Giuliano, with Poliziano and other person
ages, all in the costume of that time. In the
Marriage Feast of Jacob and Rachel he has introduced two graceful dancing figures. In the
Recognition of Joseph he has painted a profusion
of rich architectural decoration — palaces, colon-
nades, balconies, and porticoes, in the style of the
time; and in the distance we have, instead of
the Egyptian Pyramids, a view of the Cathedral
of Pisa!

Soon after the completion of the last compartment, the Queen of Sheba's visit to Solomon (of
which, unhappily, scarce a fragment remains), Benozzo Gozzoli died, at Pisa, in his seventy-eighth
year. The grateful and admiring Pisans, among
whom he had resided for sixteen years in great
honor and esteem, had presented him, in the course
of his work, with a vault or sepulchre just beneath
the compartment which contains the history of
Joseph; and in this spot he lies buried, with an
inscription purporting that his best monument
consists in the works around. Benozzo left an
only daughter, who after his death inherited the
modest little dwelling which he had purchased for
himself on the Carraia di San Francesco.

Benozzo's principal works, being in fresco, re
main attached to the walls on which they were

painted. Those only of the Campo Santo are engraved. A picture in distemper of St. Thomas Aquinas is in the Louvre (No. 1033), and is the same mentioned by Vasari as having been painted for the Cathedral of Pisa.

ANDREA CASTAGNO,

Born 1403, died 1477;

AND

LUCA SIGNORELLI,

Born 1440, died 1521.

Towards the close of the fifteenth century, we find Lorenzo de' Medici, *the Magnificent*, master of the Florentine republic, as it was still denominated, though now under the almost absolute power of one man. The mystic and spiritual school of Angelico and his followers no longer found admirers in the city of Florence, where the study of classical literature, and the enthusiastic admiration of the Medici for antique art, led to the cultivation and development of a style wholly different; the paint ers, instead of confining themselves to scriptural events and characters, began at this time to take their subjects from mythology and classical history. Meantime, the progress made in the knowledge of form, the use of colors, and all the technical appliances of the art, prepared the way for the appear·ance of those great masters who in the succeeding century carried painting in all its departments to the highest perfection, and have never yet been surpassed.

(102)

About 1460, a certain Neapolitan painter, named Antonello da Messina, having travelled into the Netherlands, learned there from Johan v. Eyk and his scholars the art of managing oil-colors. Being at Venice on his return, he communicated the secret to a Venetian painter, Domenico Veneziano, with whom he had formed a friendship, and who, having acquired considerable reputation, was called to Florence to assist Andrea di Castagno in painting a chapel in Santa Maria Novella. Andrea, who had been a scholar of Masaccio, was one of the most famous painters of the time, and a favorite of the Medici family. On the occasion of the conspiracy of the Pazzi, when the Archbishop of Pisa and his confederates were hung by the magistrates from the windows of the palace, Andrea was called upon to represent, on the walls of the Podestà, this terrible execution — "fit subject for fit hand;" and he succeeded so well, that he obtained the surname of Andrea *degl' Impiccati*, which may be translated Andrea *the hangman*. He afterwards earned a yet more infamous designation — Andrea *the assassin*. Envious of the reputation which Domenico had acquired by the beauty and brilliance of his colors, he first, by a show of the most devoted friendship, obtained his secret, and then seized the opportunity when he accompanied Domenico one night to serenade his mistress, and stabbed him to the heart. He contrived to escape suspicion, and allowed one or two innocent persons to suffer for his crime; but on his death-bed, ten years afterwards, he confessed his guilt, and has been consigned to merited infamy. Very few works of this painter remain. Four are in the Berlin Museum; they are much praised by Lanzi, but, however great their merit, it is difficult to get rid of the associations of disgust and horror connected with the character of the man. It is remarkable that none of his remaining pictures are painted in oil-colors, but all are in distemper, as if he had feared to avail himself of the secret acquired by such flagitious means, and the knowledge of which, though not the practice, became general before his death.

In the year 1471 Sixtus IV. became pope. Though by no means endued with a taste for art, he resolved to emulate the Medici family, whose example and patronage had diffused the fashion, if not the feeling, throughout all Italy; and having built that beautiful chapel in the Vatican called by his name, and since celebrated as the *Sistine* Chapel, the next thing was to decorate it with appropriate paintings. On one side of it was to be represented the history of Moses; on the other, the history of Christ; the old law and the new law, the Hebrew and the Christian dispensation, thus placed in contrast and illustrating each other. As there were no distinguished painters at that time in Rome, Sixtus invited from Florence those of the Tuscan artists who had the greatest reputation in their native country. The first of these was Sandro (that is, Alessandro) Bot-ticelli, remarkable for being one of the earliest

painters who treated mythological subjects on a
small scale as decorations for furniture, and the
first who made drawings for the purpose of being
engraved. These, as well as his religious pictures,
he treated in a fanciful, capricious style. Six of
his pictures are in the Museum at Berlin — one an
undraped Venus; and two are in the Louvre. Sandro was a pupil of the monk Fra Filippo already
mentioned, and after his death took charge of his
young son Filippino Lippi, who excelled both his
father and his preceptor, and became one of the
greatest painters of his time.* Another painter
employed by Pope Sixtus was LUCA SIGNORELLI, of
Cortona, the first who not only drew the human
form with admirable correctness, but, aided by a
degree of anatomical knowledge rare in those days,
threw such spirit and expression into the various
attitudes of his figures, that his great work, the
frescoes of the Cathedral of Orvieto, representing
the Last Judgment, were studied and even imitated
by Michael Angelo. This painter was apparently
a favorite of Fuseli, whose compositions frequently
remind us of the long limbs and animated, but
sometimes exaggerated, action of Signorelli.

* He completed the frescoes in the Chapel of the Carmine at
Florence, left unfinished by Masaccio, as already related at page
79.

DOMENICO DAL GHIRLANDAJO.

Born 1451, died 1495.

Domenico dal Ghirlandajo was also employed in the Sistine Chapel, but he was then young, and of his two pictures there one only remains, the Calling of St. Peter and St. Andrew, — so inferior to his later productions, that we do not recognize here the hand of him who became afterwards one of the greatest and most memorable painters of his time.

Domenico Corradi, or Bigordi, was born at Florence in 1451, and was educated by his father for his own profession, that of a goldsmith. In this art he acquired great skill and displayed in his designs uncommon elegance of fancy. He was the first who invented the silver ornaments in the form of a wreath or garland (*Ghirlanda*) which became a fashion with the Florentine women, and from which he obtained the name of Ghirlandajo, or *Grillandajo*, as it is sometimes written. At the age of four-and-twenty he quitted the profession of goldsmith, and became a painter. While employed in his father's workshop he had amused himself with taking the likenesses of all the persons he saw

(106)

so rapidly, and with so much liveliness and truth, as to astonish every one. The exact drawing and modelling of forms, the inventive fancy exercised in his mechanical art, and the turn for portraiture, are displayed in all his subsequent productions These were so many in number, so various in subject, and so admirable, that only a few of them can be noticed here. After he returned from Rome his first work was the painting of a chapel of the Vespucci family, in the church of Ognissanti (All Saints), in which he introduced, in 1485, the portrait of Amerigo Vespuccio the navigator, who afterwards gave his name to a new world.

Ghirlandajo painted a chapel for a certain Florentine citizen, Francesco Sassetti, in the church of the Trinità. Here he represented the whole life of Francesco's patron saint, St. Francis, in a series of pictures, full of feeling and dramatic power. As he was confined to the popular histories and traditions, which had been treated again and again by successive painters, and in which it was necessary to conform to certain fixed and prescribed rules, it was difficult to introduce any variety in the conception. Yet he has done this simply by the mere force of expression. The most excellent of these frescoes is the Death of St. Francis, surrounded by the monks of his order, in which the aged heads, full of grief, awe, resignation, are depicted with wonderful skill. At the foot of the bier is an old bishop chanting the litanies, with spectacles on his nose, which is the earliest known representation of these implements, then recently invented. On one side of the picture is the kneeling figure of Francesco Sassetti, and on the other Madonna Nera, his wife. All these histories of St. Francis are engraved in Lasinio's " Early Florentine Masters," as are also the magnificent frescoes in the choir of Santa Maria Novella, his greatest work. This he undertook for a generous and public-spirited citizen of Florence, Giovanni Tornabuoni, who agreed to repair the choir at his own cost, and, moreover, to pay Ghirlandajo one thousand two hundred gold ducats for painting the walls in fresco, and to add two hundred more if he were well satisfied with the performance.

Ghirlandajo devoted four years to his task. He painted on the right-hand wall the history of St. John the Baptist, and on the left various incidents from the life of the Virgin. One of the most beautiful represents the Birth of the Virgin. Female attendants, charming graceful figures, are aiding the mother or intent on the new-born child ; while a lady, in the elegant costume of the Florentine ladies of that time, and holding a handkerchief in her hand, is seen advancing, as if to pay her visit of congratulation. This is the portrait of Ginevra de' Benci, one of the loveliest women of the time. He has introduced her again as one of the attendants in the Visit of the Virgin to St. Elizabeth. In the other pictures he has introduced the figures of

Lorenzo de' Medici, Poliziano, Demetrio Greco, Marsilio Ficino, and other celebrated persons (of whom there are notices in Roscoe's "Life of Lorenzo de' Medici"), besides his own portrait, and those of many other persons of that time.

The idea of crowding these sacred and mystical subjects with portraits of real persons and representations of familiar objects may seem, on first view, shocking to the taste, ridiculous anachronisms, and destructive of all solemnity and unity of feeling. Such, however, is not the case, but the reverse. In the first place, the sacred and ideal personages are never portraits from nature, and are very loftily conceived in point of expression and significance. In the second place, the *real* personages introduced are seldom or never actors, merely attendants and spectators in events which may be conceived to belong to all time, and to have no especial locality ; and they have so much dignity in their aspects, the costumes are so picturesque, and the grouping is so fine and imaginative, that only the coldest and most pedantic critic could wish them absent.

When Ghirlandajo had finished this grand series of pictures, his patron, Giovanni Tornabuoni, declared himself well pleased ; but, at the same time, expressed a wish that Ghirlandajo would be content with the sum first stipulated, and forego the additional two hundred ducats. The high-minded painter, who esteemed glory and honor much more than riches, immediately withdrew his claim, saying that he cared far more to have satisfied his employer than for any amount of payment.

Besides his frescoes, Ghirlandajo painted many easel pictures in oil and in distemper. There is one of great beauty in the Louvre — the Visitation (1022), about four feet in height. But the subject he most frequently repeated was the Adoration of the Magi. In the Florence Gallery are two pictures of this subject; another of a circular form, which had been painted for the Tornabuoni family, was in the collection of Lucien Bonaparte. In the Munich Gallery there is one picture by Ghirlandajo, and in the Museum at Berlin there are six; one of them a beautiful portrait of a young girl of the Tornabuoni family, whom he has also introduced into his frescoes.

It may be said, on the whole, that the attention of Ghirlandajo was directed less to the delineation of form than to the expression of his heads, and the imitation of life and nature as exhibited in feature and countenance. He also carried the mechanical and technical part of his art to a perfection it had not before attained. He was the best colorist in fresco who had yet appeared, and his colors have stood extremely well to this day.

Another characteristic which renders Ghirlandajo very interesting as an artist was his diligent and progressive improvement; every successive production was better than the last. He was also an

excellent worker in mosaic, which, from its dura
bility, he used to call "*painting for eternity.*"

To his rare and various accomplishments as an
artist, Ghirlandajo added the most amiable qualities as a man, — qualities which obtained him the
love as well as the admiration of his fellow-citizens.
He was, says Vasari, " the delight of the age in
which he lived."   He was still in the prime of life
and in the full possession of conscious power, — so
that he was heard to wish they would give him the
walls all round the city to cover with frescoes, —
when he was seized with sudden illness, and died,
at the age of forty-four, to the infinite grief of his
numerous scholars, by whom he was interred, with
every demonstration of mournful respect, in the
church of Santa Maria Novella, in the year 1495.
His two brothers, Davide and Benedetto, were also
painters, and assisted him in the execution of his
great works; and his son, Ridolfo Ghirlandajo,
became afterwards an excellent artist, but he belongs to a later period.

Ghirlandajo formed many scholars; among them
was the great Michael Angelo. Contemporary with
Ghirlandajo lived an artist, memorable for having
aided with his instructions both Michael Angelo and
Lionardo da Vinci. This was Andrea Verrocchio
(born 1432, died 1488), who was a goldsmith, and
sculptor in marble and bronze, and also a painter,
though in painting his works are few and little
known. He drew admirably, and is celebrated

through the celebrity of the artists formed in his school. Among them was Lionardo da Vinci. He is said to have been the first who took casts in plaster from life as aids in the study of form. In the collection of Miss Rogers, the sister of the poet, there is a portrait in profile, by Verrocchio, of a Florentine lady of rank, rather hard and severe in the execution and drawing, yet with a certain simple elegance — a look of high breeding — which is very striking.

ANDREA MANTEGNA.

For a while we must leave beautiful Florence and
her painters, who were striving after perfection by
imitating what they saw in nature, — the common
appearances of the objects, animate and inanimate,
around them, — and turn to another part of Italy,
where there arose a man of genius who pursued a
wholly different course ; at least, he started from a
different point ; and who exercised for a time a great
influence on all the painters of Italy, including
those of Florence. This was ANDREA MANTEGNA,
particularly interesting to English readers, as his
most celebrated work, the Triumph of Julius Cæsar,
is now preserved in the palace of Hampton Court,
and has formed part of the royal collection ever
since the days of Charles I.

ANDREA MANTEGNA was the son of very poor and
obscure parents, and born near Padua in 1430.*
All we learn of his early childhood amounts to this :

* The dates of Mantegna's birth and death were long subjects of
uncertainty and controversy. According to some authors, he was
born in 1451, and died in 1517 ; but the best and latest authorities
are now agreed upon the dates as given in the text.

that he was employed in keeping sheep, and, being conducted to the city, entered — we know not by what chance — the school of FRANCESCO SQUARCIONE.

About the middle of this century, from which time we date the revival of letters in Europe, the study of the Greek language and a taste for the works of the classical authors had become more and more diffused through Italy. We are told that " to write Latin correctly, to understand the allusions of the best authors, to learn the rudiments at least of Greek, were the objects of every cultivated mind." Classical literature was particularly studied at the University of Padua. Squarcione, a native of that city, and by profession a painter, was early smitten with this passion for *the antique.* He not only travelled over all Italy, but visited Greece in search of the remains of ancient art. Of those which he could not purchase or remove he obtained casts or copies ; and, returning to Padua, he opened there a school or academy for painters — not, indeed, the most celebrated nor the most influential, but at that time the best attended in Italy. Squarcione numbered one hundred and thirty-seven pupils, and was considered the best teacher of his time. Yet of all this crowd of students the names of three only are preserved, and of these only one has attained lasting celebrity. By Squarcione himself we hear only of one undoubted picture displaying great talent ; but it appears that he painted little, em ployed his scholars to execute what works were confided to him, and gave himself up to the business of instruction.

ANDREA MANTEGNA was only known in the academy of Squarcione as a poor boy, whose talent and docility rendered him a favorite with his master. He worked early and late, copying with assiduity the models which were set before him, drawing from the fragments of statues, the busts, the bas-reliefs, ornaments, and vases, with which Squarcione had enriched his academy. At the age of nineteen Andrea painted his first great picture, in which he represented the four evangelists; his imagination and his pencil familiarized only with the forms of classical art, he gave to these sacred personages the air and attitude of heathen philosophers, but they excited nevertheless great applause.

At this time the Venetian JACOPO BELLINI, father of the two great Bellini, of whom we shall have to speak presently, arrived in Padua, where he was employed to paint some pictures. He was considered as the rival of Squarcione, both as a painter and teacher. Andrea was captivated by the talents and conversation of the Venetian; and yet more attracted by the charms of his daughter Nicolasa, whose hand he asked and obtained from her father. Jacopo Bellini was of opinion that he who had given such early proofs of assiduity and ability must ultimately succeed; and, though Andrea was still poor and but little known, and the Bellini fam

ily already rich and celebrated, he did not hesitate
to bestow his daughter on the youthful and modest
suitor. This marriage, and what he regarded as
the revolt of his favorite disciple, so enraged Squarcione that he never forgave the offence. Andrea
having soon after completed a picture which excelled his first, his old master attacked it with the
most merciless severity, and publicly denounced its
faults. The figures, he said, were stiff, were cold
—without life, without nature ; and observed sar-
castically that Andrea should have painted them
white, like marble, and then the color would have
harmonized with the drawing. This criticism came
with a particularly ill grace from him who had
taught the very principles he now condemned, and
Andrea felt it bitterly. The Italian annotator of
Vasari remarks, very truly, that excessive praise
often turns the brain of the weak man, and renders
the man of genius slothful and careless ; but that
severe and unjust censure, while it crushes mediocrity, acts as a spur and excitement to real genius.
Andrea showed that he had sufficient strength of
mind to rise superior to both praise and censure ;
he felt with disgust and pain the malignity of his
old master ; but he knew that much of his criticism
was just. Instead of showing any sense of injury
or discouragement, he set to work with fresh ardor.
He drew and studied from nature, instead of confining himself to the antique ; he imitated the fresher
and livelier coloring of his new relations, the Bellini

and his next picture, which represented a legend of St. Christopher, was so superior to the last, that it silenced the open cavilling of Squarcione, though it could not extinguish his animosity, perhaps rather added to it ; for Andrea had introduced among the numerous figures in his fresco that of Squarcione himself, and the likeness was by no means a flattering one. Notwithstanding the admiration which these and other works excited in his native city, the enmity of his old master seems to have rendered Padua intolerable as a residence. Andrea therefore went to Verona, where he executed several frescoes and some smaller pictures; and, being invited to Mantua by Ludovico Gonzaga, he finally entered the service of that prince. The native courtesy of Andrea's manners, as well as his acquired knowledge and his ability in his profession, recommended him to his new patron, who loaded him with honors and favors.

Some years after he had taken up his residence in Mantua, and had executed for the Marquis Ludovico and his son and successor Frederigo several works which yet remain, Andrea was invited to Rome by Pope Innocent VIII., to paint for him a chapel in the Belvedere. The Marquis of Mantua permitted him to depart but for a time only ; the permission was accompanied by gifts and by letters of recommendation to the pontiff ; and, the more to show the esteem in which the painter was held, he bestowed on him the honor of knighthood.

Mantegna, on his arrival in Rome, set himself to work with his characteristic diligence and enthusiasm, and covered the walls and the ceiling with a multiplicity of subjects, executed, says Vasari, with the delicacy of miniatures. These beautiful paintings existed till late in the last century, when Pius VI. destroyed the chapel to make room for his new museum. While Andrea was employed at Rome by Pope Innocent, a pleasant and characteristic incident occurred, which does honor both to him and to the pope. His holiness was at this time much occupied and disturbed by state affairs; and it happened that the payments were not made with the regularity which Andrea desired. The pope sometimes visited the artist at his work, and one day he asked him the meaning of a certain female figure on which he was painting. Andrea replied, with a significant look, that he was trying to represent *Patience*. The pope, understanding him at once, replied, "If you would place Patience in fitting company, you should paint *Discretion* at her side." Andrea took the hint, and said no more; and when his work was completed, the pope not only paid him the sums stipulated, but rewarded him munificently besides. About the year 1487 he returned to Mantua, where he built himself a magnificent house, painted inside and outside by his own hand, and in which he resided, in great esteem and honor, until his death in 1506. He was buried in the church of his patron saint, St. Andrew, where his monument in bronze and several of his pictures may yet be seen.

The existing works of Andrea Mantegna are so numerous, that we must content ourselves with recording only the most remarkable, and the occasions on which they were painted.

In the year 1476, Andrea executed for his friend and patron, the Marquis Ludovico Gonzaga, the famous frieze representing in nine compartments the triumph of Julius Cæsar after his conquest of Gaul. These were placed round the upper part of a hall in the palace of San Sebastiano, at Mantua, which Ludovico had lately erected. They hung in this palace for a century and a half. When Mantua was sacked and pillaged, in 1629, they, with many other pictures, escaped; the Duke Carlo Gonzaga, reduced to poverty by the vices and prodigality of his predecessors, and the wars and calamities of his own time, sold his gallery of pictures to our King Charles I. for twenty thousand pounds; and these and other works of Andrea Mantegna came to England with the rest of the Mantuan collection. When King Charles' pictures were sold by the Parliament after his death, the Triumph of Julius Cæsar was purchased for one thousand pounds; but, on the return of Charles II., it was restored to the royal collection, how or by whom does not appear. The nine pictures now hang in the palace of Hampton Court. They are painted in distemper on twilled linen, which has been stretched on frames

and originally placed against the wall with ornamented pilasters dividing the compartments. In
their present faded and dilapidated condition, hurried and uninformed visitors will probably pass
them over with a cursory glance ; yet, if we except
the Cartoons of Raphael, Hampton Court contains
nothing so curious and valuable as this old frieze
of Andrea Mantegna, which, notwithstanding the
frailty of the material on which it is executed, has
now existed for three hundred and sixty-seven years,
and, having been frequently engraved, is celebrated
all over Europe.

Andrea retained through his whole life that taste
for the forms and effects of sculpture which had
given to all his earlier works a certain hardness,
meagreness, and formality of outline, neither agreeable in itself nor in harmony with pictorial illusion ;
but in the Triumph of Julius Cæsar the combination of a sculptural style with the aims and beauties
of painting was not, as we usually find it, misplaced
and unpleasing ; it was fitted to the designed purpose, and executed with wonderful success ; the innumerable figures move one after another in a long
and splendid procession, as in an ancient bas-relief,
but colored lightly, in a style resembling the antique paintings at Pompeii. Originally it appears
that the nine compartments were separated from
each other by sculptured pilasters. In the first
picture, or compartment, we have the opening of
the procession ; trumpets, incense burning, stand-

ards borne aloft by the victorious soldiers. In the
second picture, we have the statues of the gods carried off from the temples of the enemy ; battering-
rams, implements of war, heaps of glittering armor
carried on men's shoulders, or borne aloft in char-
iots. In the third picture, more splendid trophies
of a similar kind ; huge vases filled with gold coin,
tripods, &c. In the fourth, more such trophies,
with the oxen crowned with garlands for the sacrifice. In the fifth picture are four elephants adorned
with rich garlands of fruits and flowers, bearing on
their backs magnificent candelabra, and attended
by beautiful youths. In the sixth are figures bearing vases, and others displaying the arms of the
vanquished. The seventh picture shows us the
unhappy captives, who, according to the barbarous
Roman custom, were exhibited on these occasions
to the scoffing and exulting populace. There is
here a group of female captives of all ages, among
them a young, dejected, bride-like figure, a woman
carrying her infant children, and a mother leading
by the hand her little boy, who lifts up his foot as
if he had hurt it; this group is particularly pointed
out by Vasari, who praises it for its nature and its
grace. In the eighth picture, we have a group of
singers and musicians, and among them is seen a
youth whose unworthy office it was to mock at the
wretched captives, in which he is assisted by a
chorus of the common people ; a beautiful youth
with a tambourine is ·distinguished by singular

spirit and grace. In the last picture appears the conqueror, Julius Cæsar, in a sumptuous chariot richly adorned with sculptures in the antique style He is surrounded and followed by a crowd of figures, and among them is seen a youth bearing aloft a standard, on which is inscribed Cæsar's memorable words, *Veni, Vidi, Vici* — " I came, I saw, I conquered."

The inconceivable richness of fancy displayed in this triumphal procession, the numbers of figures and objects of every kind, the propriety of the antique costumes, ornaments, armor, &c,, with the scientific manner in which the perspective is managed, the whole being adapted to its intended situation far above the eye, so that the under surfaces of the objects are alone visible (as would be the case when viewed from below), the upper surfaces vanishing into air ; all these merits combined render this series of pictures one of the grandest works of the fifteenth century, worthy of the attention and admiration of all beholders.*

When the great Flemish painter, Rubens, was at Mantua in 1606, he was struck with astonishment on viewing these works and made a fine copy in a reduced form of the fifth compartment. *Copy*, however, it cannot properly be called ; it is rather a *version* in the manner of Rubens, the style of the

* In the British Museum there is a fine set of the wood-cuts in chiaro-scuro, executed by Andrea Andreani, about 1599, when the original frieze still kept its place in the palace at Mantua.

whole, and even some of the circumstances, being
altered. This fine picture is now in the possession
of Mr. Rogers, the poet.

Another of the most celebrated of Mantegna's
works is the great picture now in the Louvre, at
Paris, and called by the Italians "*la Madonna
della Vittoria*," the Madonna of Victory. The
occasion on which it was painted recalls a great
event in history, the invasion of Italy by Charles
VIII., of France. Of all the wars undertaken by
ambitious and unprincipled monarchs, whether in-
stigated by revenge, by policy, or by rapacious thirst
of dominion, this invasion of Italy, in 1495, was the
most flagitious in its injustice, its folly, and its cru-
elty; it was also the most retributive in its results.
Charles, after ravaging the whole country from the
Alps to Calabria, found himself obliged to retreat,
and on the banks of the Taro was met by Gian-
Francesco, Marquis of Mantua, the son and successor of Frederigo, at the head of an army. On
the part of the Italians it was rather a victory
missed than a victory won; for the French continued their retreat across the Alps, and the loss of
the Italians was immense. The Marquis of Mantua,
however, chose to consider it as a victory. He built
a church on the occasion, and commanded Andrea
Mantegna to paint a picture for the high altar,
which should express at once his devotion and his
gratitude. Considering the subject and the occasion, the French must have had a particular and

malicious pleasure in placing this picture in the Louvre, where it now hangs, at the upper end of that immense gallery.

It represents in the centre, under a canopy or arbor composed of garlands of foliage and fruit, and seated on a throne, the Virgin Mary, who holds on her knees the infant Saviour. On her right stand the archangel Michael and St. Maurice in complete armor. On the left are the patron saints of Mantua, St. Longinus and St. Andrew, with the infant St. John. More in front, on each side, are the Marquis of Mantua and his wife, the celebrated and accomplished Isabella d'Este, who, kneeling, return thanks for the so-called victory over the French. The figure of the Marchesa Isabella is still, in the French catalogue of the Louvre, styled St. Elizabeth, an error pointed out long since by Lanzi and others. This picture was finished in the year 1500, when Andrea was seventy. In beauty and softness of execution it exceeds all his other works, while in the poetical conception of the whole, the grandeur of the saints, and the expression in the countenance of Gonzaga as he gazes upwards in a transport of devotion, it is worthy of his best years. In the Louvre are three other pictures by Andrea Mantegna. One is the Crucifixion of our Saviour, a small picture, remarkable for containing his own portrait in the figure of the soldier seen half-length in front. Another, an allegorical subject, represents the Vices flying before Wisdom, Chastity, and

Philosophy, while Justice, Fortitude, and Temper-
ance, return from above, once more to take up
their habitation among men. Another picture, of
exceeding beauty, represents the Muses dancing to
the sound of Apollo's lyre. Mars, Venus, and
Cupid, stand on a rocky height, looking upon them,
while Vulcan is seen at a distance threatening his
faithless consort. In this little picture Mantegna
seems inspired by the very spirit of Greek art. The
Muses are designed with exquisite taste and feeling. It is probably the chef-d'œuvre of the artist
in his own particular style, that for which his
natural turn of mind and early studies under Squarcione had fitted him. In general his religious pictures are not pleasing ; and many of his classical
subjects have a tasteless meagreness in the forms,
which is quite opposed to all our conceptions of
beauty and greatness of style ; but he has done
grand things. Besides the works already men
tioned, there are four pictures in the Museum, at
Berlin, and others at Vienna, Florence, and Naples.
Of many disciples formed by Andrea Mantegna, not
one attained to any fame or influence in his art.
They all exaggerated his manner and defects, as is
usual with scholars who follow the manner of their
master. His two sons were both artists, studious
and respectable men, but neither of them inherited
the genius of their father. Ariosto, in a famous
stanza of his great poem (" Orlando Furioso,"
cxxxiii., st. 2), in which he has commemorated all

the leading painters of his own time, places the
name of Andrea Mantegna between those of Leonardo da Vinci and Gian Bellini :

> " E quei che furo a nostri di, o son ora,
>   Leonardo, Andrea Mantegna, Gian Bellino,
>   Duo Dossi, e quel, che a par sculpe, o colora
>   Michel piu che mortal Angel divino ;
>   Bastiano, Raffael, Titian ch' honora
>   Non men Cador, che quei Venezia e Urbino ;
>   E gli altri di cui tal opra si vede
>   Qual della prisca età si legge, e crede."

> " Lo ! Leonardo ! Gian' Bellino view,
>   Two Dossi, and Mantegna reached by few,
>   With these an angel, Michael, styled divine,
>   In whom the sculptor and the painter join :
>   Sebastian, Titian, Raphael, three that grace
>   Cadora, Venice, and Urbino's race :
>   Each genius that can past events recall
>   In living figures on the storied wall."

THE INVENTION OF ENGRAVING ON WOOD AND COPPER: 1423—1452.

ANDREA MANTEGNA was not only eminent as a
painter ; he owed much of his celebrity and his
influence over the artists of that age to the multiplication and diffusion of his designs by copper-
plate engraving, an art unknown till his time
He was one of the first who practised it —- certainly
the first painter who engraved his own designs.

In these days, when we cannot walk through the

streets even of a third-rate town without passing
shops with their windows filled with engravings
and prints; when not our books only, but the
newspapers that lie on our tables, are illustrated;
when the *Penny Magazine* can place a little print
after Mantegna at once before the eyes of fifty
thousand readers; when every beautiful work of
art as it appears is multiplied and diffused by hundreds and thousands of copies; when the talk is
rife of wondrous inventions by which such copies
shall reproduce themselves to infinitude, without
change or deterioration, we find it difficult to throw
our imagination back to a time when such things
were not.

What printing did for literature, engraving on
wood and copper has done for painting — not only
diffused the designs and inventions of artists, which
would otherwise be confined to one locality, but in
many cases preserved those which would otherwise
have perished altogether. It is interesting to remember that three inventions to which we owe such
infinite instruction and delight were almost simul-
taneous. The earliest known impression of an engraving on wood is dated 1423; the earliest impression from an engraved metal plate was made
about 1452; and the first printed book, properly
so called, bears date, according to the best authorities, 1455.

Stamps for impressing signatures and characters
on paper, in which the required forms were cut

upon blocks of wood, we find in use in the earliest times. Seals for convents and societies, in which the distinctive devices or letters were cut hollow upon wood or metal, were known in the fourteenth century. The transition seems easy to the next application of the art, and thence, perhaps, it has happened that the name of the man who made this step is lost. All that is certainly known is, that the first wood-blocks for the purpose of pictorial representations were cut in Germany, in the province of Suabia; that the first use made of the art was for the multiplication of playing-cards, which about the year 1418 or 1420 were manufactured in great quantities at Augsburg, Nuremberg, and Venice; and that the next application of the art was devotional. It was used to multiply rude figures of saints, which were distributed among the common people. The earliest wood-cut known is a coarse figure of St. Christopher, dated 1423. This curiosity exists in the library of Earl Spencer, at Althorpe. Another impression, which is declared by connoisseurs to be a little later, is in the Royal Library at Paris, where it is framed and hung up for the inspection of the curious. Rude, ill-drawn, grotesque, — printed with some brownish fluid, on the coarsest ill-colored paper, — still it is impossible to look at it without some of the curiosity, interest, and reverence, with which we regard the first printed book, though it must be allowed that, in comparison with this first sorry specimen of a

wood-cut, the first *book* was a beautiful performance.

Up to a late period, the origin of engraving on
copper was involved in a like obscurity, and volumes of controversy have been written on the subject; some claiming the invention for Germany,
others for Italy. At length, however, the indefatigable researches of antiquarians and connoisseurs,
aided by the accidental discovery in 1794 of the
first impression from a metal plate, have set the
matter at rest. If to Germany belongs the invention of engraving on wood, the art of copper-plate
engraving was beyond all doubt first introduced
and practised at Florence; yet here again the invention seems to have arisen out of a combination
of accidental circumstances, rather than to belong
of right to one man. The circumstances, as well
as we can trace them, were these :

The goldsmiths of Italy, and particularly of Florence, were famous, in the fifteenth century, for
working in *Niello*. They traced with a sharp point
or graver on metal plates, generally of silver, all
kinds of designs, sometimes only arabesques, sometimes single figures, sometimes elaborate and complicated designs from sacred and profane history.
The .ines thus cut or *scratched* were filled up with a
black mass of sulphate of silver, so that the design
traced appeared very distinct, contrasted with the
white metal. In Italy the substance used in filling
up the lines was called from its black color, in

Latin *nigellum*, and in Italian *niello*. In this manner church plate, as chalices and reliquaries, also dagger-sheaths, sword-hilts, clasps, buttons, and many other small silver articles, were ornamented. In Sir John Soane's Museum there is an old MS. book, of which the binding exhibits some beautiful specimens of niello-work of the fifteenth century. Those who practised the art were called *niellatori*.

According to Vasari's account, Maso Finiguerra was a skilful goldsmith, living in Florence. He became celebrated for the artistic beauty of his designs and workmanship in niello. Finiguerra is said to be the first to whom it accidentally occurred to try the effect of his work, and preserve a memorandum of his design in the following manner: Previous to filling up the engraved lines with the *niello*, which was a final process, he applied to them a black fluid easily removed, and then laying a piece of damp paper on the plate or object, and pressing or rubbing it forcibly, the paper imbibed the fluid from the tracing, and presented a facsimile of the design, which had the appearance of being drawn with a pen. That Finiguerra was the first or the only worker in *niello* who used this method of trying the effect of the work is more than doubtful ; but it is certain that the earliest known impression of a niello plate is the impression from a pax * now existing in the church of S. Giovanni

---

* A pax, or pix, is the name given to the vessel in which the consecrated bread or wafer of the sacrament was deposited. This vessel was usually of the richest workmanship, often enriched with gems.

at Florence executed by Finiguerra, and representing the subject we have often alluded to — the Coronation of the Virgin by her Son, the Redeemer, in presence of Saints and Angels. It contains nearly thirty minute figures, most exquisitely designed This relic is preserved in the Royal Library at Paris, where it was discovered lying among some old Italian engravings by the Abbé Zani. The date of the work is fixed beyond all dispute ; for the record of the payment of sixty-six gold ducats (thirty-two pounds sterling) to Maso Finiguerra for this identical pax still exists, dated 1452. The only existing impression from it must have been made previously, perhaps a few weeks or months before. It is now, like the first wood-cut, framed and hung up in the Royal Library at Paris for the inspection of the curious.

Another method of trying the effect of niello-work before it was quite completed was by taking the impression of the design, not on paper, but on sulphur, of which some curious and valuable speci- mens remain. After seeing several impressions of niello plates of the fifteenth century, we are no longer surprised to find skilful goldsmiths converted into excellent painters and sculptors. In our own time, this art, after having been forgotten since the sixteenth century, when it fell into disuse, has been very successfully revived by Mr. Wagner, a gold- smith of Berlin, now residing at Paris.

We have no evidence that it occurred to Maso

Finiguerra, or any other niello-worker, to engrave designs on plates of copper for the express purpose of making and multiplying impressions of them on paper. The first who did this as a trade or profession was Baccio Baldini, who, about 1467, employed several painters, particularly Sandro Botticelli and Filippino Lippi, to make designs for him to engrave. Andrea Mantegna caught up the idea with a kind of enthusiasm. He made the first experiment when about sixty, and, according to Lanzi, he engraved, during the sixteen remaining years of his life, not less than fifty plates. Of these about thirty are now known to collectors, and considered genuine. Among them are his own designs for the Triumph of Julius Cæsar (the fifth, sixth, and seventh compartments only).

Familiar as we now are with all kinds of copper plate and wood engraving, there are persons who do not understand clearly the difference between them. Independent of the difference of the material on which they are executed, the grand distinction between the two arts is this : that the copper-plate engraver cuts out the lines by which the impression is produced, which are thus left hollow, and afterwards filled up with ink ; the impression is produced by laying a piece of wet paper on the plate, and passing them together under a heavy and perfectly even roller. The method of the engraver on wood is precisely the reverse. He cuts away all the surrounding surface of the block of wood, and leaves

the lines which are to produce the impression
prominent. They are afterwards blackened with
ink like a stamp, and the impression taken with a
common printing-press.

When Andrea Mantegna made his first essays in
engraving on copper, he does not seem to have used
a press or roller. Perhaps he was unacquainted with
that implement. At all events, the early impressions of his plates have evidently been taken by
merely laying the paper on the copper-plate, and
then rubbing it over with the hand ; and they are
very faint and spiritless, compared with the later
impressions taken with a press

THE BELLINI.

A. D. 1421 to A. D. 1516.

JACOPO BELLINI, the father, had studied painting under Gentile da Fabriano, of whom we have spoken as the scholar, or at least the imitator, of the famous monk, Angelico da Fiesole. To express his gratitude and veneration for his instructor, Jacopo gave the name of Gentile to his eldest son. The second and most famous of the two was christened Giovanni (John) ; in the Venetian dialect, *Gian Bellini*.

The sister of the Bellini being married to Andrea Mantegna, who exercised for forty years a sort of patriarchal authority over all the painters of northern Italy, it is singular that he should have had so little influence over his Venetian relatives. It is true the elder brother, Gentile, had always a certain leaning to Mantegna's school, and was fond of studying from a mutilated antique Venus which he kept in his studio. But the genius of his brother Gian Bellini was formed altogether by other influ-

(134)

euces. The commercial intercourse between Venice and Germany brought several pictures and painters of Germany and the Netherlands into Venice. In the island of Murano, at Venice, dwelt a family called the Vivarini, who had carried on the art of painting from generation to generation, and who had associated with them some of the early Flemings. Thus it was that the painters of the first Venetian school became familiarized with a style of coloring more rich and vivid than was practised in any other part of Italy. They were among the first who substituted oil-painting for distemper. To these advantages the elder Bellini added the knowledge of drawing and perspective taught in the Paduan school, and the religious and spiritual feeling which they derived from the example and instruction of Gentile da Fabriano. In these combined elements Gian Bellini was educated, and founded the Venetian school, afterwards so famous and so prolific in great artists.

The two brothers were first employed together in an immense work, which may be compared in its importance and its object to the contemplated decoration of our houses of parliament. They were commanded to paint the Hall of Council in the palace of the Doge, with a series of pictures representing the principal events (partly legendary and fictitious, partly authentic) of the Venetian wars with the Emperor Frederic Barbarossa (1177) ; the combats and victories on the Adriatic, the recon-

ciliation of the Emperor with Pope Alexander III.
in the Place of St. Mark, when Frederic held the
stirrup of the pope's mule; the Doge Ziani receiving from the pope the gold ring with which he
espoused the Adriatic in token of perpetual dominion over it; and other memorable scenes dear to
the pride and patriotism of the Venetians.

These were painted in fourteen compartments
round the hall. What remains to us of the works
of the two brothers renders it a subject of lasting
regret that these frescoes, and others still more
valuable, were destroyed by fire in 1577.

In 1452 Constantinople was taken by the Turks,
an event which threw the whole of Christendom
into consternation, not unmixed with shame. The
Venetians were the first to resume their commercial
relations with the Levant; they sent an embassy
to the Turkish Sultan to treat for the redemption
of the Christian prisoners, and negotiate a peace.
This was happily concluded in 1454, under the auspices of the Doge, old Francesco Foscari.* It was
on this occasion that the Sultan Mohammed II.,
having seen some Venetian pictures, desired that
the Venetian government would send him one of
their painters. The Council of Ten, after some de-
liberation, selected for this service Gentile Bellini,
who took his departure accordingly in one of the

* The story of the two Foscari is the subject of a tragedy by Lord
Byron. The taking of Constantinople is the subject of one of the
most beautiful tragedies of Joanna Baillie.

state galleys, and on arriving at Constantinoplo
was received with great honor. During his residence there he painted the portrait of the Sultan
and one of his favorite sultanas; and he took an
opportunity of presenting to the Sultan, as a token
of homage from himself, a picture of the head of
John the Baptist after decapitation. The Sultan
admired it much, but criticized, with the air of a
connoisseur, the appearance of the neck. He observed that the shrinking of the severed nerves was
not properly expressed. As Gentile Bellini did not
appear to feel the full force of this criticism, the
Sultan called in one of his slaves, commanded the
wretch to kneel down, and, drawing his sabre, cut
off his head with a stroke, and thus gave the astonished and terrified painter a practical lesson in
anatomy. It may be easily believed that after this
horrible scene Gentile became uneasy till he had
obtained leave of departure; and the Sultan at
length dismissed him, with a letter of strong recommendation to his own government, a chain of gold,
and other rich presents. After his return to Venice
he painted some remarkable pictures; among them
one representing St. Mark preaching at Alexandria,
in which he has painted the men and women of
Alexandria in rich Turkish costumes, such as he
had seen at Constantinople. This curious picture
is now in the Academy at Milan, and is engraved
in Rosini's " Storia della Pittura." A portrait of
Mohammed II., painted by Gentile Bellini, is said

to be in England.   All the early engravings of the grim Turkish conqueror which now exist are from the portraits painted by Bellini.   He died in 1501, at the age of eighty.

A much more memorable artist in all respects was his brother Gian Bellini.   His works are divided into two classes, — those which he painted before he adopted the process of oil-painting, and those executed afterwards.   The first have great sweetness and elegance and purity of expression, with, however, a certain timidity and dryness of manner ; in the latter we have a foretaste of the rich Venetian coloring, without any diminution of the grave simple dignity and melancholy sweetness of expression which distinguished his earlier works. Between his sixty-fifth and his eightieth year he painted those pictures which are considered as his chefs-d'œuvre, and which are now preserved in the churches at Venice and in the Gallery of the Academy of Arts in that city.

It has been said that Gian Bellini introduced himself disguised into the room of Antonella da Messina when he was painting at Venice, and stole from him the newly-discovered secret of mixing the colors with oils instead of water.   It is a consolation to think that this story does not rest on any evidence worthy of credit.   Antonella had divulged his secret to several of his friends, particularly to Domenico Veneziano, afterwards murdered by An- drea Castagno.   Besides, the character of Bellini

renders it unlikely that he would have been guilty
of such a perfidious trick

Gian Bellini is said to have introduced at Venice
the fashion of portrait-painting. Before his time
the likenesses of living persons had been frequently
painted, but they were almost always introduced
into pictures of large subjects. Portraits, properly
so called, were scarcely known till his time; then,
and afterwards, every noble Venetian sat for his picture—generally the head only, or half-length. Their
houses were filled with family portraits, and it became a custom to have the effigies of their doges and
those who distinguished themselves in the service of
their country painted by order of the state and hung
in the ducal palace, where many of them are still
to be seen. Up to the latest period of his life Gian
Bellini had been employed in painting for his coun-
trymen only religious pictures or portraits, or subjects of Venetian history; the classical taste which
had spread through all the states of Italy had not
yet penetrated to Venice. But towards the end of
his life, when nearly ninety, he was invited to Ferrara to paint in the palace of the duke a dance of
bacchanals. On this occasion he made the acquaintance of Ariosto, who mentions him with honor among
the painters of his time (see p. 126).

There is at the palace of Hampton Court a very
curious little head of Bellini, certainly genuine,
though much injured. It is inscribed underneath,
Johanes Bellini ipse. We have lately acquired for

our National Gallery a most curious and genuine portrait of one of the old doges, painted by Bellini. It is somewhat hard in the execution, but we cannot look at it without feeling that we could swear to the truth of the resemblance. In the Louvre at Paris are three pictures ascribed to Gian Bellini. One contains his own portrait and that of his brother Gentile, heads only ; the former is dark, the latter fair ; both wear a kind of cap or *beret*. Another, about six feet in length, represents the reception of a Venetian ambassador at Constantinople. A third is a Virgin and Child. The first-mentioned is by Gentile, and the two last uncertain. In the Berlin Museum are seven pictures by him, all considered genuine, and all are painted on panel and *in oils*. They belong, therefore, to his latest and best period.

Gian Bellini died in 1516. He had formed many disciples, and among them two whose glory in these later times had almost eclipsed that of their great teacher and precursor — GIORGIONE and TITIAN. Another, far less famous, but of whom some beautiful pictures still exist at Venice, was Cima da Cornegliano.

THE UMBRIAN SCHOOL

PIETRO PERUGINO.

Born 1446, died 1524.

THE fame of PERUGINO rests more on his having been the master and instructor of Raphael, than on his own works or worth. Yet he was a great and remarkable man in his own day: interesting in ours as the representative of a certain school of art immediately preceding that of Raphael. Francesco Francia has left behind him a name perhaps less known and celebrated, but far more revered.

The territory of Umbria in Italy comprises that mountainous region of the Ecclesiastical States now called the Duchy of Spoleto. Perugia, Foligno, Assisi, and Spoleto, were among its principal towns; and the whole country, with its retired valleys and isolated cities, was distinguished in the middle ages as the peculiar seat of religious enthusiasm. It was here that St. Francis of Assisi preached and prayed, and gathered around him his fervid, self-denying votaries. Art, as usual, reflected the habits and feelings of the people; and here Gentile da Fabriano, the beloved friend of Angelico da Fiesole, exercised a particular influence. No less than thirteen or fourteen Umbrian painters, who flourished between the time of Gentile and that of Raphael, are mentioned in Passavant's " Life of Raphael." This mystical and spiritual direction of art extended itself to Bologna, and found a worthy interpreter in Francesco Francia. We shall, however, speak first of Perugino.

Pietro Vannucci was born at a little town in Umbria, called Citta della Pieve, and he was known for the first thirty years of his life as Pietro della Pieve ; after he had settled at Perugia, and had obtained there the rights of citizenship, he was called Pietro di Perugia, or IL PERUGINO, by which name he is best known.

We know little of the early life and education of Perugino ; his parents were respectable, but poor. His first instructor is supposed to have been Nicolo Alunno. At this time (about 1470) Florence was considered as the head-quarters of art and artists ; and the young painter, at the age of five-and-twenty, undertook a journey to Florence, as the most certain path to excellence and fame.

Vasari tells us that Pietro was excited to industry by being constantly told of the great rewards and honors which the professors of painting had earned in ancient and in modern times, and also by the pressure of poverty. He left Perugia in a state of absolute want, and reached Florence, where he pursued his studies for many months with unwearied diligence, but so poor meanwhile that he had not even a bed to sleep on. He studied in the chapel of Masaccio in the Carmine, which has been already mentioned; received some instruction in drawing and modelling from Andrea Verrocchio; and was a friend and fellow-pupil of Lionardo da Vinci. They are thus mentioned together in a contemporary poem written by Giovanni Santi, the father of the great Raphael:

> " Due giovin par d' etate e par d' amori,
>   Lionardo da Vinci e 'l Perusino
>   Pier della Pieve, che son divin Pittori."

That is,

> " Two youths, equal in years, equal in affection,
>   Lionardo da Vinci and the Perugian
>   Peter della Pieve, both divine painters."

But, though " par d' etate e par d' amori," they certainly were not equal in gifts. Perugino dwindles into insignificance when we think of the triumphant and universal powers of Lionardo. But this is anticipating.

There can be no doubt that Perugino possessed genius and feeling, but confined and shadowed by certain moral defects; it was as if the brightness of his genius kept up a continual struggle with the meanness of his soul, to be in the end overpowered and held down by the growing weakness and debasement. Yet when young in his art a pure and gentle feeling guided his pencil; and in the desire to learn

in the fixed determination to improve and to excel,
his calm sense and his calculating spirit stood him
in good stead. There was a famous convent near
Florence, in which the monks — not lazy nor ignorant, as monks are usually described — carried on
several arts successfully, particularly the art of
painting on glass. Perugino was employed to paint
some frescoes in their convent, and also to make
designs for the glass-painters. In return, he learned
how to prepare and to apply many colors not yet in
general use; and the lucid and vigorous tints to
which his eye became accustomed in their workshop
certainly influenced his style of coloring. He gradually rose in estimation; painted a vast number of
pictures and frescoes for the churches and chapels
of Florence, and particularly an altar-piece of great
beauty for the famous convent of Vallombrosa. In
this he represented the Assumption of the Virgin,
who is soaring to heaven in the midst of a choir of
angels, while the twelve Apostles beneath look upwards with adoration and astonishment. This excellent picture is preserved in the Academy of the
Fine Arts at Florence, and near it is the portrait
of the Abbot of Vallombrosa by whose order it was
painted. Ten years after Perugino had first entered
Florence a poor, nameless youth, he was called to
Rome by Pope Sixtus IV. to assist with most of the
distinguished painters of that time in painting the
famous Sistine Chapel. All the frescoes of Peru
gino except two were afterwards effaced to make

room for Michael Angelo's Last Judgment. Those
which remain show that the style of Perugino at
this time was decidedly Florentine, and quite distinct from his earlier and later works. They represent the Baptism of Christ in the River Jordan, and
Christ delivering the Keys to St. Peter. While at
Rome he also painted a room in the palace of Prince
Colonna. When he returned to Perugia he resumed
the feeling and manner of his earlier years, combined
with better drawing and coloring, and his best pictures were painted between 1490 and 1502. His
principal work, however, was the hall of the *Col-
lege del Cambio* (that is, Hall of Exchange) at Perugia, most richly and elaborately painted with
frescoes, which still exist. The personages introduced exhibit a strange mixture of the sacred and
profane. John the Baptist and other saints, Isaiah,
Moses, Daniel, David, and other prophets, are fig-
ured on the walls with Fabius Maximus, Socrates,
Pythagoras, Pericles, Horatius Cocles, and other
Greek and Roman worthies. Other pictures painted
in Perugia are remarkable for the simplicity, grace,
and dignity, of his Virgins, the infantine sweetness
of the children and cherubs, and the earnest, ardent
expression in the heads of his saints.

Perugino, in the very beginning of the sixteenth
century, was certainly the most popular painter of
his time: a circumstance which, considering that
Raphael, Francia, and Lionardo da Vinci, were all
working at the same time, would surprise us, did

we not know that contemporary *popularity* is not generally the recompense of the most distinguished genius. In fact, Perugino has produced some of the weakest and worst, as well as some of the most exquisite pictures in the world. He undertook an immense number of works, and employed his schol- ars and assistants to execute them from his designs. A passion, of which perhaps the seeds were sown in his early days of poverty and misery, had taken possession of his soul. He was no longer excited to labor by a spirit of piety or the generous ambition to excel, but by a base and insatiable thirst for gain. All his late pictures, from the year 1505 to his death, betray the influence of this mean passion. He aimed at nothing beyond mechanical dexterity, and to earn his money with as little expense of time and trouble as possible; he became more and more feeble, mannered, and monotonous, continually re- peating the same figures, actions, and heads, till his very admirers were wearied; and on his last visit to Florence, Michael Angelo, who had never done him justice, pronounced him, with contempt, "*Goffo nell' arte,*" that is, a mere bungler; for which affront Pietro summoned him before the magistrates, but came off with little honor. He was no longer what he had been. Such was his love of money, or such his mistrust of his family, that when moving from place to place he carried his beloved gold with him; and being on one occa sion robbed of a large sum, he fell ill, and was like

to die of grief. It seems, however, hardly consist-
ent with the mean and avaricious spirit imputed to
him, that, having married a beautiful girl of Perugia, he took great delight in seeing her arrayed, at
home and abroad, in the most costly garments, and
sometimes dressed her with his own hands. To the
reproach of avarice — too well founded — some writers have added that of irreligion ; nay, two centuries after his death they showed the spot where he
was buried in unconsecrated ground under a few
trees, near Fontignano, he having refused to receive
the last sacraments. This accusation has been refuted ; and in truth there is such a divine beauty
in some of the best pictures of Perugino, such exquisite purity and tenderness in his Madonnas, such
an expression of enthusiastic faith and devotion in
some of the heads, that it would be painful to believe that there was no corresponding feeling in his
heart. In one or two of his pictures he had reached
a degree of sublimity worthy of him who was the
master of Raphael, but the instances are few.

In our National Gallery there is a little Madonna
and Child by Perugino. The Virgin is seen half-
length, holding the infant Christ, who is standing in
front and grasps in his little hand one of the tresses
of her long, fair hair ; the young St. John is seen
half-length on the left, looking up with joined
hands. It is an early picture, painted before his
first residence at Florence and before he had made
his first essays in oil. It is very feeble and finical

in the execution, but very sweet and simple in the expression.

In the Louvre at Paris there is a curious allegorical picture by Perugino, representing the Combat of Love and Chastity ; many figures in a landscape It seems a late production — feeble and tasteless ; and the subject is precisely one least adapted to the painter's style and powers.

In almost every collection on the continent there are works of Perugino, for he was so popular in his lifetime that his pictures were as merchandise, and sold all over Italy.

Pietro Perugino died in 1524. He survived Raphael four years ; and he may be said, during the last twenty-five years of his life, to have survived himself.

His scholars were very numerous, but the fame of all the rest is swallowed up in that of his great disciple RAPHAEL. Bernardino di Perugia, called PINTURICCHIO, was rather an assistant than a pupil He has left some excellent works.

FRANCESCO RAIBOLINI, CALLED IL FRANCIA.

Born 1450, died 1517.

THERE existed throughout the fourteenth and fifteenth centuries a succession of painters in Bologna, known in the history of Italian art as the *early* Bolognese school, to distinguish it from the *later* school, which the Carracci founded in the same city — a school altogether dissimilar in spirit and feeling. The chief characteristic of the former was the fervent piety and devotion of its professors. In the *sentiment* of their works they resembled the Umbrian school, but the *manner* of execution is different. One of these early painters, Lippo (or Filippo) di Dalmasio, was so celebrated for the beauty of his Madonnas, that he obtained the name of *Lippo dalle Madonne.* He greatly resembled the Frate Angelico in life and character, but was inferior as an artist. To his heads of the Virgin he gave an expression of saintly beauty, purity, and tenderness, which two hundred years later excited the admiration and emulation of Guido. Lippo died about 1409. Passing over some other names, we come to that of the greatest painter of the early Bologna school, FRANCESCO RAIBOLINI.

(149)

He was born in 1450; being just four years younger than his contemporary Perugino. Like many other painters of that age, already mentioned, he was educated for a goldsmith, and learned to design and model correctly. Francesco's master in the arts of working in gold and niello * was a certain Francia, whose name, in affectionate gratitude to his memory, he afterwards adopted, signed it on his pictures, and is better known by it than by his own family name. Up to the age of forty, Francesco Francia pursued his avocation of goldsmith, and became celebrated for the excellence of his workmanship in chasing gold and silver, and the exquisite beauty and taste of his niellos. He also excelled in engraving dies for coins and medals, and was appointed superintendent of the mint in his native city of Bologna, which office he held till his death.

We are not told how the attention of Francia was first directed to the art of painting. It is said that the sight of a beautiful picture by Perugino awakened the dormant talent; that he learned drawing from Marco Zoppo, one of the numerous pupils of Squarcione, and that for many months he entertained in his house certain artists who initiated him into the use of colors, &c. However this may be, his earliest picture is dated 1490, when he was in his fortieth year. It exists at present in the gallery

* For an account of the art of working in niello, and the invention to which it led, see p. 129.

at Bologna, and represents his favorite subject, so often repeated, a Madonna and Child, enthroned and surrounded by saints and martyrs. This picture, which, if it be a first production, may well be termed wonderful as well as beautiful, excited so much admiration, that Giovanni Bentivoglio, then lord of Bologna, desired him to paint an altar-piece for his family chapel in the church of San Giacomo. This second essay of his powers excited in the strongest degree the enthusiasm of his fellow-citizens. The people of Bologna were distinguished among the other states of Italy for their patronage of native talent ; they now exulted in having produced an artist who might vie with those of Florence, or Perugia, or Venice.

The vocation of Francia was henceforth determined. He abandoned his former employment of goldsmith and niello-worker, and became a painter by choice and by profession. During the next ten years he improved progressively in composition and in color, still retaining the simple and beautiful sentiment which had from the first distinguished his works. His earliest pictures are in oil ; but his success encouraged him to attempt fresco, and in this style, which required a grandeur of conception and a breadth and rapidity of execution for which his laborious and diminutive works in gold and niello could never have prepared his mind or hand, he appears to have succeeded at once. He was first employed by Bentivoglio to decorate one of the chambers in his palace with the story of Judith and Holofernes; and he afterwards executed in the chapel of St. Cecilia a series of frescoes from the legend of that saint. "The composition," says Kugler, "is extremely simple, without any superfluous figures; the action dramatic and well conceived. We have here the most noble figures, the most beautiful and graceful heads, a pure taste in the drapery, and masterly backgrounds." It should seem that the merits here enumerated include all that constitutes perfection. Unhappily, these fine specimens of Francia's art are falling into ruin and decay.

The style of Francia at his best period is very distinct from that of Perugino, whom he resembles, however, so far as to show that the pictures of the latter were the first objects of his emulation and imitation. In the works of Perugino there is a melancholy verging frequently on sourness and harshness, or fading into insipidity. Francia, in his richer and deeper coloring, his ampler forms, and the cheerful, hopeful, affectionate expression in his heads, reminds us of the Venetian school.

His celebrity in a short period had extended through the whole of Lombardy. Not only his native city, but Parma, Modena, Cesena, and Ferrara, were emulous to possess his works. Even Tuscany, so rich in painters of her own, had heard of Francia. The beautiful altar-piece which has enriched our National Gallery since the year

1841 was painted at the desire of a nobleman of Lucca

This altar-piece is composed of two separate pictures. The larger compartment contains eight figures rather less than life. In the centre on a raised throne are seated the Virgin and her mother St. Anne. The Virgin is attired in a red tunic, and a dark blue mantle, which is drawn over the head. She holds in her lap the Infant Christ, to whom St. Anne is presenting a peach. The expression of the Virgin is exceedingly pure, calm, and saintly, yet without the seraph-like refinement which we see in some of Raphael's Madonnas. The head of the aged St. Anne is simply dignified and maternal. At the foot of the throne stands the little St. John, holding in his arms the cross of reeds and the scroll inscribed " Ecce Agnus Dei " (*Behold the Lamb of God!*) On each side of the throne are two saints. To the right of the Virgin stands St. Paul, holding a sword, the instrument of his martyrdom ; and St. Sebastian bound to a pillar and pierced with arrows. On the left, St. Lawrence with the emblematical gridiron and palm-branch, and another saint, probably St. Frediano. The heads of these saints want elevation of form, the brow in all being rather low and narrow ; but the prevailing expression is simple, affectionate, devout, full of faith and hope. The background is formed of two open arches adorned with sculpture, the blue sky beyond ; and lower down, between St. Paul and St. Sebastian, is seen a glimpse of a beautiful landscape. The draperies are grand and ample ; the coloring, rich and warm ; the execution, most finished in every part. On the cornice of the raised throne, or pedestal, is inscribed FRANCIA AURIFEX BONONIENSIS P. (that is, painted by Francia, goldsmith of Bologna), but no date It measures six feet and a half high by six feet wide.

Over this square picture was placed the lunette, or arch, which now hangs on the opposite side of the room. It represents the subject called in Italian a *Pietà*, — the Dead Redeemer supported on the knees of the Virgin mother. An angel clothed in green drapery supports the drooping head of the Saviour. Another angel in red drapery kneels at his feet. Grief in the face of the sorrowing mother — in the countenances of the angels reverential sorrow and pity — are most admirably expressed.

This altar-piece was painted by Francia about the year 1500, for the Marchesa Buonvisi of Lucca, and placed in the chapel of the Buonvisi family, in the church of San Frediano. It remained there till lately purchased by the Duke of Lucca, who sent it with other pictures to be disposed of in England. The two pieces were valued at four thousand pounds ; after some negotiation, our government obtained them for the National Gallery at the price of three thousand five hundred pounds.

The works of Francia were, until lately, confined to the churches of Bologna and other cities of Lombardy ; now they are to be found in all the

great collections of Europe, that of the Louvre excepted, which does not contain a single specimen
The Bologna Gallery contains six, the Berlin Mu
seum three, of his pictures.* In the Florentine
Gallery is an admirable portrait of a man holding
a letter in his hand. In the Imperial Gallery at
Vienna there is a most exquisite altar-piece, the
same size and style as the one in the National
Gallery, but still mcre beautiful and poetical. The
Virgin and Child are seated on the throne in the
midst of a charming landscape ; St. Francis standing on one side, and St. Catherine on the other.
The Gallery at Munich contains a picture by him,
perhaps the most charming he ever painted. It
represents the Infant Saviour lying on the grass
amid roses and flowers ; the Virgin stands before
him, looking down with clasped hands, and in an
ecstasy of love and devotion, on her divine Son
The figures are rather less that life. A small but
very beautiful picture by Francia, a Madonna and
Child, is now in the possession of Mr. Frankland
Lewis.

It is pleasant to be assured that the life and character of Francia were in harmony with his genius.
Vasari describes him as a man of comely aspect, of
exemplary morals, of amiable and cheerful manners ; in conversation so witty, so wise, and so
agreeable, that in discourse with him the saddest

* One of these (No. 253) is a repetition of the Pietà in our
National Gallery.

man would have felt his melancholy dissipated, his
cares forgotten ; adding that he was loved and ven
erated not only by his family and fellow-citizens,
but by strangers and the princes in whose service
he was employed.   A most interesting circumstance
in the life of Francia was his friendship and corres
pondence with the youthful Raphael, who was
thirty-four years younger than himself.   There is
extant a letter which Raphael addressed to Francia
in the year 1508.   In this letter, which is expressed
with exceeding kindness and deference, Raphael
excuses himself for not having painted his own
portrait for his friend, and promises to send it soon.
He presents him with his design for the Nativity,
and requests to have in return Francia's design for
the Judith,* to be placed among his most precious
treasures ; he alludes, but discreetly, to the grief
which Francia must have felt when his patron
Bentivoglio was exiled from Bologna by Pope
Julius II., and he concludes, affectionately, " Continue to love me as I love you, with all my heart."
Raphael afterwards, according to his promise, sent
his portrait to his friend, and Francia addressed
to him a very pretty sonnet, in which he styles
him, as if prophetically, the " painter above all
painters : "

" Tu solo il Pittor sei de' Pittori."

About the year 1516 Raphael sent to Bologna

* This drawing is said to exist in the collection of the Archduke
Charles, at Vienna. See Passavant.

his famous picture of the St Cecilia, surrounded
by other Saints, which had been commanded by a
lady of the house of Bentivoglio, to decorate the
church of St. Cecilia, the same church in which
Francia had painted the frescoes already mentioned.
Raphael, in a modest and affectionate letter, recommended the picture to the care of his friend
Francia, entreating him to be present when the
case was opened, to repair any injury it might have
received in the carriage, and to correct anything
which seemed to him faulty in the execution.
Francia zealously fulfilled his wishes ; and when he
beheld this masterpiece of the divinest of painters,
burst into transports of admiration and delight,
placing it far above all that he had himself accomplished. As he died a short time afterwards, it
was said that he had sickened of envy and despair
on seeing himself thus excelled, and in his native
city his best works eclipsed by a young rival.
Vasari tells this story as a tradition of his own
time ; his expression is " *come alcuni credono* " (as
some believe) ; but it rests on no other evidence,
and is so contrary to all we know of the gentle and
generous spirit of Francia, and so inconsistent with
the sentiments which for many years he had cher-
ished and avowed for Raphael, that we may set it
aside as unworthy of all belief. The date of
Francia's death has been a matter of dispute ; but
it appears certain, from state documents lately discovered at Bologna, that he died Master of the Mint

in that city, on the 6th of January, 1517, being
then in his sixty-eighth year. His son Giacomo
became an esteemed painter in his father's style.
In the Berlin Gallery there are six pictures by his
hand ; and one by Giulio Francia, a cousin and
pupil of the elder Francia.

FRA BARTOLOMEO, CALLED ALSO BACCIO DELLA PORTA AND IL FRATE.

Born 1469, died 1517.

BEFORE we enter on the golden age of painting, —that splendid era which crowded into a brief quarter of a century (between 1505 and 1530) the greatest names and most consummate productions of the art,— we must speak of one more painter, justly celebrated. Perugino and Francia (of whom we have spoken at length) and FRA BARTOLOMEO, of whom we are now to speak, were still living at this period; but they belonged to a previous age, and were informed, as we shall show, by a wholly different spirit. They contributed in some degree to the perfection of their great contemporaries and successors, but they owed the sentiment which inspired their own works to influences quite distinct from those which prevailed during the next half-century. The last of these elder painters of the first Italian school was FRA BARTOLOMEO.

He was born in the little town of Savignano, in the territory of Prato, near Florence. Of his family little is known, and of his younger years nothing, but that, having shown a disposition to the art of

design, he was placed under the tuition of Cosimo
Roselli, a very good Florentine painter ; and that
while receiving his instructions he resided with
some relations who dwelt near one of the gates of
the city (La Porta San Piero). Hence, for the first
thirty years of his life, he was known among his
companions by the name of Baccio della Porta ;
Baccio being the Tuscan diminutive of Bartolomeo.
While studying in the *atelier* of Cosimo Roselli.
Baccio formed a friendship with Mariotto Albertinelli, a young painter about his own age. It was
on both sides an attachment almost fraternal
They painted together, sometimes on the same picture, and in style and sentiment were so similar
that it has become difficult to distinguish their
works. Baccio was, however, more particularly
distinguished by his feeling for softness and har
mony of color, and the tender and devout ex
pression of his religious pictures. From his earli
est years he appears to have been a religious enthu
siast ; and this turn of mind not only characterized
all the productions of his pencil, but involved him
in a singular manner with some of the most remarkable events and characters of his time.

Lorenzo de' Medici, called Lorenzo the Magnificent, was then master of the liberties of Florence. The revival of classical learning, the study
of the antique sculptures (diffused, as we have related, by the school of Padua, and rendered still
more a fashion by the influence and popularity of

Andrea Mantegna, already old, and Michael Angelo, then a young man), was rapidly corrupting
the simple and pious taste which had hitherto prevailed in art, even while imparting to it a more
universal direction, and a finer feeling for beauty
and sublimity in the abstract. At the same time,
and encouraged for their own purposes by the
Medici family, there prevailed with this pagan
taste in literature and art a general laxity of
morals, a license of conduct, and a disregard of all
sacred things, such as had never, even in the darkest ages of barbarism, been known in Italy. The
papal chair was during that period filled by two
popes, the perfidious and cruel Sixtus IV., and the
yet more detestable Alexander VI. (the infamous
Borgia). Florence, meantime, under the sway of
Lorenzo and his sons, became one of the most
magnificent, but also one of the most dissolute of
cities.

The natural taste and character of Bartolomeo
placed him far from this luxurious and licentious
court; but he had acquired great reputation by
the exquisite beauty and tenderness of his Madonnas, and he was employed by the Dominicans of
the convent of St. Mark to paint a fresco in their
church representing the Last Judgment. At this
time Savonarola, an eloquent friar in the convent,
was preaching against the disorders of the times,
the luxury of the nobles, the usurpation of the
Medici, and the vices of the popes, with a fearless

11

fervor and eloquence which his hearers ar d himself
mistook for direct inspiration from heaven. The
influence of this extraordinary man increased daily,
and among his most devoted admirers and disciples
was Bartolomeo. In a fit of perplexity and re-
morse, caused by an eloquent sermon of Savonarola,
he joined with many others in making a sacrifice
of ail the books and pictures which related to
heathen poetry and art on which they could lay
their hands. Into this funeral pyre, which was
kindled in sight of the people in one of the principal streets of Florence, Bartolomeo flung all those
of his designs, drawings, and studies, which represented either profane subjects or the human figure
undraped, and he almost wholly abandoned the
practice of his art for the society of his friend and
spiritual pastor. But the talents, the enthusiasm,
the popularity of Savonarola, had marked him for
destruction. He was excommunicated by the pope
for heresy, denounced by the Medici, and at length
forsaken by the fickle people who had followed,
obeyed, almost adored him as a saint. Bartolomeo
happened to be lodged in the convent of St. Mark
when it was attacked by the rabble and a party of
nobles. The partisans of Savonarola were massa-
cred, and Savonarola himself carried off to torture
and to death. Our pious and excellent painter was
not remarkable for courage. Terrified by the
tumult and horrors around him, he hid himself,
vowing, if he escaped the danger, to dedicate him

self to a religious life. Within a few weeks the unhappy Savonarola, after suffering the torture was publicly burned in the Grand Piazza of Florence ; and Bartolomeo, struck with horror at the fate of his friend, — a horror which seemed to paralyze all his faculties, — took the vows and became a Dominican friar, leaving to his friend Albertinelli the task of completing those of his frescoes and pictures which were left unfinished.

He passed the next four years of his life without touching a pencil, in the austere seclusion of his convent. At the end of this period the entreaties and commands of his Superior induced Bartolomeo to resume the practice of his art, and from this time he is known as Fra Bartolomeo di San Marco, and by many writers he is styled simply Il Frate (*the Friar*) ; in Italy he is scarcely known by any other designation.

Timid by nature, and tormented by religious scruples, he at first returned to his easel with languor and reluctance ; but an incident occurred which reäwakened all his genius and enthusiasm. Young Raphael, then in his twenty-first year, and already celebrated, arrived in Florence. He visited the Frate in his cell, and between these kindred spirits a friendship ensued which ended only with death, and to which we partly owe the finest works of both. Raphael, who was a perfect master of perspective, instructed his friend in the more complicated rules of the science, and Fra Bartolomeo in return initiated Raphael into some of his methods of coloring.

It was not, however, in the merely mechanical processes of art that these two great painters owed most to each other. It is evident, on examining his works, that Fra Bartolomeo's greatest improvement dates from his acquaintance with Raphael; that his pictures from this time display more energy of expression — a more intellectual grace : while Raphael imitated his friend in the softer blending of his colors, and learned from him the art of arranging draperies in an ampler and nobler style than he had hitherto practised ; in fact, he had just at this time caught the sentiment and manner of Bartolomeo so completely, that the only great work he executed at Florence (the Madonna del Balda-chino, in the Palazzo Pitti) might be at the first glance mistaken for a composition of the Frate. Richard-son, an excellent writer and first-rate authority, observes that " at this time Fra Bartolomeo seems to have been the greater man, and might have been *the* Raphael, had not Fortune been determined in favor of the other." It is not, however, Fortune alone which determines these things ; and of Raphael we might say, as Constance said of her son, that " at his birth Nature and Fortune joined to make him great." But this is digressing, and we must now return to the personal history of the Frate.

About the year 1513 Bartolomeo obtained leave of the Superior of his convent to visit Rome. He

had heard so much of the grand works on which
Raphael and Michael Angelo were employed by
Leo X., that he could no longer repress the wish to
behold and judge with his own eyes these wonderful productions.   He was also engaged to paint in
the church of St. Sylvester, on Monte Cavallo. But
the air of Rome did not agree with him.   He, indeed, renewed his friendship with Raphael, and
they spent many hours and days in each other's
society ; but Raphael had by this time so far out-
run him in every kind of excellence, and what he
saw around him in the Vatican and in the Sistine
Chapel so far surpassed his previous conceptions,
that admiration and astonishment seemed to swal-
low up the feeling of emulation.   There was no
envy in his gentle and pious mind ; but he could not
paint, he could not apply himself.   A cloud fell
upon his spirits, which was attributed partly to
indisposition ; and he returned to Florence, leaving
at Rome only two unfinished pictures — figures of
St. Peter and St. Paul, which Raphael undertook to
finish for him, and, in the midst of his own great
and multifarious works, found time to complete.
It is said that while Raphael was painting on the
head of St. Peter, two of his friends, who were cardinals, and not remarkable for the sanctity of their
lives, stood conversing with him, and thought
either to compliment him, or perhaps rouse him to
contradiction, by criticizing the work of Bartolomeo.   One of them observed that the coloring was

much *too red*. To which Raphael replied, with that graceful gayety which blunts the edge of a sarcasm, "May it please your Eminences, the holy apostle here represented is blushing in heaven, as he certainly would do were he now present, to behold the church he founded on earth governed by such as you!"

On returning to Florence, Fra Bartolomeo resumed his pencil, and showed that his journey to Rome had not been in vain. His finest works, the St. Mark, now in the Pitti Palace, and the famous Madonna di Misericordia at Lucca, were executed after his return. Every picture subsequently painted displayed increasing vigor; and he was still in the full possession of his powers when he was seized with a fever and dysentery, caused, it is said, by eating too many figs, and died in his convent, October 8, 1517, being then in his forty-eighth year.

The personal character of Fra Bartolomeo is impressed on all his works. He was deficient, as we have seen, in physical courage and energy; but in his disposition enthusiastic, devout, and affectionate. Tenderness and a soft regular beauty characterize his female heads; his saints have a mild and serious dignity. He is very seldom grand or sublime in conception, or energetic in movement and expression; the pervading sentiment in all his best pictures is *holiness*. He particularly excelled in the figures of boy-angels, which he introduced into

most of his groups, sometimes playing on musical instruments, seated at the feet of the Virgin, or
bearing a canopy over her head, but, however employed, always full of infantine grace and candor.
He is also famed for the rich architecture he introduced into his pictures, and for the grand and
flowing style of his draperies. It was his opinion
that every object should be painted, if possible,
from nature ; and, for the better study and arrangement of the drapery, he invented those wooden
figures with joints (called lay-figures) which are
now to be found in the studio of every painter, and
which have been of incalculable service in art.

His pictures are not commonly met with. Lucca,
Florence, and Vienna, possess the three finest.

The first of these, at Lucca, is perhaps the most
important of all his works. It is called the Madonna della Misericordia, and represents the Virgin,
a grand and beautiful figure, standing on a raised
platform with outstretched arms, pleading for
mercy for mankind; around her are groups of sup-
pliants, who look up to her as *she* looks up to
heaven, where, throned in judgment, is seen her
divine Son. Wilkie, in one of his letters from
Italy (1827), dwells upon the beauty of this noble
picture, and says that it combines the merits of
Raphael, of Titian, of Rembrandt, and of Rubens!
" Here," he says, " a monk in the retirement of
his cloister, shut out from the taunts and criticism
of the world, seems to have anticipated in his early

time all that his art could arrive at in its most advanced maturity; and this he has been able to do without the usual blandishments of the more recent periods, and with all the higher qualities peculiar to the age in which he lived." *

This is very high praise, particularly from such a man as Wilkie. The mere outline engraving in Rosini's "Storia della Pittura" will show the beauty of the composition; and the testimony of Wilkie with regard to the magical coloring is sufficient.

The St. Mark in the Pitti Palace is a single figure, seated, and holding his Gospel in his hand. It is so remarkable for its grandeur and simplicity as to have been frequently compared with the remains of Grecian art. For this picture a Grand-Duke of Tuscany (Ferdinand II.) paid twelve hundred pounds, nearly two hundred years ago; which, according to the present value of money, would be equal to about three thousand pounds.

In the Imperial Gallery at Vienna is the Presentation in the Temple, a picture of wonderful dignity and beauty, and well known by the fine engravings which exist of it. The figures are rather less than life.

In the Louvre at Paris are two very fine pictures: a Madonna enthroned, with several figures, life-size, which was painted as an altar-piece for his own convent of St. Mark, and afterwards sent as a

* Life of Sir David Wilkie, vol. ii., p. 451.

present to Francis I.; the other is an Annunciation.

In the Grosvenor Gallery there is a divine little
picture, in which the Infant Christ is represented
reclining on the lap of the Virgin, and holding the
cross, which the young St. John, stretching forth
his arms, appears anxious to take from him.

The Berlin Gallery contains only one of his pic
tures; the Dresden Gallery, not one. His works are
best studied in his native city of Florence, to which
they are chiefly confined.

Fra Bartolomeo had several scholars, none of
whom were distinguished, except a nun of the monastery of St. Catherine, known as Suor Plautilla,
who very successfully imitated his style, and has
left some beautiful pictures.

LIONARDO DA VINCI.

We now approach the period when the art of painting reached its highest perfection, whether considered with reference to poetry of conception, or the mechanical means through which these conceptions were embodied in the noblest forms. Within a short period of about thirty years, that is, between 1490 and 1520, the greatest painters whom the world has yet seen were living and working together. On looking back, we cannot but feel that the excellence they attained was the result of the efforts and aspirations of a preceding age ; and yet these men were so great in their vocation, and so individual in their greatness, that, losing sight of the linked chain of progress, they seemed at first to have had no precursors, as they have since had no peers. Though living at the same time, and most of them in personal relation with each other, the direction of each mind was different — was peculiar ; though exercising in some sort a reciprocal influence, this influence never interfered with the most decided originality. These wonderful artists who would have been remarkable men in their time, though they had never touched a pencil, were Lionardo da Vinci, Michael Angelo, Raphael, Correggio, Giorgione, Titian, in Italy ; and in Germany, Albert Durer. Of these men, we might say, as of Homer and Shakspeare, that they belong to no particular age or country, but to all time, and to the universe. That they flourished together within one brief and brilliant period, and that each carried out to the highest degree of perfection his own peculiar aims, was no casualty ; nor are we to seek for the causes of this surpassing excellence merely in the history of the art as such. The causes lay far deeper, and must be referred to the history of human culture. The fermenting activity of the fifteenth century found its results in the extraordinary development of human intelligence in the commencement of the sixteenth century. We often hear in these days of "the spirit of the age ; " but in that wonderful age three mighty spirits were stirring society to its depths : — the spirit of bold investigation into truths of all kinds, which led to the Reformation ; the spirit of daring adventure, which led men in search of new worlds beyond the eastern and the western oceans ; and the spirit of art, through which men soared even to the "seventh heaven of invention."

Lionardo da Vinci seems to present in his own person a *résumé* of all the characteristics of the age in which he lived. He was *the* miracle of that age of miracles. Ardent and versatile as youth,

patient and persevering as age; a most profound
and original thinker; the greatest mathematician
and most ingenious mechanic of his time; architect
chemist, engineer, musician, poet, painter ! — we
are not only astounded by the variety of his natural
gifts and acquired knowledge, but by the practical direction of his amazing powers.* The extracts
which have been published from MSS. now existing
in his own handwriting show him to have anticipated, by the force of his own intellect, some of the
greatest discoveries made since his time. These
fragments, says Mr. Hallam,† "are, according to
our common estimate of the age in which he lived,
more like revelations of physical truths vouchsafed
to a single mind, than the superstructure of its
reasoning upon any established basis. The discoveries which made Galileo, Kepler, Castelli, and
other names illustrious — the system of Copernicus
— the very theories of recent geologists, are anticipated by Da Vinci within the compass of a few
pages, not perhaps in the most precise language,
or on the most conclusive reasoning, but so as to
strike us with something like the awe of preternatural knowledge. In an age of so much dog-

* The Italian writers thus sum up the qualifications of Lionardo,
with an array of discriminative epithets not easily translated : —
"*Valente* musico e poeta ; *ingegnoso* mecanico ; *profondo* geom-
etra e matematico ; *egregio* architetto ; *esimio* idraulico ; *eccelente*
plasticatore e *sommo* pittore.'
† " History of the Literature of Europe.

matism, he first laid down the grand principle of
Bacon, that experiment and observation must be
the guides to just theory in the investigation of
nature. If any doubt could be harbored, not as to
the right of Lionardo da Vinci to stand as the first
name of the fifteenth century, which is beyond all
doubt,* but as to his originality in so many discoveries, which probably no one man, especially in such
circumstances, has ever made, it must be by an
hypothesis not very untenable, that some parts of
physical science had already attained a height
which mere books do not record."

It seems at first sight almost incomprehensible
that, thus endowed as a philosopher, mechanic,
inventor, discoverer, the fame of Lionardo should
now rest on the works he has left as a painter.
We cannot, within these limits, attempt to explain
why and how it is that as the man of science he has
been naturally and necessarily left behind by the
onward march of intellectual progress, while as the
poet-painter he still survives as a presence and a
power. We must proceed at once to give some
account of him in the character in which he exists
to us and for us — that of the great artist.

Lionardo was born at Vinci, near Florence, in
the Lower Val d'Arno, on the borders of the territory of Pistoia.   His father, Piero da Vinci, was

---

* When we think of Lionardo's contemporary, Columbus, we feel
inclined, if not to dispute this fiat of the great historian, at least to
ponder on it, and those ponderings lead us far.

an advocate of Florence — not rich, but in independent circumstances, and possessed of estates in
land. The singular talents of his son induced Piero
to give him, from an early age, the advantage of the
best instructors. As a child, he distinguished himself by his proficiency in arithmetic and mathematics. Music he studied early, as a science as
well as an art. He invented a species of lyre for
himself, and sung his own poetical compositions to
his own music — both being frequently extempora-
neous. But his favorite pursuit was the art of
design in all its branches; he modelled in clay or
wax, or attempted to draw every object which struck
his fancy. His father sent him to study under Andrea Verrocchio (of whom we have already given
some account),* famous as a sculptor, chaser in
metal, and painter. Andrea, who was an excellent
and correct designer, but a bad and hard colorist,
was soon after engaged to paint a picture of the
Baptism of our Saviour. He employed Lionardo,
then a youth, to execute one of the angels. This
he did with so much softness and richness of color
that it far surpassed the rest of the picture ; and
Verocchio from that time threw away his palette,
and confined himself wholly to his works in sculpture and design ; " enraged," says Vasari, " that
a child should thus excel him." †

* See p. 111.
† This picture is now preserved in the Academy at Florence. The
first angel on the right is that which was painted by Lionardo.

The youth of Lionardo thus passed away in the pursuit of science and of art. Sometimes he was deeply engaged in astronomical calculations and investigations; sometimes ardent in the study of natural history, botany, and anatomy; sometimes intent on new effects of color, light, shadow, or expression, in representing objects animate or inanimate. Versatile, yet persevering, he varied his pursuits, but he never abandoned any. He was quite a young man when he conceived and demonstrated the practicability of two magnificent projects. One was, to lift the whole of the church of San Lorenzo, by means of immense levers, some feet higher than it now stands, and thus supply the deficient elevation;* the other project was, to form the Arno into a navigable canal, as far as Pisa, which would have added greatly to the commercial advantages of Florence.†

It happened about this time that a peasant on the estate of Piero da Vinci brought him a circular piece of wood, cut horizontally from the trunk of a very large old fig-tree, which had been lately felled, and begged to have something painted on it as an ornament for his cottage. The man being an especial favorite, Piero desired his son Lionardo to grat-

* Wild as this project must have appeared, it was not perhaps impossible. In our days, the Sunderland Light-house was lifted from its foundations, and removed to a distance of several yards.

† This project was carried into execution two hundred years later.

ify his request; and Lionardo, inspired by that wildness of fancy which was one of his characteristics, took the panel into his own room, and resolved to astonish his father by a most unlooked-for proof of his art. He determined to compose something which should have an effect similar to that of the Medusa on the shield of Perseus. and almost petrify beholders. Aided by his recent studies in natural history, he collected together from the neighboring swamps and the river-mud all kinds of hideous reptiles, as adders, lizards, toads, serpents; insects, as moths, locusts; and other crawling and flying, obscene and obnoxious things; and out of these he compounded a sort of monster, or chimera, which he represented as about to issue from the shield, with eyes flashing fire, and of an aspect so fearful and abominable that it seemed to infect the very air around. When finished, he led his father into the room in which it was placed, and the terror and horror of Piero proved the success of his attempt. This production, afterwards known as the Rotello del Fico,* from the material on which it was painted, was sold by Piero secretly for one hundred ducats, to a merchant, who carried it to Milan, and sold it to the duke for three hundred. To the poor peasant thus cheated of his Rotello, Piero gave a wooden shield, on which was painted a heart transfixed by a dart; a device better suited to his taste and comprehension. In the

* *Rotello* means a shield or buckler; *Fico*, a fig-tree.

subsequent troubles of Milan, Lionardo's picture disappeared, and was probably destroyed, as an object of horror, by those who did not understand its value as a work of art.

The anomalous monster represented on the Rotello was wholly different from the Medusa, afterwards painted by Lionardo, and now existing in the Florence Gallery. It represents the severed head of Medusa, seen foreshortened, lying on a fragment of rock. The features are beautiful and regular ; the hair already metamorphosed into serpents —

> " which curl and flow,
> And their long tangles in each other lock,
> And with unending involutions show
> Their mailéd radiance."

Those who have once seen this terrible and fascinating picture can never forget it. The ghastly head seems to expire, and the serpents to crawl into glittering life, as we look upon it.

During this first period of his life, which was wholly passed in Florence and its neighborhood. Lionardo painted several other pictures, of a very different character, and designed some beautiful cartoons of sacred and mythological subjects, which showed that his sense of the beautiful, the elevated, and the graceful, was not less a part of his mind, than that eccentricity and almost perversion of fancy which made him delight in sketching ugly,

12

exaggerated caricatures, and representing the deformed and the terrible.

Lionardo da Vinci was now about thirty years old, in the prime of his life and talents. His taste for pleasure and expense was, however, equal to his genius and indefatigable industry ; and, anxious to secure a certain provision for the future, as well as a wider field for the exercise of his various talents, he accepted the invitation of Ludovico Sforza il Moro, then regent, afterwards Duke of Milan, to reside in his court, and to execute a colossal equestrian statue of his ancestor Francesco Sforza. Here begins the second period of his artistic career, which includes his sojourn at Milan, that is, from 1483 to 1499.

Vasari says that Lionardo was invited to the court of Milan for the Duke Ludovico's amusement, " as a musician and performer on the lyre, and as the greatest singer and *improvisatore* of his time ; " but this is improbable. Lionardo, in his long letter to that prince, in which he recites his own qualifications for employment, dwells chiefly on his skill in engineering and fortification, and sums up his pretensions as an artist in these few brief words : " I understand the different modes of sculpture in marble, bronze, and terra-cotta. In painting, also, I may esteem myself equal to any one, let him be who he may." Of his musical talents he makes no mention whatever, though undoubtedly these, as well as his other social accomplishments, his hand some person, his winning address, his wit and eloquence, recommended him to the notice of the prince, by whom he was greatly beloved, and in whose service he remained for about seventeen years. It is not necessary, nor would it be possible here, to give a particular account of all the works in which Lionardo was engaged for his patron,* nor of the great political events in which he was involved, more by his position than by his inclination; for instance, the invasion of Italy by Charles VIII. of France, and the subsequent invasion of Milan by Louis XII., which ended in the destruction of the Duke Ludovico. We shall only mention a few of the pictures he executed. One of these, the portrait of Lucrezia Crivelli, is now in the Louvre (No. 1091). Another was the Nativity of our Saviour, in the imperial collection at Vienna; but the greatest work of all, and by far the grandest picture which, up to that time, had been executed in Italy, was the Last Supper, painted on the wall of the refectory, or dining-room, of the Dominican convent of the Madonna delle Grazie. It occupied the painter about two years. Of this magnificent creation of art only the mouldering remains are now visible. It has been so often repaired, that almost every vestige of the original painting is annihilated; but, from the multiplicity

---

* Of these, the canal of the Martesana, as well from its utility as from the difficulties he surmounted in its execution, would have been sufficient to immortalize him.

of descriptions, engravings, and copies that exist no picture is more universally known and celebrated.

The moment selected by the painter is described in the twenty-sixth chapter of St. Matthew, twenty-first and twenty-second verses : " And as they did eat, he said, Verily, I say unto you, that one of you shall betray me : and they were exceeding sorrowful, and began every one of them to say unto him, Lord, is it I ? " The knowledge of character displayed in the heads of the different apostles is even more wonderful than the skilful arrangement of the figures and the amazing beauty of the workmanship. The space occupied by the picture is a wall twenty-eight feet in length, and the figures are larger than life. The best judgment we can now form of its merits is from the fine copy executed by one of Lionardo's best pupils, Marco Uggione, for the Certosa at Pavia, and now in London, in the collection of the Royal Academy. Eleven other copies, by various pupils of Lionardo, painted either during his lifetime or within a few years after his death, while the picture was in perfect preservation, exist in different churches and collections.

Of the grand equestrian statue of Francesco Sforza, Lionardo never finished more than the model in clay, which was considered a masterpiece. Some years afterwards (in 1499), when Milan was invaded by the French, it was used as a target by the Gascon bowmen, and completely destroyed. The profound anatomical studies which Lionardo made for this work still exist.

In the year 1500, the French being in possession of Milan, his patron Ludovico in captivity, and the affairs of the state in utter confusion, Lionardo returned to his native Florence, where he hoped to reëstablish his broken fortunes, and to find employment. Here begins the third period of his artistic life, from 1500 to 1513, that is, from his forty-eighth to his sixtieth year. He found the Medici family in exile, but was received by Pietro Soderini (who governed the city as "*Gonfalonicre perpetuo*") with great distinction, and a pension was assigned to him as painter in the service of the republic.

Then began the rivalry between Lionardo and Michael Angelo, which lasted during the remainder of Lionardo's life. The difference of age (for Michael Angelo was twenty-two years younger) ought to have prevented all unseemly jealousy. But Michael Angelo was haughty, and impatient of all superiority, or even equality ; Lionardo, sensitive, capricious, and naturally disinclined to admit the pretensions of a rival, to whom he could say, and *did* say, " I was famous before you were born ! " With all their admiration of each other's genius, their mutual frailties prevented any real good-will on either side. The two painters competed for the honor of painting in fresco one side of the great Council-hall in the Palazzo Vecchio at

Florence. Each prepared his cartoon ; each, emu
lous of the fame and conscious of the abilities of his
rival, threw all his best powers into his work.
Lionardo chose for his subject the Defeat of the
Milanese general, Niccolò Piccinino, by the Florentine army in 1440. One of the finest groups represented a combat of cavalry disputing the possession
of a standard. "It was so wonderfully executed,
that the horses themselves seemed animated by the
same fury as their riders ; nor is it possible to describe the variety of attitudes, the splendor of the
dresses and armor of the warriors, nor the incredible skill displayed in the forms and actions of the
horses."

Michael Angelo chose for his subject the moment
before the same battle, when a party of Florentine
soldiers bathing in the Arno are surprised by the
sound of the trumpet calling them to arms. Of
this cartoon we shall have more to say in treating
of his life. The preference was given to Lionardo
da Vinci. But, as Vasari relates, he spent so much
time in trying experiments, and in preparing the
wall to receive oil-painting, which he preferred to
fresco, that in the interval some changes in the
government intervened, and the design was abandoned. The two cartoons remained for several
years open to the public, and artists flocked from
every part of Italy to study them. Subsequently
they were cut up into separate parts, dispersed, and
lost. It is curious that of Michael Angelo's com

position only one small copy exists; of Lionardo's
not one. From a fragment which existed in his
time, but which has since disappeared, Rubens
made a fine drawing, which was engraved by Ede-
linck, and is known as the Battle of the Standard.

It was a reproach against Lionardo, in his own
time, that he began many things and finished few;
that his magnificent designs and projects, whether
in art or mechanics, were seldom completed. This
may be a subject of regret, but it is unjust to make
it a reproach. It was in the nature of the man
The grasp of his mind was so nearly superhuman
that he never, in anything he effected, satisfied himself or realized his own vast conceptions. The most
exquisitely finished of his works, those that in the
perfection of the execution have excited the wonder
and despair of succeeding artists, were put aside
by him as unfinished sketches. Most of the pictures now attributed to him were wholly or in part
painted by his scholars and imitators from his cartoons. One of the most famous of these was designed for the altar-piece of the church of the convent called the Nunziata. It represented the
Virgin Mary seated in the lap of her mother, St.
Anna, having in her arms the infant Christ, while
St. John is playing with a lamb at their feet; St.
Anna, looking on with a tender smile, rejoices in
her divine offspring. The figures were drawn with
such skill, and the various expressions proper to
each conveyed with such inimitable truth and grace,

that, when exhibited in a chamber of the convent
the inhabitants of the city flocked to see it, and for
two days the streets were crowded with people,
" as if it had been some solemn festival ; " but the
picture was never painted, and the monks of the
Nunziata, after waiting long and in vain for their
altar-piece, were obliged to employ other artists
The cartoon, or a very fine repetition of it, is now
in the possession of our Royal Academy, and it
must not be confounded with the St. Anna in the
Louvre, a more fantastic and apparently an earlier
composition.

Lionardo, during his stay at Florence, painted
the portrait of Ginevra Benci, already mentioned,
in the memoir of Ghirlandajo, as the reigning
beauty of her time ; and also the portrait of Mona
Lisa del Giocondo, sometimes called La Joconde.
On this last picture he worked at intervals for four
years, but was still unsatisfied. It was purchased
by Francis I. for four thousand golden crowns, and
is now in the Louvre. We find Lionardo also engaged by Cæsar Borgia to visit and report on the
fortifications of his territories, and in this office he
was employed for two years. In 1514 he was invited to Rome by Leo X., but more in his character
of philosopher, mechanic, and alchemist, than as a
painter. Here he found Raphael at the height of
his fame, and then engaged in his greatest works
— the frescoes of the Vatican. Two pictures which
Lionardo painted while at Rome — the Madonna

of St. Onofrio, and the Holy Family, painted for Filiberta of Savoy, the pope's sister-in-law (which is now at St. Petersburg) — show that even this veteran in art felt the irresistible influence of the genius of his young rival. They are both *Raffael-lesque* in the subject and treatment.

It appears that Lionardo was ill-satisfied with his sojourn at Rome. He had long been accustomed to hold the first rank as an artist wherever he resided; whereas at Rome he found himself only one among many who, if they acknowledged his greatness, affected to consider his day as past. He was conscious that many of the improvements in the arts which were now brought into use, and which enabled the painters of the day to produce such extraordinary effects, were invented or introduced by himself. If he could no longer assert that measureless superiority over all others which he had done in his younger days, it was because he himself had opened to them new paths to excellence. The arrival of his old competitor Michael Angelo, and some slight on the part of Leo X., who was annoyed by his speculative and dilatory habits in executing the works intrusted to him, all added to his irritation and disgust. He left Rome, and set out for Pavia, where the French king Francis I. then held his court. He was received by the young monarch with every mark of respect, loaded with favors, and a pension of seven hundred gold crowns settled on him for life At the famous conference between Francis I. and Leo X. at Bologna, Lionardo attended his new patron, and was of essential service to him on that occasion. In the following year, 1516, he returned with Francis I. to France, and was attached to the French court as principal painter. It appears, however, that during his residence in France he did not paint a single picture. His health had begun to decline from the time he left Italy ; and, feeling his end approach, he prepared himself for it by religious meditation, by acts of charity, and by a most conscientious dis tribution by will of all his worldly possessions to his relatives and friends. At length, after pro-tracted suffering, this great and most extraordinary man died at Cloux, near Amboise, on the 2d of May, 1519, being then in his sixty-seventh year. It is to be regretted that we cannot wholly credit the beautiful story of his dying in the arms of Francis I., who, as it is said, had come to visit him on his death-bed. It would, indeed, have been, as Fuseli expressed it, "an honor to the king, by which Destiny would have atoned to that monarch for his future disaster at Pavia," had the incident really happened, as it has been so often related by biographers, celebrated by poets, represented with a just pride by painters, and willingly believed by all the world ; but the well-authenticated fact that the court was *on that day* at St. Germain-en-Laye whence the royal ordinances are dated, renders the story, unhappily, very doubtful

We have mentioned a few of the genuine works of Lionardo da Vinci; they are exceedingly rare It appears certain that not one-third of the pictures attributed to him and bearing his name were the production of his own hand, though they were the creation of his mind, for he generally furnished the cartoons or designs from which his pupils executed pictures of various degrees of excellence.

Thus the admirable picture in our National Gallery of Christ disputing with the Doctors, though undoubtedly designed by Lionardo, is supposed by some to be executed by his best scholar, Bernardino Luini; by others it is attributed to Francesco Melzi. Those ruined pictures which bear his name at Windsor and at Hampton Court are from the Milanese school.*

Of nine pictures in the Louvre attributed to Lionardo, three only—the St. John, and the two famous portraits of the Mona Lisa and Lucrezia Crivelli — are considered genuine. The others are from his designs and from his school.

In the Florentine Gallery, the Medusa is certainly genuine; but the famous Herodias holding the dish to receive the head of John the Baptist was probably painted from his cartoon by Luini.

* The Falconer, at Windsor, I believe to be by Holbein, and it is curious that this is not the first nor only Holbein which has been attributed to Lionardo. There is one in the Liverpool Institute, and I have known others.

His own portrait, in the same gallery (in the Salle des Peintres), is wonderfully fine ; indeed, the finest of all, and the one which at once attracts and fixes attention.

In the Milan collections are many pictures attributed to him. A few are in private collections in England. Lord Ashburton has an exquisite group of the Infant Christ and St. John playing with a lamb ; and there is a small Madonna in Lord Shrewsbury's gallery at Alton Towers.

But it is the MS. notes and designs left behind him that give us the best idea of the indefatigable industry of this "myriad-minded man," and the almost incredible extent of his acquirements. In the Ambrosian Library at Milan there are twelve huge volumes of his works relative to arts, chemistry, mathematics, &c. ; one of them contains a collection of anatomical drawings, which the celebrated anatomist Dr. Hunter described as the most wonderful things of the kind for accuracy and beauty that he had ever beheld. In the Royal Library at Windsor there are three volumes of MSS. and drawings, containing a vast variety of subjects — portraits, heads, groups, and single figures ; fine anatomical studies of horses ; a battle of elephants, full of spirit ; drawings in optics, hydraulics, and perspective ; plans of military machines, maps and surveys of rivers ; beautiful and accurate drawings of plants and rocks, to be introduced into his pictures ; musical airs noted in his own hand, perhaps his own compositions ; anatomical subjects, with elaborate notes and explanations. In the Royal Library at Paris there is a volume of philosophical treatises, from which extracts have been published by Venturi. In the Holkham Collection is a MS. treatise on hydraulics. The " Treatise on Painting," by Lionardo da Vinci, has been translated from the original Italian into French, English, and German, and is the foundation of all that has since been written on the subject, whether relating to the theory or to the practice of the art. His MSS. are particularly difficult to read or decipher, as he had a habit of writing from right to left, instead of from left to right. What was his reason for this singularity has not been explained.

The scholars of Lionardo da Vinci, and those artists formed in the Academy which he founded in Milan, under the patronage of Ludovico il Moro, comprise that school of art known as the Milanese, or Lombard School. They are distinguished by a lengthy and graceful style of drawing, a particular amenity and sweetness of expression (which in the inferior painters degenerated into affectation and a sort of vapid smile), and particularly by the transparent lights and shadows — the *chiaroscuro*, of which Lionardo was the inventor or discoverer. The most eminent painters were Bernardino Luini ; Marco Uggione, or D'Oggioni ; Antonio Beltraffio ; Francesco Melzi ; and

Andrea Salai.   All these studied under the immediate tuition of Lionardo, and painted most of the
pictures ascribed to him.   Gaudenzio Ferrari and
Cesare da Sesto imitated him, and owed their
celebrity to his influence.

MICHAEL ANGELO.

Born 1474, died 1564.

WE have spoken of Lionardo da Vinci. Michael Angelo, the other great luminary of art, was twenty-two years younger ; but the more severe and reflective cast of his mind rendered their difference of age far less in effect than in reality. It is usual to compare Michael Angelo with Raphael, but he is more aptly compared with Lionardo da Vinci. All the great artists of that time, even Raphael himself, were influenced more or less by these two extraordinary men, but they exercised no influence on each other. They started from opposite points ; they pursued throughout their whole existence, and in all they planned and achieved, a course as different as their respective characters. It would be very curious and interesting to carry out the comparison in detail ; to show the contrast in organization, in temper, in talent, in taste, which existed between men so highly and so equally endowed ; but our limits forbid this indulgence. We shall, therefore, only observe here that, considered as artists, they emulated each other in variety of power, but that Lionardo was more the painter than the sculptor and architect, Michael Angelo was more the sculptor and architect than the painter. Both sought true inspiration in Nature, but they beheld her with different eyes. Lionardo, who designed admirably, appears to have seen no *outline* in objects and labored all his life to convey, by color and light and shade, the impression of beauty and the illusive effect of rotundity. He preferred the use of oil to fresco, because the mellow smoothness and transparency of the vehicle was more capable of giving the effects he desired. Michael Angelo, on the contrary, turned his whole attention to the definition of *form*, and the expression of life and power through action and movement; he regarded the illusive effects of painting as meretricious and beneath his notice, and despised oil-painting as a style for women and children. Considered as men, both were as high-minded and generous as they were gifted and original; but the former was as remarkable for his versatile and social accomplishments, his love of pleasure and habits of expense as the latter for his stern, inflexible temper, and his temperate, frugal, and secluded habits.

Michael Angelo Buonaroti was born at Settignano, near Florence, in the year 1474. He was descended from a family once noble — even amongst the noblest of the feudal lords of northern Italy — the Counts of Canossa; but that branch of it represented by his father, Luigi Lionardo Buonaroti Simoni, had for some generations become poorer

and poorer, until the last descendant was thankful
to accept an office in the law, and had been nomi
nated magistrate or mayor (*Podesta*) of Chiusi.
In this situation he had limited his ambition to
the prospect of seeing his eldest son a notary or
advocate in his native city. The young Michael
Angelo showed the utmost distaste for the studies
allotted to him, and was continually escaping from
his home and from his desk to haunt the ateliers
of the painters, particularly that of Ghirlandajo,
who was then at the height of his reputation, and
of whom some account has been already given.

The father of Michael Angelo, who found his
family increase too rapidly for his means, had destined some of his sons for commerce (it will be
recollected that in Genoa and Florence the most
powerful nobles were merchants or manufacturers),
and others for civil or diplomatic employments. But
the fine arts, as being at that time productive of
little honor or emolument, he held in no esteem,
and treated these tastes of his eldest son sometimes
with contempt, and sometimes even with harshness.
Michael Angelo, however, had formed some friend-
ships among the young painters, and particularly
with Francesco Granacci, one of the best pupils of
Ghirlandajo ; he contrived to borrow models and
drawings, and studied them in secret with such
persevering assiduity and consequent improvement
that Ghirlandajo, captivated by his genius, undertook to plead his cause to his father, and at length

13

prevailed over the old man's family pride and prej-
udices. At the age of fourteen, Michael Angelo
was received into the studio of Ghirlandajo as a
regular pupil, and bound to him for three years ;
and such was the precocious talent of the boy, that
instead of being paid for his instruction, Ghirlandajo undertook to pay the father, Lionardo Buonaroti, for the first, second, and third years, six,
eight, and twelve golden florins, as payment for the
advantage he expected to derive from the labor of
the son. Thus was the vocation of the young artist
decided for life.

At that time Lorenzo the Magnificent reigned
over Florence. He had formed in his palace and
gardens a collection of antique marbles, busts,
statues, fragments, which he had converted into
an academy for the use of young artists, placing
at the head of it as director a sculptor of some
eminence, named Bertoldo. Michael Angelo was
one of the first who, through the recommendation
of Ghirlandajo, was received into this new academy, afterwards so famous and so memorable in the
history of art. The young man, then not quite
sixteen, had hitherto occupied himself chiefly in
drawing ; but now, fired by the beauties he beheld
around him, and by the example and success of a
fellow-pupil, Torregiano, he set himself to model in
clay, and at length to copy in marble what was
before him ; but, as was natural in a character
and genius so steeped in individuality, his copies

became not so much imitations of form as original
embodyings of the leading idea, and Lorenzo de'
Medici, struck by his extraordinary power, sent for
his father and offered to attach the boy to his own
particular service, and to undertake the entire care
of his education. The father consented, on condition of receiving for himself an office under the
government; and thenceforth Michael Angelo was
lodged in the palace of the Medici, and treated by
Lorenzo as his son.

Such sudden and increasing favor excited the
envy and jealousy of his companions, particularly
of Torregiano, who, being of a violent and arrogant
temper (that of Michael Angelo was by no means
conciliating), sought every means of showing his
hatred. On one occasion, a quarrel having ensued
while they were at work together, Torregiano turned
in fury and struck his rival a blow with his mallet,
which disfigured him for life. His nose was flat-
tened to his face, and Torregiano, having by this
" sacrilegious stroke " gratified his hatred, was
banished from Florence.

It is fair, however, to give Torregiano's own account of this incident as he related it to Benvenuto
Cellini, many years afterwards. " This Buonaroti
and I, when we were young men, went to study in
the church of the Carmelites, in the chapel of Masaccio. It was customary with Buonaroti to rally
those who were learning to draw there. One day,
among others, a sarcasm of his having stung me te

the quick, I was extremely irritated, and, doubling my fist, gave him such a violent blow on the nose that I felt the bone and cartilage yield as if they had been made of paste, and the mark I then gave him he will carry to his grave."

Thus it appears that the blow was not unprovoked, and that Michael Angelo, even at the age of sixteen, indulged in that contemptuous arrogance and sarcastic speech which, in his maturer age, made him so many enemies. But to return.

Michael Angelo continued his studies under the auspices of Lorenzo; but just as he had reached his eighteenth year he lost his generous patron, his second father, and was thenceforth thrown on his own resources. It is true that the son of Lorenzo, Piero de' Medici, continued to extend his favor to the young artist, but with so little comprehension of his genius and character, that on one occasion, during a severe winter, he sent him to form a statue of snow for the amusement of his guests.

Michael Angelo, while he yielded, perforce, to the caprices of his protector, turned the energies of his mind to a new study — that of anatomy — and pursued it with all that fervor which belonged to his character. His attention was at the same time directed to literature, by the counsels and conversations of a very celebrated scholar and poet, then residing in the court of Piero — Angelo Poliziano; and he pursued at the same time the cultivation of his mind and the practice of his art. Engrossed

by his own studies, he was scarcely aware of what
was passing around him, nor of the popular intrigues which were preparing the ruin of the
Medici. Suddenly this powerful family were flung
from sovereignty to temporary disgrace and exile;
and Michael Angelo, as one of their retainers, was
obliged to fly from Florence, and took refuge in the
city of Bologna. During the year he spent there
he found a friend who employed him on some works
of sculpture; and on his return to Florence he executed a Cupid in marble, of such beauty that it
found its way into the cabinet of the Duchess of
Mantua as a real antique. On the discovery that
the author of this beautiful statue was a young man
of two-and-twenty, the Cardinal San Giorgio invited him to Rome, and for some time lodged him
in his palace. Here Michael Angelo, surrounded
and inspired by the grand remains of antiquity,
pursued his studies with unceasing energy. He
produced a statue of Bacchus, which added to his
reputation; and the group of the dead Christ on
the knees of his Virgin Mother (called *the Pietà*),
which is now in the church of St. Peter's, at Rome.*

* This Pietà is the only work whereon Michael Angelo inscribed
his name, which he has carved distinctly on the girdle of the Virgin.
The circumstance which induced him to do this is curious. Some
time after the group was fixed in its place, he was standing before it
considering its effect, when two strangers entered the church, and
began, even in his hearing, to dispute concerning the author of the
work, which they agreed in exalting to the skies as a masterpiece
One of them, who was a Bolognese, insisted that it was by a sculptor

This last, being frequently copied and imitated, obtained him so much applause and reputation, that
he was recalled to Florence. to undertake several
public works, and found himself once more established in his native city about the year 1504.

Hitherto we have seen Michael Angelo wholly
devoted to the study and practice of sculpture; but
soon after his return to Florence he was called upon
to compete with Lionardo da Vinci in executing the
cartoons for the frescoes with which it was intended
to decorate the walls of the Palazzo Vecchio, or
town-hall of Florence. The cartoon of Lionardo
has been already described. That of Michael Angelo represented an incident which occurred during
the siege of Pisa,—a group of Florentine soldiers
bathing in the Arno hear the trumpet which proclaims a sortie of the enemy, and spring at once to
the combat.　He chose this subject, perhaps, as
affording ample opportunity to exhibit his peculiar
and wonderful skill in designing the human figure.
All is life and movement. The warriors, some
already clothed, but the greater part undressed,
hasten to obey the call to battle; they are seen
clambering up the banks—buckling on their armor
—rushing forward, hurriedly, eagerly. There are,
altogether, about thirty figures, the size of life,

of Bologna, whom he named. Michael Angelo listened in silence,
and the next night, when all slept, he entered the church, and by
the light of a lantern engraved his name, in deep, indelible characters, where it might best be seen.

drawn with black chalk, and relieved with white.
This cartoon was regarded by his contemporaries as
the most perfect of his works ; that is, in respect to
the execution merely : as to subject, sentiment,
and character, it would not certainly rank with the
finest of his works ; for, with every possible variety
of gesture and attitude, exhibited with admirable
and lifelike energy and the most consummate
knowledge of form, there was only one expression
throughout, and that the least intellectual, majestic, or interesting — the expression of hurry and
surprise. While this great work existed, it was a
study for all the young artists of Italy. But
Michael Angelo, who had suffered in person from
the jealousy of one rival, was destined to suffer yet
more cruelly from the envy of another. It is said
that Bandinelli, the sculptor, profited by the
troubles of Florence to tear in pieces this monument
of the glory and genius of a man he detested ; but
in doing so he has only left an enduring stain upon
his own fame. A small old copy of the principal
part of the composition exists in the collection of
the Earl of Leicester, at Holkham, and has been
finely engraved by Schiavonetti.

The next work in which Michael Angelo was engaged was the tomb of Pope Julius II., who, while
living, had conceived the idea of erecting a most
splendid monument to perpetuate his memory. For
this work, which was never completed, Michael
Angelo executed the famous statue of Moses, seated,

grasping his flowing beard with one hand, and with the other sustaining the tables of the law. While employed on this tomb, the pope commanded him to undertake also the decoration of the ceiling of the Sistine Chapel. The reader may remember that Pope Sixtus IV., in the year 1473, erected his famous chapel, and summoned the best painters of that time, Signorelli, Cosimo Roselli, Perugino, and Ghirlandajo, to decorate the interior. But down to the year 1508 the ceiling remained without any ornament; and Michael Angelo was called upon to cover this enormous vault, a space of one hundred and fifty feet in length by fifty in breadth, with a series of subjects, representing the most important events connected, either literally or typically, with the fall and redemption of mankind.

No part of Michael Angelo's long life is so interesting, so full of characteristic incident, as the his tory of his intercourse with Pope Julius II., which began in 1505, and ended only with the death of the pope, in 1513.

Michael Angelo had at all times a lofty idea of his own dignity as an artist, and never would stoop either to flatter a patron or to conciliate a rival. Julius II., though now seventy-four, was as impatient of contradiction, as fiery in temper as full of magnificent and ambitious projects, as if he had been in the prime of life. In his service was the famous architect Bramante, who beheld with jealousy and alarm the increasing fame of Michael

Angelo and his influence with the pontiff, and set himself by indirect means to lessen both. He insinuated to Julius that it was ominous to erect his own mausoleum during his lifetime, and the pope gradually fell off in his attentions to Michael Angelo, and neglected to supply him with the necessary funds for carrying on the work. On one occasion, Michael Angelo, finding it difficult to obtain access to the pope, sent a message to him to this effect, " that henceforth, if his holiness desired to see him, he should send to seek him elsewhere ; " and the same night, leaving orders with his servants to dispose of his property, he departed for Florence. The pope dispatched five couriers after him with threats, persuasions, promises, — but in vain. He wrote to the Gonfaloniere Soderini, then at the head of the government of Florence, commanding him, on pain of his extreme displeasure, to send Michael Angelo back to him ; but the inflexible artist absolutely refused. Three months were spent in vain negotiations. Soderini, at length, fearing the pope's anger, prevailed on Michael Angelo to return, and sent with him his relation Cardinal Soderini to make up the quarrel between the high contending powers. The pope was then at Bologna, and at the moment when Michael Angelo arrived he was at supper. He desired him to be brought into his presence, and, on seeing him, exclaimed, in a transport of fury, " Instead of obeying our commands and coming to us, thou hast waited till we came in search of thee! " (Bologna being much nearer to Florence than to Rome.) Michael Angelo fell on his knees, and entreated pardon with a loud voice. " Holy father," said he, " my offence has not arisen from an evil nature; I could no longer endure the insults offered to me in the palace of your holiness! " He remained kneeling, and the pope continued to bend his brows in silence, when a certain bishop in attendance on the Cardinal Soderini, thinking to mend the matter, interfered with excuses, representing that " Michael Angelo — poor man! — had erred through ignorance ; that artists were wont to presume too much on their genius," and so forth. The irascible pope, interrupting him with a sharp blow across the shoulders with his staff, exclaimed, " It is thou that art ignorant and presuming, to insult him whom we feel ourselves bound to honor. Take thyself out of our sight! " And, as the terrified prelate stood transfixed with amazement, the pope's attendants forced him out of the room. Julius then, turning to Michael Angelo, gave him his forgiveness and his blessing, and commanded him never again to leave him, promising him on all occasions his favor and protection. This extraordinary scene took place in November, 1506.

The work on the tomb was not, however, immediately resumed. Michael Angelo was commanded to execute a colossal statue of the pope, to be erected in front of the principal church of Bologna.

He threw into the figure and attitude so much of the haughty and resolute character of the original, that Julius, on seeing the model, asked him, with a smile, whether he intended to represent him as blessing or as cursing. To which Michael Angelo prudently replied, that he intended to represent his holiness as admonishing the inhabitants of Bologna to obedience and submission. " And what," said the pope, well pleased, " wilt thou put in the other hand ? " — " A book, may it please your holiness." — " A book, man! " exclaimed the pope: " put rather a sword. Thou knowest I am no scholar." The fate of this statue, however we may lament it, was fitting and characteristic. A few years afterwards, the populace of Bologna rebelled against the popedom, flung down the statue of Julius, and out of the fragments was constructed a cannon, which, from its origin, was styled *La Giuliana*.

On his return to Rome, Michael Angelo wished to have resumed his work on the mausoleum ; but the pope had resolved on the completion of the Sistine Chapel. He commanded Michael Angelo to undertake the decoration of the vaulted ceiling, and the artist was obliged, though reluctantly, to obey. At this time the frescoes which Raphael and his pupils were painting in the chambers of the Vatican had excited the admiration of all Rome. Michael Angelo, who had never exercised himself in the mechanical part of the art of fresco, invited from Florence several painters of eminence, to execute his designs under his own superintendence, but they could not reach the grandeur of his conceptions, which became enfeebled under their hands ; and, one morning, in a mood of impatience, he destroyed all that they had done, closed the doors of the chapel against them, and would not thenceforth admit them to his presence. He then shut himself up, and proceeded with incredible perseverance and energy to accomplish his task alone ; he even prepared his own colors with his own hands. He began with the end towards the door; and in the two compartments first painted (though not first in the series), the Deluge, and the Vineyard of Noah, he made the figures too numerous and too small to produce their full effect from below, — a fault which he corrected in those executed subsequently. When almost half the work was completed, the pope insisted on viewing what was done, and the astonishment and admiration it excited rendered him more and more eager to have the whole completed at once. The progress, however, was not rapid enough to suit the impatient temper of the pontiff. On one occasion, he demanded of the artist *when* he meant to finish it, to which Michael Angelo replied, calmly, " When I can." —" When thou canst ! " exclaimed the fiery old pope. " Thou hast a mind that I should have thee thrown from the scaffold ! " At length, on the day of All Saints, 1512, the ceiling was uncovered to public view. Michael Angelo had employed on the paint'ng only, without reckoning the time spent in preparing the cartoons, twenty-two months, and he received in payment three thousand crowns.

To describe this grand work in all 'its details, would occupy many pages. It will give some idea of its immensity to say that it contains in all upwards of two hundred figures, the greater part of colossal size; and that with regard to invention, grandeur, and expression, it has been a school for study, and a theme for wonder, during three successive ages. In the centre of the ceiling are four large compartments and five small ones. In the former are represented the Creation of the Sun and Moon; the Creation of Adam, perhaps the most majestic design that was ever conceived by the genius of man; the Fall and the Expulsion from Paradise; the Deluge. In the five small compartments are represented the Gathering of the Waters (Gen. 1: 9); the Almighty separating Light from Darkness; the Creation of Eve; the Sacrifice of Noah, and Noah's Vineyard. Around these, in the curved part of the ceiling, are the Prophets and the Sibyls who foretold the birth of Christ. These are among the most wonderful forms that modern art has called into life. They are all seated and employed in contemplating books or antique rolls of manuscript, with genii in attendance. These mighty beings sit before us, looking down with solemn meditative aspects, or upwards with inspired looks that see into futurity All their forms are massive and

sublime, all are full of varied and individual char
acter.

Beneath these again are a series of groups representing the earthly genealogy of Christ, in which
the figures have a repose, a contemplative grace and
tenderness, which place them among the most interesting of all the productions of Michael Angelo.
These and the figure of Eve in the Fall show how
intense was his feeling of beauty, though he frequently disdained to avail himself of it. In the
four corners of the ceiling are representations of
the miraculous deliverance of the people of Israel, in
allusion to the general redemption of man by the
Saviour, namely, Holofernes vanquished by Judith,
David overcoming Goliath, the Brazen Serpent, and
the Punishment of Haman.

There is a small print in Kugler's Hand-book,
which will give a general idea of the arrangement
of this famous ceiling. There is one on a large
scale by Piroli, and a still larger one by Cunego,
which, if accessible, will answer the purpose better. In our National School of Design, at Somerset
House, there is an admirable colored drawing lately
brought from Rome by Mr. L. Grüner, which will
convey a very correct idea not merely of the arrangement of the subjects and figures, but of the
harmonious disposition of the colors — a merit not
usually allowed to Michael Angelo.

The collection of engravings after Michael Angelo
in the British Museum is very imperfect, but it con

tains some fine old prints from the Prophets, which should be studied by those who wish to understand the true merit of this great master, of whom Sir Joshua Reynolds said that " to kiss the hem of his garment, to catch the slightest of his perfections. would be glory and distinction enough for an ambitious man ! "

When the Sistine Chapel was completed Michael Angelo was in his thirty-ninth year ; fifty years of a glorious though troubled career were still before him.

Pope Julius II. died in 1513, and was succeeded by Leo X., the son of Lorenzo the Magnificent. As a Florentine and his father's son, we might naturally have expected that he would have gloried in patronizing and employing Michael Angelo ; but such was not the case. There was something in the stern, unbending character, and retired and abstemious habits of Michael Angelo, repulsive to the temper of Leo, who preferred the graceful and amiable Raphael, then in the prime of his life and genius. Hence arose the memorable rivalry between Michael Angelo and Raphael, which on the part of the latter was merely generous emulation, while it must be confessed that something like bitterness and envy, or at least scorn, mingled with the feelings of Michael Angelo. The pontificate of Leo X., an interval of ten years, was the least productive period of his life. He was sent to Florence, to superintend the building of the church of San Lorenzo and the completion of Santa Croce ; but he differed with the pope on the choice of the marble, quarrelled with the officials, and scarcely anything was accomplished. Clement VII., another Medici, was elected pope in 1523. He was the son of that Giuliano de' Medici who was assassinated by the Pazzi in 1478. He had conceived the idea of con secrating a chapel in the church of San Lorenzo, to receive the tombs of his ancestors and relations, and which should be adorned with all the splendors of art. Michael Angelo planned and built the chapel, and for its interior decoration designed and exe- cuted six of his greatest works in sculpture. Two are seated statues : one representing Lorenzo de' Medici, Duke of Urbino, who died young, in 1519, living only to be the father of Catherine de' Medici (and, as it has been well said, " had an evil spirit assumed the human shape to propagate mischief, he could not have done better ") ; the other, oppo- site, his cousin Giuliano de' Medici, who was as weak as Lorenzo was vicious. The other four are colossal recumbent figures, entitled the Night, the Morning, the Dawn, and the Twilight ; though why so called, and why these figures were intro- duced in such a situation — what was the inten- tion, the meaning of the artist — does not seem to be understood by any of the critics on art who have written on the subject. The statue of Lorenzo is almost awful in its sullen grandeur. He looks down in a contemplative attitude ; hence the ap

pellation by which the figure is known in Italy —
Il Pensièro (*Thought* or *Meditation*). But there is
mischief in the look — something vague, ominous,
difficult to be described. Altogether it well-nigh
realizes our idea of Milton's Satan brooding over
his infernal plans for the ruin of mankind. Mr.
Rogers styles it truly "the most real and unreal
thing that ever came from the chisel." And his
description of the whole chapel is as vivid as poetry
and as accurate as truth could make it :

> " Nor then forget that chamber of the dead
> Where the gigantic shades of Night and Day,
> Turned into stone, rest everlastingly.
>   There from age to age
> Two ghosts are sitting on their sepulchres.
> That is the Duke Lorenzo.   Mark him well !
> He meditates ; his head upon his hand.
> What from beneath his helm-like bonnet scowls ?
> Is it a face, or but an eyeless skull ?
> 'T is lost in shade — yet, like the basilisk,
> It fascinates and is intolerable."

While Michael Angelo was engaged in these works
his progress was interrupted by events which threw
all Italy into commotion. Rome was taken and
sacked by the Constable de Bourbon, in 1537. The
Medici were once more expelled from Florence, and
Michael Angelo, in the midst of these strange vicissitudes, was employed by the republic to fortify his
native city against his former patrons. Great as
an engineer as in every other department of art and

science, he defended Florence for nine months. At length the city was given up by treachery, and, fearing the vengeance of the conquerors, Michael Angelo fled and concealed himself; but Clement VII. was too sensible of his merit to allow him to remain long in disgrace and exile. He was par-doned, and continued ever afterwards in high favor with the pope, who employed him on the sculptures in the chapel of San Lorenzo during the remainder of his pontificate.

Clement VII. was succeeded by Pope Paul III.. of the Farnese family, in 1534. This pope, though nearly seventy when he was elected, was as anxious to immortalize his name by great undertakings as any of his predecessors had been before him. His first wish was to complete the decoration of the interior of the Sistine Chapel, left unfinished by Julius II. and Leo X. He summoned Michael Angelo, who endeavored to excuse himself, pleading other engagements; but the pope would listen to no excuses which interfered with his sovereign power to dissolve all other obligations; and thus the artist found himself, after an interval of twenty years, most reluctantly forced to abandon sculpture for painting; and, as Vasari expresses it, he con-sented to serve Pope Paul only because he *could* not do otherwise.

In representing the Last Judgment on the wall of the upper end of the Sistine Chapel, Michael

Angelo only adhered to the original plan as it had been adopted by Julius II., and afterwards by Clement VII.

In the centre of this vast composition he has placed the figure of the Messiah in the act of pronouncing the sentence of condemnation, " Depart from me, ye accursed, into everlasting fire ; " and by his side the Virgin Mary : around them, on each side, the apostles, the patriarchs, the prophets, and a company of saints and martyrs : above these are groups of angels bearing the cross, the crown of thorns, and other instruments of the passion of our Lord ; and further down another group of angels holding the book of life, and sounding the awful trumpets which call up the dead to judgment. Below, on one side, the resurrection and ascent of the blessed ; and, on the other, demons drag down the condemned to everlasting fire. The number of figures is at least two hundred. Those who wish to form a correct idea of the composition and arrangement should consult the engravings. Several, of different sizes and different degrees of excellence, are in the British Museum.

There can be no doubt that Michael Angelo's Last Judgment is the grandest picture that ever was painted — the greatest effort of human skill, as a creation of art ; yet is it full of faults in taste and sentiment ; and the greatest fault of all is in the conception of the principal personage, the Messiah as judge. The figure, expression, attitude, are all nnworthy — one might almost say *vulgar* in the worst sense; for is there not both profaneness and vulgarity in representing the merciful Redeemer of mankind, even when he " comes to judgment," as inspired merely by wrath and vengeance?—as a thick-set athlete, who, with a gesture of sullen anger, is about to punish the wicked with his fist? It has been already observed that Michael Angelo borrowed the idea of the two figures of the Virgin and Christ from the old fresco of Orcagna in the Campo Santo; but in improving the drawing he has wholly lost and degraded the sentiment. In the groups of the pardoned, as Kugler has well observed, we look in vain for " the glory of heaven — for beings bearing the stamp of divine holiness and renunciation of human weakness. Everywhere we meet with the expression of human passion human efforts; we see no choir of solemn, tranquil forms — no harmonious unity of clear, grand lines produced by ideal draperies; but in their stead a confused crowd of naked bodies in violent attitudes, unaccompanied by any of the characteristics made sacred by holy tradition." On the other hand, the groups of the condemned, and the astonishing energy and variety of the struggling and suspended forms, are most fearful; and it is quite true that when contemplated from a distance the whole representation fills the mind with wonder and mysteri ous horror. It was intended to represent the defeat and fall of the rebel angels on the opposite wall

(above and on each side of the principal door) but
this was never done; and the *intention* of Michael
Angelo in the decoration of the Sistine Chapel remains incomplete. The picture of the Last Judg
ment was finished and first exhibited to the people
on Christmas day, 1541, under the pontificate of
Paul III. Michael Angelo was then in his sixty-
seventh year, and had been employed on the painting and cartoons nearly nine years.

The same Pope Paul III. had, in the mean time,
constructed a beautiful chapel, which was called
after his name the chapel *Paolina*, and dedicated
to St. Peter and St. Paul. Michael Angelo was
called upon to design the decorations. He painted
on one side the Conversion of St. Paul, and on the
other the Crucifixion of St. Peter. But these fine
paintings — of which existing old engravings (to be
found in the British Museum) give a better idea than
the blackened and faded remains of the original
frescoes — were from the first ill-disposed as to the
locality, and badly lighted, and at present they
excite little interest compared with the more famous
works in the Sistine.

During the period that Michael Angelo was
engaged in the decoration of the Pauline Chapel.
he executed a group in marble — the Virgin with
the dead Redeemer and two other figures — which
was never completely finished. It is now at
Florence behind the high altar of the church of

Santa Croce.   It is full of tragic grandeur and expression.*

With the frescoes in the Pauline Chapel ends Michael Angelo's career as a painter.   During the remainder of his life, a period of sixteen years, we find him wholly devoted to architecture.   His vast and daring genius finding ample scope in the completion of St. Peter's, he has left behind him in his capacity of architect yet greater marvels than he had achieved as painter and sculptor.   Who that has seen the cupola of St. Peter's soaring into the skies, but will think almost with awe of the universal and majestic intellect of the man who reared it?

There is a striking anecdote of Mrs. Siddons, which at this moment comes back upon the mind. When standing before the Apollo Belvedere, then in the gallery of the Louvre, she exclaimed, after a long pause, "How great must be the Being who created the genius which produced such a form as this!"—a thought characteristic of her mind, but

* An eye-witness has left us a very graphic description of the energy with which, even in old age, Michael Angelo handled his chisel : "I can say that I have seen Michael Angelo at the age of sixty, and with a body announcing weakness, make more chips of marble fly about in a quarter of an hour than would three of the strongest young sculptors in an hour, — a thing almost incredible to him who has not beheld it. He went to work with such impetuosity and fury of manner, that I feared almost every moment to see the block split into pieces. It would seem as if, inflamed by the idea of greatness which inspired him, this great man attacked with a species of fury the marble which concealed the statue." — *Blaise de Vigenère.*

more fitly inspired by the works of Michael Angelo
than by those of any artist the world has yet seen.
They bear impressed upon them a character of greatness, of durability, of sublimity of invention, and
consummate skill in contrivance, which fills the contemplative mind, and leads it irresistibly from the
created up to the Creator.

As our subject is painting, not architecture, we
shall not dwell much on this period of the life of
Michael Angelo. In the year 1544, being then in
his seventy-second year, he was appointed to the
office of chief architect of St. Peter's by Pope Paul
III., and he continued to discharge it through the
pontificates of Julius III., Pius IV., and Pius V.
He accepted the office with reluctance, pleading his
great age, and the obstacles and difficulties he was
likely to meet with from the jealousies and intrigues
of his rivals, and the ignorance and intermeddling
of the pope's officials. He solemnly called heaven
to witness that it was only from a deep sense of duty
that he yielded to the pope's wishes ; and he proved
that this was no empty profession by constantly re-
fusing any salary or remuneration. Notwithstanding the difficulties he encountered, the provocations
and the disgusts most intolerable to his haughty
and impatient spirit, he held on his way with a stern
perseverance till he had seen his great designs so far
carried out that they could not be wholly abandoned
or perverted by his successors.*

* This, however, applies only to the stupendous dome. His design

When his sovereign the Grand Duke of Florence endeavored, by the most munificent offers and promises, to attract him to his court, he constantly pleaded that to leave his great work unaccomplished would be, on his part, "a *sin*, a *shame* and the ruin of the greatest religious monument in Christian Europe." Michael Angelo considered that he was engaged in a work of piety, and for this reason, "for his own honor and the honor of God," he refused all emolument.

It appears, from the evidence of contemporary writers, that in the last years of his life the ac knowledged worth and genius of Michael Angelo, his wide-spread fame, and his unblemished integrity, combined with his venerable age and the haughtiness and reserve of his deportment to invest him with a sort of princely dignity. It is recorded that when he waited on Pope Julius III. to receive his commands, the pontiff rose on his approach, seated him, in spite of his excuses, on his right hand: and while a crowd of cardinals, prelates, ambassadors, were standing round at humble distance, carried on the conference, as equal with equal. The Grand Duke Cosmo I. always uncovered in his presence, and stood with his hat in his hand while speaking to him.

One of the most beautiful anecdotes recorded of Michael Angelo in his later years, and one of the very few amiable traits in his character was his

for the façade, and even the original form of the church, having been subsequently altered.

strong and generous attachment to his old servant
Urbino. One day, as Urbino stood by him while he
worked, he said to him, "My poor Urbino! what
wilt thou do when I am gone?"—"Alas!" replied
Urbino. "I must then seek another master!"—
"No," replied Michael Angelo, "that shall never
be!" and he immediately presented him with two
thousand crowns, thus rendering him independent
of himself and others. Urbino, however, continued
in his service; and when seized with his last illness,
Michael Angelo, the stern, the sarcastic, the over-
bearing Michael Angelo, nursed him with the tenderness and patience of a mother, sleeping in his
clothes on a couch that he might be ever near him.
The old man died, at last, leaving his master almost
inconsolable. "My Urbino is dead," he writes to
Vasari, "to my infinite grief and sorrow. Living,
he served me truly, and in his death he taught me
how to die. I have now no other hope than to
rejoin him in Paradise!"

The arrogance imputed to Michael Angelo seems
rather to have arisen from a contempt for others,
than from any overweening opinion of himself. He
was too proud to be vain. He had placed his standard of perfection so high, that to the latest hour
of his life he considered himself as striving after that
ideal excellence which had been revealed to him, but
to which he conceived that others were blind or indifferent. In allusion to his own imperfections, he
made a drawing, since become famous, which repre

sents an aged man in a go-cart, and underneath the words "*Ancora impara*" (still learning)

He continued to labor unremittingly, and with the same resolute energy of mind and purpose, till the gradual decay of his strength warned him of his approaching end. He did not suffer from any particular malady, and his mind was strong and clear to the last. He died at Rome, on the 17th of February, 1563, in the eighty-ninth year of his age. A few days before his death, he dictated his will in these few, simple words : "I bequeath my soul to God, my body to the earth, and my possessions to my nearest relations." His nephew, Lionardo Buonaroti, who was his principal heir, by the orders of the Grand Duke Cosmo had his remains secretly conveyed out of Rome and brought to Florence; they were with due honors deposited in the church of Santa Croce, under a costly monument, on which we may see his noble bust surrounded by three very commonplace and ill-executed statues representing the arts in which he excelled — Painting, Sculpture, and Architecture. They might have added *Poetry ;* for Michael Angelo was so fine a poet that his productions would have given him fame, though he had never peopled the Sistine with his giant creations, nor "*suspended the Pantheon in the air.*" * The

* The dome of the Pantheon, which appears self-sustained, had, from the time of Augustus Cæsar, attracted the wonder and admiration of all beholders, as a marvel of scientific architecture. Michael

object to which his poems are chiefly addressed,
Vittoria Colonna, Marchioness of Pescara, was the
widow of the celebrated commander who overcame
Francis I. at the battle of Pavia ; herself a poetess,
and one of the most celebrated women of her time for
beauty, talents, virtue, and piety. She died in 1547.
Several of Michael Angelo's sonnets have been translated by Wordsworth, and a selection of his poems,
with a very learned and eloquent introduction, has
been published by Mr. John Edward Taylor, in a
little volume entitled " Michael Angelo a Poet."

It must be borne in recollection that the pictures
ascribed to Michael Angelo in catalogues and picture galleries are in every instance copies made by
his scholars from his designs and models. Only one
easel picture is acknowledged as the genuine production of his hand. It is a Holy Family in the
Florentine gallery, which as a composition is very
exaggerated and ungraceful, and in color hard and
violent. It is painted in distemper, varnished ; not
in oils, as some have supposed.

MARCELLO VENUSTI was continually employed in
executing small pictures from celebrated cartoons of
Michael Angelo ; and the diminutive size, and soft,
neat, delicate execution, form a singular contrast
with the sublimity of the composition and the grand
massive drawing of the figures. One of these subjects is the Virgin seated at the foot of the Cross,

Angelo had said, on some occasion, " I will take the Pantheon and
suspend it in air ; " and he did so.

holding on her lap the dead Redeemer, whose arms
are supported by two angels : innumerable dupli-
cates and engravings exist of this composition (one
exquisite example is in the Queen's gallery in Buck-
ingham Palace) ; also of the Christ on the Cross,
with the Virgin and St. John standing and two angels looking out of the sky behind, with an expression of intense anguish (one of these, a very fine
example, was lately sold in the Lucca gallery). Another is Il Silenzio, *The Silence.* The Virgin is represented with the infant Christ lying across her knee,
with his arm hanging down ; she has a book in one
hand ; behind her on one side is the young St. John
in the panther's skin, with his finger on his lips ; on
the other, St. Joseph. The Annunciation, in which
the figure of the Virgin is particularly majestic, is a
fourth. Copies of these subjects, with trifling varia-
tions, are to be found in many galleries, and the
engravings of all are in the British Museum.

SEBASTIAN DEL PIOMBO was another artist who
painted under the direction and from the cartoons
of Michael Angelo ; and the most famous example
of this union of talent is the Raising of Lazarus,
in our National Gallery. "Sebastian," says Lanzi,
" was without the gift of invention, and in compositions of many figures slow and irresolute ; " but
he was a consummate portrait painter, and a most
admirable colorist. A Venetian by birth, he had
learned the art of coloring under Giorgione. On
coming to Rome in 1518, he formed a close intimacy

with Michael Angelo ; the tradition is, that Michael Angelo associated Sebastiano with himself, and gave him the cartoons of his grand designs, to which the Venetian was to lend the magical hues of his pallette for the purpose of crushing Raphael. If this tradition be true, the failure was signal and deserved ; but luckily we are not *obliged* to believe it. It rests on no authority worthy of credit.

GIACOPO PONTORMO painted the Venus and Cupid now at Hampton Court, from a famous cartoon of Michael Angelo ; and also a Leda, which is in the National Gallery, and of which the cartoon, by Michael Angelo, is in our Royal Academy.

But the most celebrated and the most independent among the scholars and imitators of Michael Angelo was DANIEL DA VOLTERRA, whose most famous work is the Taking down the Saviour from the Cross, with a number of figures full of energy and movement.

GIORGIO VASARI was a pupil and especial favorite of Michael Angelo ; he was a painter and architect of second-rate merit. He has, however, earned himself an immortality by his admirable biography of the painters, sculptors, and architects of Italy, from the earliest times to the death of Michael Angelo, whom he survived only ten years. A large picture by Vasari, representing the six great poets of Italy, is in the gallery of Mr. Hope.

It is not necessary to say anything here of the painters who, in the middle of the sixteenth century, and in the lifetime of Michael Angelo, imi

tated his manner. They were mere journeymen,
and, indeed, imitated him most abominably; mis-
taking extravagance for sublimity, exaggeration for
grandeur, and distortion and affectation for energy
and passion, — a wretched set! But, before we
leave Florence, we must speak of one more artist,
whose proper place is here, because he was a Florentine, and because he combined in a singular manner the characteristics of the three great men of
whom we have last spoken, — Lionardo da Vinci, Fra
Bartolomeo, and Michael Angelo, — without exactly
imitating or equalling any one of them. This was
Andrea del Sarto, a great artist; but who would
have been a far greater artist had he been a better
man.

ANDREA DEL SARTO.

Andrea Vannucchi was the son of a tailor (in Italian *Sarto*) ; hence the appellation by which he was early known, and has since become celebrated. He was born in 1478, and, like many others, began life as a goldsmith and chaser in metal, but, soon turning his attention to painting, and studying indefatigably, he attained so much excellence that he was called in his own time " Andrea senza errori," that is, Andrea *the Faultless*. He is certainly one of the most fascinating of painters ; but in all his pictures, even the finest, while we are struck by the elegance of the heads and the majesty of the figures, we feel the want of any real elevation of sentiment and expression. It would be difficult to point out any picture of Andrea del Sarto which has either simplicity or devotional feeling.

A man possessed of genius and industry, loving his art, and crowned with early fame and success, ought to have been through life a prosperous and a happy man. Andrea was neither. He was miserable, unfortunate, and contemned, through his own fault or folly. He loved a beautiful woman of infamous character, who was the wife of a hatter; and on the death of her husband, in spite of her bad reputation and the warnings of his best friends, he married her. From that hour he never had a quiet heart, or home, or conscience. He had hitherto supported his old father and mother. She prevailed on him to forsake them. His friends stood aloof, pitying and despising his degradation. His scholars (and formerly the most promising of the young artists of that time had been emulous for the honor of his instructions) now fell off, unable to bear the detestable temper of the woman who governed his house. Tired of this existence, he accepted readily an invitation from Francis I., who, on his arrival at Paris, loaded him with favor and distinction; but after a time, his wife, finding she had no longer the same command over his purse or his proceedings, summoned him to return. He had entered into such engagements with Francis I. that this was not easy: but, as he pleaded his domestic position, and promised, and even took an oath on the Gospel, that he would return in a few months, bringing with him his wife, the king gave him license to depart, and even intrusted him with a large sum of money to be expended in certain specified objects.

Andrea hastened to Florence, and there, under the influence of his infamous wife, he embezzled the money, which was wasted in his own and her extravagance; and he never returned to France to keep his oath and engagements. But, though he had been weak and wicked enough to commit this crime, he had sufficient sensibility to feel acutely the disgrace which was the consequence. It preyed on his mind, and embittered the rest of his life. The avarice and infidelity of his wife added to his sufferings. He continued to paint, however, and improved to the last in correctness of style and beauty of color.

In the year 1530 he was attacked by a contagious disorder. Abandoned on his death-bed by the woman to whom he had sacrificed honor, fame, and friends, he died miserably, and was buried hastily, and without the usual ceremonies of the church, in the same convent of the Nunziata which he had adorned with his works.

Andrea del Sarto can only be estimated as a painter by those who have visited Florence. Fine as are his oil-pictures, his paintings in fresco are still finer. One of these, a Repose of the Holy Family, has been celebrated, for the last two centuries, under the title of the *Madonna del Sacco*, because Joseph is represented leaning on a sack. There are engravings of it in the British Museum.

The cloisters of the convent of the Nunziata, and a building called the Scalzo, at Florence, contain his most admired works. His finest picture in oil is in the Florence Gallery, in the cabinet called the Tribune, where it hangs behind the Venus de' Medici. It represents the Virgin seated on a

throne, with St. John the Baptist standing on one
side, and St. Francis on the other; a picture of
wonderful majesty and beauty. In general his
Madonnas are not pleasing. They have, with great
beauty, a certain vulgarity of expression ; and in
his groups he almost always places the Virgin on
the ground, either kneeling or sitting. His only
model for all his females was his wife ; and even
when he did not paint from her, she so possessed
his thoughts that unconsciously he repeated the
same features in every face he drew, whether Virgin, or saint, or goddess. Pictures by Andrea del
Sarto are to be found in almost all galleries, but
very fine examples of his art are rare out of Florence. The picture in our National Gallery attributed to him is very unworthy of his reputation.
Those at Hampton Court are not better. There is
a fine portrait at Windsor, called the Gardener of
the Duke of Florence, attributed to him ; and a
female head, a sketch full of nature and power. In
the Louvre is the picture of Charity, No. 85,
painted for Francis I. when Andrea was at Fontainebleau in 1518, and three others. Lord West-
minster, Lord Lansdowne, Mr. Munroe of Park-
street, and Lord Cowper in his collection at Panshanger, possess the finest examples of Andrea del
Sarto which are in England. At Panshanger there
is a very fine portrait of Andrea del Sarto by himself. He is represented as standing by a table at
which he has been writing, and looking up from

the letter which lies before him. The figure is half-
length, and the countenance noble, but profoundly
melancholy. One might fancy that he had been
writing to his wife.

RAPHAEL SANZIO D'URBINO.

Born 1483, died 1520.

Wᴇ have spoken at length of two among the great men who influenced the progress of art in the beginning of the sixteenth century, — Lionardo da Vinci and Michael Angelo. The third and greatest name was that of RAPHAEL.

In speaking of this wonderful man we shall be more diffuse and enter more into detail than usual. How can we treat, in a small compass, of him whose fame has filled the universe? In the history of Italian art he stands alone, like Shakspeare in the history of our literature; and he takes the same kind of rank — a superiority not merely of degree but of quality. Everybody has heard of RAPHAEL: every one has attached some associations of excel lence and beauty, more or less defined, to that familiar name; but it is necessary to have studied profoundly the history of art, and to have an inti- mate acquaintance with the productions of contem- porary and succeeding artists, to form any just idea of the wide and lasting influence exercised by this harmonious and powerful genius. His works have been an inexhaustible storehouse of ideas to paint-

(228)

ers and to poets. Everywhere in art we find his
traces. Everywhere we recognize his forms and
lines, borrowed or stolen, reproduced, varied, imitated — never improved. Some critic once said,
" Show me any sentiment or feeling in any poet,
ancient or modern, and I will show you the same
thing either as well or better expressed in Shakspeare." In the same manner one might say,
" Show me in any painter, ancient or modern, any
especial beauty of form, expression, or sentiment,
and in some picture, drawing, or print, after
Raphael, I will show you the same thing as well or
better done, and *that* accomplished which others
have only sought or attempted." To complete our
idea of this rare union of greatness and versatility
as an artist with all that could grace and dignify
the man, we must add such personal qualities as
very seldom meet in the same individual — a bright,
generous, genial, gentle spirit ; the most attractive
manners, the most winning modesty,

> " His heavenly face the mirror of his mind ;
> His mind a temple for all lovely things
> To flock to, and inhabit ;" —

and we shall have a picture in our fancy more
resembling that of an antique divinity, a young
Apollo, than a real human being. There was a
vulgar idea at one time prevalent that Raphael was
a man of vicious and dissipated habits, and even
died a victim to his excesses. This slander has

been silenced forever by indisputable evidence to the contrary, and now we may reflect with pleasure that nothing rests on surer evidence than the admirable qualities of Raphael ; that no earthly renown was ever so unsullied by reproach, so justified by merit, so confirmed by concurrent opinion, so established by time. The short life of Raphael was one of incessant and persevering study. He spent one-half of it in acquiring that practical knowledge, and that mechanical dexterity of hand, which were necessary before he could embody in forms and colors the rich creations of his wonderful mind ; and when he died, at the age of thirty-seven, he left behind him two hundred and eighty-seven pictures, and five hundred and seventy-six drawings and studies. If we reflect for one moment, we must be convinced that such a man *could* not have been idle and dissipated ; for we must always take into consideration that an excelling painter must be not only a poet in mind, but a ready and perfect artificer ; and that, though nature may bestow the " genius and the faculty divine," only time, practice, assiduous industry, can give the exact and cunning hand. " An author," as Richardson observes, " must *think*, but it is no matter what character he writes ; he has no care about that, if what he writes be legible. A curious mechanic's hand must be exquisite ; but his thoughts may be at liberty." The painter must think and invent with his fancy, and what his fancy invents his hand must acquire the power to execute, or vain is his power of creative thought. It has been observed — though Raphael was unhappily an exception — that painters are generally long-lived and healthy; and that, of all the professors of science and art, they are the least liable to alienation of mind or morbid effects of the brain. One reason may be, that through the union of the opposite faculties of the excursive fancy and mechanic skill, — head and hand balancing each other, — a sort of harmony in their alternate or coëfficient exercise is preserved habitually, which reäcts on the whole moral and physical being. As Raphael carried to the highest perfection the union of those faculties of head and hand which constitute the complete artist, so this harmony pervaded his whole being, and nothing deformed or discordant could enter there. In all the portraits which exist of him, from infancy to manhood, there is a divine sweetness and repose. The little cherub face of three years old is not more serene and angelic than the same features at thirty. The child whom father and mother, guardian and step-mother, caressed and idolized in his loving innocence, was the same being whom we see in the prime of manhood subduing and reigning over all hearts, so that, to borrow the words of a contemporary, " not only all men, but the very brutes, loved him : " the only very distinguished man of whom we read who lived and died without an enemy or a detractor !

Raphael Sanzio or Santi was born in the city of Urbino. on Good Friday, in the year 1483. His father, Giovanni Santi, was a painter of no mean talent, who held a respectable rank in his native city, and was much esteemed by the Dukes Frederigo and Guidobaldo of Urbino, both of whom played a very important part in the history of Italy between 1474 and 1494. The name of Raphael's mother was Magia, and the house in which he was born is still standing, and regarded by the citizens of Urbino with just veneration. He was only eight years old when he lost his mother, but his father's second wife, Bernardina, well supplied her place. and loved him and tended him as if he had been her own son. His father was his first instructor, and very soon the young pupil was not only able to assist him in his works, but showed such extraordinary talent that Giovanni deemed it right to give him the advantage of better teaching than his own. Perugino was the most celebrated master of that time, and Giovanni travelled to Perugia to make arrangements for placing Raphael under his care ; but before these arrangements were completed this good father died, in August, 1494. His wishes were, however, carried into execution by his widow and by his wife's brother, Simone Ciarla ; and Raphael was sent to study under Perugino, in 1495, being then twelve years old.

He remained in this school till he was nearly twenty, and was chiefly employed in assisting his

master. A few pictures painted between his sixteenth and twentieth year have been authenticated
by careful research, and are very interesting from
being essentially characteristic. There is, of course,
the manner of his master Perugino, but mingled
with some of those qualities which were particularly his own, and which his after life developed
into excellence; and nothing in these early pictures
is so remarkable as the gradual improvement of his
style, and his young predilection for his favorite subject, the Madonna and Child. The most celebrated
of all his pictures painted in the school of Perugino
was one representing the Marriage of the Virgin
Mary to Joseph — a subject which is very common
in Italian art, and called Lo Sposalizio (the Espousals). This beautiful picture is preserved in the
Gallery at Milan. There is a large and fine engraving of it by Longhi, which can be seen in any good
print-shop. In the same year that he painted this
picture (1504), Raphael visited Florence for the
first time. He carried with him a letter of recommendation from Giovanna, Duchess of Sora, and
sister of the Duke of Urbino, to Soderini, who had
succeeded the exiled Medici in the government of
Florence. In this letter the duchess styles him "a
discreet and amiable youth," to whom she was
attached for his father's sake and for his own good
qualities, and she requests that Soderini will favor
and aid him in his pursuits. Raphael did not remain long at Florence in this first visit, but he made

the acquaintance of Fra Bartolomeo and Ridolfo Ghirlandajo, and saw some cartoons by Lionardo da Vinci and Michael Angelo, which filled his mind with new and bold ideas both of form and composition. In the following year he was employed in executing several large pictures for various churches at Perugia. One of these, a large altar-piece, painted for the church of the Servite, is now at Blenheim ; it is full of beauty and dignity. Beneath it was a little picture of St. John preaching in the Wilderness, which is in the possession of Lord Lansdowne. About the same time he painted for himself a lovely little miniature called the Dream of the Young Knight, in which he represents a youth armed, who sees in a vision two female figures, one alluring him to pleasure, the other, with a book and sword, inviting him to study and to strive for excellence. This is now in England, in the possession of Lady Sykes. It has been lately engraved in an exquisite style by Mr. L. Grüner.

When he had finished these and other works, he returned to Florence, and remained there till 1508.

Some of the most exquisite of his works may be referred to this period of his life, that is, before he was five-and-twenty.

One of these is the Madonna sitting under the Palm-tree, while Joseph presents flowers to the Infant Christ. This may be seen in the Bridgewater Gallery. A second is the Madonna in the possession of Earl Cowper, and now at Panshanger

Another is the famous Madonna in the Florentine Gallery, called the Madonna del Cardellino (the Virgin of the Goldfinch), because the little St. John is presenting a goldfinch to the Infant Christ. Another, as famous, now in the Louvre, called La Belle Jardinière, because the Madonna is seated in a garden amid flowers, with Christ standing at her knee. The St. Catherine in our National Gallery was also painted about the same period; and the little picture of St. George and the Dragon, which Guidobaldo, Duke of Urbino, sent as a present to Henry VII., and which is now at St. Petersburg. In this picture St. George is armed with a lance, and has the Garter round his knee, with the inscription "Honi soit qui mal y pense." There is another little St. George in the Louvre, in which the saint is about to slay the dragon with a sword. And there are, besides, two or three large altar-pieces and some beautiful portraits; in all about thirty pictures painted during the three years he spent at Florence.

RAPHAEL AT ROME.

In his twenty-fifth year, when Fra Bartolomeo, Lionardo da Vinci, and Michael Angelo, were all at the height of their fame, and many years older than himself, the young Raphael had already become celebrated from one end of Italy to the other. At this time Julius II. was pope. Of his extraordinary and energetic character we have already

spoken at length, in the life of Michael Angelo
At the age of seventy he was revolving plans for
the aggrandizement of his power and the embellish-
ment of the Vatican which it would have taken a
long life to realize. Conscious that the time before
him was to be measured by months rather than by
years, and ambitious to concentrate in his own person all the glory that must ensue from such magnificent works, he listened to no obstacles, he would
endure no delays, he spared no expense, in his undertakings. Bramante, the greatest architect, and
Michael Angelo, the greatest sculptor, in Italy, were
already in his service. Lionardo da Vinci was then
employed in public works at Florence, and could
not be engaged; and he therefore sent for Raphael
to undertake the decoration of those halls in the
Vatican which Pope Nicholas V. and Sixtus IV.
had begun and left unfinished. The invitation, or
rather order, of the pope, was as usual so urgent and
so peremptory, that Raphael hurried from Florence,
'eaving his friends Bartolomeo and Ghirlandajo to
complete his unfinished pictures, and immediately
on his arrival at Rome he commenced the greatest
of his works, the Chambers (*Camere*) of the Vatican.

In general, when Raphael undertook any great
work illustrative of sacred or profane history, he
did not hesitate to ask advice of his learned and
literary friends on points of costume or chronology. But when he began his paintings in the

Vatican he was wholly unassisted, and the plan which he laid before the pope, and which was immediately approved and adopted, shows that the grasp and cultivation of his mind equalled his powers as a painter. He dedicated this first saloon, called in Italian the Camera della Segnatura, t) the glory of those high intellectual pursuits which may be said to embrace in some form or other all human culture — he represented Theology, Poetry, Philosophy, and Jurisprudence.

And first on the ceiling he painted in four circles four allegorical female figures with characteristic symbols, throned amid clouds, and attended by beautiful genii. Of these, the figure of Poetry is distinguished by superior grandeur and inspiration. Beneath these figures and on the four sides of the room he painted four great pictures, each about fifteen feet high by twenty or twenty-five feet wide, the subjects illustrating historically the four allegorical figures above. Under Theology he placed the composition called *La Disputa*, that is, the argument concerning the holy sacrament. In the upper part is the heavenly glory, the Redeemer in the centre, beside him the Virgin mother. On the right and left, arranged in a semicircle, patriarchs, apostles, and saints, all seated ; all full of character, dignity, and a kind of celestial repose befitting their beatitude. Angels are hovering round ; four of them, surrounding the emblematic Dove, hold the Gospels. In the lower half of the picture are

assembled the celebrated doctors and teachers of the
Church, grand, solemn, meditative figures; some
searching their books, some lost in thought, some
engaged in colloquy sublime.   And on each side, a
little lower, groups of disciples and listeners, every
head and figure a study of character and expression,
— all different, all full of nature, animation, and
significance ; and thus the two parts of this magnificent composition, the heavenly beatitude above, the
mystery of faith below, combine into one comprehensive whole.   This picture contains about fifty
full-length figures.

Under Poetry we have Mount Parnassus. Apollo
and the Muses are seen on the summit.   On one
side, near them, the epic and tragic poets, Homer,
Virgil, Dante.   (Ariosto had not written his poem
at this time, and Milton and Tasso were yet unborn.)
Below, on each side, are the lyrical poets, Petrarch,
Sappho, Corinna, Pindar, Horace.   The arrangement, grouping, and character, are most admirable
and graceful ; but Raphael's original design for
this composition, as we have it engraved by Marc
Antonio, is finer than the fresco, in which there
are many alterations which cannot be considered as
improvements.

Under Philosophy he has placed the School of
Athens.   It represents a grand hall or portico, in
which a flight of steps separates the foreground
from the background. Conspicuous, and above the
rest, are the elder intellectual philosophers, Plato

Aristotle, Socrates : Plato characteristically pointing upwards to heaven ; Aristotle pointing to the
earth ; Socrates impressively discoursing to the listeners near him.

Then, on a lower plan, we have the Sciences and
Arts, represented by Pythagoras and Archimedes ;
Zoroaster, and Ptolemy the geographer ; while
alone, as if avoiding and avoided by all, sits Diog-
enes the Cynic. Raphael has represented the art
of painting by the figure of his master Perugino,
and has introduced a portrait of himself humbly
following him. The group of Archimedes (whose
head is a portrait of Bramante, the architect) surrounded by his scholars, who are attentively watching him as he draws a geometrical figure, is one of
the finest things which Raphael ever conceived ; and
the whole composition has in its regularity and
grandeur a variety and dramatic vivacity which
relieve it from all formality. This picture also
contains not less than fifty figures.

Law, or Jurisprudence, from the particular con-
struction of the wall on which the subject is painted,
is represented with less completeness, and is broken
up into divisions. Prudence, Fortitude, and Tem-
perance, are above ; below, on one side, is Pope
Gregory delivering the ecclesiastical law ; and on
the other, Justinian promulgating his famous code
of civil law. The whole decoration of this chamber
forms a grand allegory of the domain of human

intellect, shadowed forth in creations of surpassing beauty and dignity.

The description here given is necessarily brief and imperfect. We advise our readers to consult the engravings of these frescoes, and with the above explanation they will probably be intelligible; at all events, the wonderfully prolific genius of the painter will be appreciated, in the number of the person-ages introduced and the appropriate characters of each.

About this time Raphael painted that portrait of Julius II., of which a duplicate is in our National Gallery. No one who has studied the history of this extraordinary old man, and his relations with Michael Angelo and Raphael, can look upon it without interest. Another fine duplicate is in the gallery of Mr. Miles, at Leigh Court, near Bris-tol. The original is in the Pitti Palace at Flor ence.

Also at this time Raphael painted the portrait of himself, which is preserved in the Gallery of Painters at Florence; it represents him as a very handsome young man, with luxuriant hair and dark eyes, full lips, and a pensive yet benign counte-nance.* To this period we may also refer a num-ber of beautiful Madonnas: Lord Garvagh's, called the Aldobrandini Madonna; the Virgin of the

* There is an engraving by Pontius. The head engraved by Raphael Morghen as the portrait of Raphael is now considered to be the portrait of Bindo Altoviti. It is at Munich.

Bridgewater Gallery; the Vierge au Diademe in the Louvre; and the yet more famous Madonna di Foligno, now at Rome in the Vatican.

While employed for Pope Julius in executing the frescoes already described, Raphael found a munificent friend and patron in Agostino Chigi, a rich banker and merchant, who was then living at Rome in great splendor. He painted several pictures for him: the four Sibyls in the chapel of the Chigi family, in the church of Santa Maria della Pace, — sublime figures, full of grandeur and inspiration; and, on the wall of a chamber in his palace, that fresco the Triumph of Galatea, well known from the numerous engravings.

About the year 1510 Raphael began the decoration of the second chamber of the Vatican. In this series of compositions he represented the power and glory of the Church, and her miraculous deliverances from her secular enemies : all these being an indirect honor paid to, or rather claimed by Julius II., who made it a subject of pride that he had not only expelled all enemies from the Papal territories, but also enlarged their boundaries — by no scrupulous means. On the ceiling of this room are four beautiful pictures — the promises of God to the four Patriarchs, Noah, Abraham, Jacob, and Moses. On the four side walls, the Expulsion of Heliodorus from the Temple at Jerusalem; the Miracle of Bolsena, by which, as it was said, heretics were silenced; Attila, King of the Huns, terrified by the apparition of St. Peter and St. Paul; and St. Peter delivered from Prison. Of these the Heliodorus is one of the grandest and most poetical of all Raphael's creations: the group of the celestial warrior trampling on the prostrate Heliodorus, with the avenging spirits rushing, floating along, air-borne, to scourge the despoiler, is wonderful for its supernatural powers; it is a vision of beauty and terror.

Before this chamber was finished, Julius II. died, and was succeeded by Leo X. in 1513.

Though the character of Pope Leo X. was in all respects different from that of Julius, he was not less a patron of Raphael than his predecessor had been; and certainly the number of learned and accomplished men whom he attracted to his court, and the enthusiasm for classical learning which prevailed among them, strongly influenced those productions of Raphael which date from the accession of Leo. They became more and more allied to the antique, and less and less imbued with that pure religious spirit which we find in his earlier works.

Cardinal Bembo, Cardinal Bibiena, Count Castiglione, the poets Ariosto and Sanazzaro, ranked at this time among Raphael's intimate friends. With his celebrity his riches increased; he built himself a fine house in that part of Rome called the Borgo, between St. Peter's and the Castle of St. Angelo; he had numerous scholars from all parts of Italy, who attended on him with a love and reverence and duty far beyond the lip-and-knee homage which waits on princes ; and such was the influence of his benign and genial temper, that all these young men lived in the most entire union and friendship with him and with each other, and his school was never disturbed by those animosities and jealousies which before and since have disgraced the schools of art of Italy. All the other painters of that time were the friends rather than tho rivals of the supreme and gentle Raphael, with the single exception of Michael Angelo.

About the period at which we are now arrived, the beginning of the pontificate of Leo X., Michael Angelo had left Rome for Florence, as it has been related in his life. Lionardo da Vinci came to Rome, by the invitation of Leo, attended by a train of scholars, and lived on good terms with Raphael, who treated the venerable old man with becoming deference. Fra Bartolomeo also visited Rome about 1513, to the great joy of his friend. We find Raphael at this time on terms of the tenderest friendship with Francia, and in correspondence with Albert Durer, for whom he entertained the highest admiration.

Under Leo X. Raphael continued his great works in the Vatican. He began the third hall or *camera* in 1515. The ceiling of this chamber had been painted by his master Perugino for Sixtus IV. ; and Raphael, from a feeling of respect for his old master, would not remove or paint over his work. On the sides of the room he represented the principal events in the lives of Pope Leo III. and Pope Leo IV., shadowing forth under their names the glory of his patron Leo X. Of these pictures, the most remarkable is that which is called in Italian L'Incendio del Borgo (the Fire in the Borgo). The story says that this populous part of Rome was on fire in the time of Leo IV., and that the conflagration was extinguished by a miracle. In the hurry, confusion, and tumult, of the scene; in the men escaping half naked; in the terrified groups assembled in the foreground; in the women carrying water; we find every variety of attitude and emotion, expressed with a perfect knowledge of form; and some of the figures exhibit the influence of Michael Angelo's ceiling of the Sistine Chapel, already described. This fresco, though so fine in point of drawing, is the worst *colored* of the whole series; the best in point of color are the Heliodorus and the Miracle of Bolsena.

The last of the chambers in the Vatican is the Hall of Constantine, painted with scenes from the life of that emperor. The whole of these frescoes having been executed by the scholars of Raphael, from his designs and cartoons, we shall not dwell on them here, only observing that an excellent reduced copy of the finest of all, the Battle of Constantine and Maxentius, may be seen at Hampton Court.

While Raphael, assisted by his scholars, was designing and executing the large frescoes in the Vatican, he was also engaged in many other works. His fertile mind and ready hand were never idle, and the number of *original* creations of this wonderful man, and the rapidity with which they succeeded each other, are quite unexampled.   Among his most celebrated and popular compositions is the series of subjects from the Old Testament, called " Raphael's Bible ; " these were comparatively small pictures, adorning the thirteen cupolas of the " Loggie " of the Vatican.   These " Loggie " are open galleries, running round three sides of an open court ; and the gallery on the second story is the one painted under Raphael's direction.   Up the sides and round the windows are arabesque orna. ments, festoons of fruit, flowers, animals, all combined and grouped together with the most exquisite and playful fancy.   They have been much injured by time, yet more by the barbarous treatment of the French soldiery when Rome was sacked in 1527, and worst of all by unskilful attempts at restoration.   The pictures in the cupolas, being out of reach, are better preserved.   Sacred subjects were never represented in so beautiful, so poetical, and so intelligible a manner as by Raphael ; but, as the copies and engravings of these works are innumerable, and easily met with, we shall not enter into a particular description of them ; very good copies of several may be seen at the National School of Design at Somerset House.*

There was still another great work for the Vatican intrusted to Raphael. The interior of the Sistine Chapel had been ornamented round the lower walls with paintings in imitation of tapestries Leo X. resolved to substitute real draperies of the most costly material; and Raphael was to furnish the subjects and drawings, which were to be copied in the looms of Flanders, and worked in a mixture of wool, silk, and gold. Thus originated the famous CARTOONS OF RAPHAEL.

They were originally eleven in number, to fit the ten compartments into which the wall was divided by as many pilasters, and the space over the altar. Eight were large, one larger than the rest, and two small. Of the eleven cartoons designed by Raphael, four are lost, and seven remain, which are now in the Royal Gallery at Hampton Court. As they rank among the greatest productions of art, and have been for some time freely thrown open to the public, we shall give a detailed account of them here from various sources,† and add some remarks

---

* A set of excellent engravings from the series, in a fine free style, and of a large size, and all executed at Rome after the original frescoes, is now publishing by Parker, in the Strand, at the extraordinary low price of six engravings for nine shillings. The subjects, the size, and the fine taste of the execution, render them admirable ornaments for the walls of a school-room or study.

† See Passavant's "Rafael;" Kugler's "Handbuch;" Bunsen's "Stadt Rom;" Murray's "Handbook to the Public Gal

which may enable the uninitiated to form a judgment of their characteristic merits, as well as to appreciate duly the privilege which in a wise, as well as a right royal and gracious spirit, has lately been conceded to the people.

The intention in the whole series of subjects was to express the mission, the sufferings, and the triumph, of the Christian church. The Death of the First Martyr, and the Acts of the two great Apostles, St. Peter and St. Paul, were ranged along the sides to the right and left of the high altar; while over the altar was the Coronation of the Virgin, a subject which, as we have already seen, was always symbolical of the triumph of religion. In the original arrangement the tapestries hung in the following order : *

On the left of the altar — 1. The Miraculous Draught of Fishes (that is, the Calling of Peter) ; 2. The Charge to Peter; 3. The Stoning of Stephen ; 4. The Healing of the Lame Man ; 5. The Death of Ananias.

On the right of the altar — 1. The Conversion of St. Paul ; 2. Elymas struck Blind ; 3. Paul and

leries of Art;" and a very clever account of the Cartoons which appeared in the *Penny Magazine* some years ago. From all these works extracts have been freely taken, and put together so as to form a correct and complete description both of the Cartoons and the Tapestries.

* Subsequently, when the whole of the wall was painted by Michael Angelo with the Last Judgment, this order was changed, and the tapestry of the Crowning of the Virgin entirely removed.

Barnabas at Lystra ; 4. Paul preaching at Athens·
5. Paul in Prison.   All along underneath ran a
rich border in chiaro'scuro, of a bronze color, relieved with gold, representing on a smaller scale
incidents in the life of Leo X., with ornamental
arabesques, groups of sporting genii, fruits, flowers,
&c. ; and the pilasters between the tapestries were
also adorned with rich arabesques. Old engravings
exist of some of these designs, which are among the
most beautiful things in Italian art; as full of
grandeur and grace as they are exquisitely fanciful
and luxuriant.

The large cartoons of this series which are lost
are, the Stoning of Stephen ; the Conversion of St.
Paul ; Paul in his Dungeon at Philippi ; and the
Crowning of the Virgin.

The seven which remain to us are arranged at
Hampton Court without any regard either to their
original arrangement or to chronological order.
Beginning at the door by which we enter, they succeed each other thus :

1. The Death of Ananias.

"Thou hast not lied unto men, but unto God." — Acts 5.

Nine of the Apostles stand together on a raised
platform; St. Peter in the midst, with uplifted
hands, is in the act of speaking; on the right
Ananias lies prostrate on the earth, while a young
man and woman, on the left, are starting back.

with ghastly horror and wonder in every feature;
in the background, to the left, is seen Sapphira,
who, unaware of the catastrophe of her husband
and the terrible fate impending over her, is paying
some money with one hand, while she withholds
some in the other; St. John and another Apostle
are on the left, distributing alms. The figures are
altogether twenty-four in number. Size, seventeen
feet six inches by eleven feet four inches.

As a composition, considered artistically, this
cartoon holds the first place; nothing has ever ex-
ceeded it: only Raphael himself, in some of his
other works, has equalled it in the wondrous adapt-
ation of the means employed to the end in view.
By the circular arrangement of the composition,
and by elevating the figures behind above those in
front, the whole of the personages on the scene are
brought at once to sight. The elevated position
of Peter and James, though standing back from
the foreground, and their dignified figures, contrast
strongly with the abject form of Ananias, struck
down by the hand of God, helpless, and, as it
seems, quivering in every limb. Those of the spectators who are near Ananias express their horror
and astonishment by the most various and appropriate expression.

"He falls," says Hazlitt, "so naturally, that it
seems as if a person could fall no other way; and
yet, of all the ways in which a human figure could
fall, it is probably the most expressive of a person

overwhelmed by, and in the grasp of, divine vengeance. This is in some measure the secret of
Raphael's success. Most painters, in studying an
attitude, puzzle themselves to find out what will be
picturesque, and what will be fine, and never dis-
cover it. Raphael only thought how a person
would stand or fall under such or such circumstances, and the picturesque and the fine followed
as a matter of course. Hence the unaffected force
and dignity of his style, which are only another
name for truth and nature under impressive and
momentous circumstances."

We have here an instance of that truly Shak-
spearian art by which Raphael always softens and
heightens the effect of tragic terror. St. John, at
the very instant when this awful judgment has
fallen on the hypocrite and unbeliever, has benignly
turned to bestow alms and a blessing on the poor
good man before him.*

* "It has been questioned whether the woman who is advancing
from behind was meant for Sapphira, as it is stated in the sacred
record that three hours had elapsed after the death of Ananias
before she entered the place. Notwithstanding this objection, it is
most probable that Raphael intended this figure for the wife of
Ananias; and the slight inaccuracy is more than atoned for by the
sublime moral, which shows the woman approaching the spot where
her husband had met his doom, and where her own death awaits
her, but wholly unconscious of those judgments, and absorbed in
counting that gold by which both she and her partner had been
betrayed to their fate."

2. Elymas the Sorcerer struck with Blindness.

"And now, behold, the hand of the Lord is upon thee, and thou shalt be blind, not seeing the sun for a season. And immediately there fell on him a mist and a darkness; and he went about seeking some to lead him by the hand."—Acts 13: 11.

The Proconsul Sergius, seated on his throne, beholds with astonishment Elymas struck blind by the word of the Apostle Paul, who stands on the left; an attendant is gazing with wonder in his face, while eight persons behind him are all occupied with the miraculous event which is passing before their eyes; two lictors are on the left; in all fourteen figures. Size, fourteen feet seven inches by eleven feet four inches.

This cartoon, as a composition, is particularly remarkable for the concentration of the effect and interest in the one action. The figure of St. Paul is magnificent; while the crouching, abject form of Elymas, groping his way, and blind even to his finger-ends, stands in the midst, and on him all eyes are bent.* The manner in which the impression is graduated from terror down to indifferent curiosity, while one person explains the event to another by means of gesture, are among

* A story is told of Garrick objecting to the truth of this action in the hearing of Benjamin West, who, in vindication of the painter, desired Garrick to shut his eyes and walk across the room, when he instantly stretched out his hand and began to feel his way with the exact attitude and expression here represented.

the most spirited dramatic effects Raphael ever
produced.

3. The Healing of the Lame Man at the Beau-tiful Gate of the Temple.

"Then Peter said, Silver and gold have I none, but such as I
have I give unto thee. And he took him by the right hand and
lifted him up." — Acts 3 : 6, 7.

Under the portico of the Temple of Jerusalem
stand the two Apostles Peter and John : the former
is holding by the hand a miserable, deformed cripple, who gazes up in his face with joyful, eager
wonder ; another cripple is seen on the left. Among
the people are seen conspicuous a woman with an
infant in her arms, and another leading two naked
boys, one of whom is carrying two doves as an offering. The wreathed and richly-adorned columns are
imitated from those which have been preserved for
ages in the church of St. Peter, as relics of the
Temple of Jerusalem. With regard to the composition, Raphael has been criticized for breaking it
up into parts by the introduction of the pillars ;
yet, if properly considered, this very management
is a proof of the exquisite taste of the painter, and
his attention to the object he had in view. Adher-
ing to the sense of the passage in Scripture, he
could not make all the figures refer to one principal action, the healing of the cripple ; he has
therefore, framed it in a manner between the two
columns ; and by the groups introduced into the

other two divisions he has intimated that the people were entering the temple " at the hour of prayer, being the ninth hour." It is evident, moreover, that had the shafts been perfectly straight, according to the severest law of good taste in architecture, the effect would have been extremely disagreeable to the eye ; by their winding form they harmonize with the manifold forms of the moving figures around, and they illustrate, by their elaborate elegance, the Scripture phrase, " the gate which is called Beautiful." The misery, the distortion, the ugliness of the cripple, are made as striking as possible, and contrasted with the noble head and form of St. Peter, and the benign features of St. John. The figure of the young woman with her child is a model of feminine sweetness and grace ; it is eminently, perfectly Raphaelesque, stamped with his peculiar sentiment and refinement. The bright open sky seen between the interstices of the columns harmonizes with the lightness, cheerfulness, and happy expression, of these figures. In the compartment where the miracle is taking place, there is the same correspondence of effect with sentiment ; the subdued light of the lamps burning in the depth of the recess accords well with the reverential feeling excited by the sacred transaction. Many parts of this cartoon have unfortunately been injured, and much of the harmony destroyed, yet it remains one of the most wonderful relics of art now extant.

4. The Miraculous Draught of Fishes.

"When Simon Peter saw it, he fell down at Jesus' knees, saying
Depart from me, for I am a sinful man, O Lord."— LUKE 5: 8.

On the left Christ is seated in a bark, in the act
of speaking to St. Peter, who has fallen on his knees
before him ; behind him is a youth, and a second
bark is on the right.   Two men are busied drawing
up the nets miraculously laden, while a third steers.
On the shore, in the foreground, stand three cranes ;
and in the distance are seen the people to whom
Christ had been preaching out of the ship or boat.
In this cartoon the composition is very beautiful ;
and the execution, from its mingled delicacy,
power, and precision, is supposed to be almost
entirely from Raphael's own hand.   The effect is
wonderfully bright.   In the broad, clear daylight,
and against the sky, the figures stand out in strong
relief.   The clear lake ripples round the bark, and
the figure of the Saviour, in the pale blue vest and
white mantle, appears all light, and radiant with
beneficence.   The awe, humility, and love, in the
attitude and countenance of St. Peter, are wonder
fully expressive.   The masterly drawing in the
figures of the apostles in the second boat conveys
most strongly the impression of the weight they are
attempting to raise.   In the fish and the cranes,
all painted with exquisite and minute fidelity to
nature, we trace the hand of Giovanni da Udine.
These strange, black birds have here a grand effect

"There is a certain sea-wildness about them, and, as their food was fish, they contribute mightily to express the affair in hand; they are a fine part of the scene. They serve also to prevent the heaviness which that part would otherwise have had, by breaking the parallel lines which would have been made by the boats and base of the picture." *

* "A painter is allowed sometimes to depart even from natural and historical truth. Thus, in the cartoon of the Draught of Fishes, Raphael has made a boat too little to hold the figures he has placed in it; and this is so visible, that some are apt to triumph over that great man as having nodded on that occasion, while others have pretended to excuse it by saying it was done to make the miracle appear greater; but the truth is, had he made the boat large enough for those figures, his picture would have been all boat, which would have had a disagreeable effect; and to have made his figures small enough for a vessel of that size, would have rendered them unsuitable to the rest of the set, and have made those figures appear less considerable. It is amiss as it is, but would have been worse any other way, as it frequently happens in other cases. Raphael, therefore, wisely chose this lesser inconvenience, this seeming error, which he knew the judicious would know was none, and for the rest he was above being solicitous for his reputation with them. So that, upon the whole, this is so far from being a fault, that it is an instance of the consummate judgment of that most incomparable man, which he learned in his great school, the antique, where this liberty is commonly taken in an eminent manner in the Trajan and Antoninian columns, and on many other occasions, in the finest bas-reliefs. And to note it, by the by, it seems to be a strange rashness and self-sufficiency in a spectator or a reader, when he thinks he sees an absurdity in a great author, to take it immediately for granted it is such. Surely it is a most reasonable and just prejudice in favor of a man we have always known to act with wisdom and propriety on every occasion, to suspend at least our criticism, and cast off illiberal triumph over him, and to suppose it at least possible that he might have had reasons that we are not aware of." — Richardson, p. 27.

5. Paul and Barnabas at Lystra.

"Then the priest of Jupiter which was before their city brought oxen and garlands unto the gates, and would have done sacrifice with the people; which when the apostles Barnabas and Paul heard of, they rent their clothes."—Acts 14: 13, 14.

On the left Paul and Barnabas are standing beneath a portico, and appear to recoil from the intention of the townsmen to offer sacrifice to them; the first is rending his garment and rebuking a man who is bringing a ram to be offered. On the right, near the centre, is seen a group of the people bringing forward two oxen; a man is raising an axe to strike one of them down; his arm is held back by a youth, who, having observed the abhorrent gesture of Paul, judges that the sacrifice will be offensive to him. In the foreground appears the cripple, no longer so, who is clasping his hands with an expression of gratitude; his crutches lie useless at his feet. An old man, raising part of his dress, gazes with a look of astonishment on the restored limbs. In the background, the forum of Lystra, with several temples. Towards the centre is seen a statue of Mercury, in allusion to the words in the text: "And they called Paul, Mercurius, because he was the chief speaker."

As a composition this cartoon is an instance of the consummate skill with which Raphael has contrived to bring together a variety of circumstances so combined as to make the story perfectly intelligible as a passing scene, linking it at the same

time with the past and the succeeding time. We
have the foregone moment in the appearance of
the healed cripple, and the wonder he excites ; in
the furious looks directed against the apostles by
some of the spectators we see foreshadowed the
persecution which immediately followed this act
of mistaken adoration. Every part of the grouping, the figures, the head, both in drawing and
expression, are wonderful, and have an infusion of
the antique and classical spirit most proper to the
subject. The sacrificial group of the ox, with the
figure holding its head and the man lifting the
axe, was taken from a Roman bas-relief which in
Raphael's time was in the Villa Medici, and the
idea varied and adapted to his purpose with infinite skill. The boys piping at the altar are full
of beauty, and most gracefully contrasted in character. The whole is full of movement and interest.

6. St. Paul Preaching at Athens.

"Then Paul stood in the midst of Mars' hill, and said, Ye men
of Athens, I perceive that in all things ye are too superstitious.
For as I passed by and beheld your devotions, I found an altar
with this inscription, To the unknown God." — Acts 17: 22, 23.

Paul, standing on some elevated steps, is preaching to the Athenians in the Areopagus ; behind him
are three philosophers of the different sects, the
Cynic, the Epicurean, and the Platonic ; beyond.
a group of sophists disputing among each other.
On the right are seen the half-figures of Dionysius

the Areopagite and the woman Damaris, of whom it is expressly said that they " believed and clave unto him." On the same side, in the background, is seen the statue of Mars, in front of a circular temple. In point of pictorial composition, this cartoon is one of the finest in the series. St. Paul, elevated above his auditors, grandly dignified in bearing, as one divinely inspired, lofty in stature and position, " stands like a tower." This figure of St. Paul has been imitated from the fresco of Masaccio in the Carmine at Florence. There Paul is represented as visiting St. Peter in prison. One arm only is raised, the forefinger pointing upward; he is speaking words of consolation to him through the grated bars of his dungeon, behind which appears the form of St. Peter. Raphael has taken the idea of the figure, raised the two arms, and given the whole an air of inspired energy wanting in the original. The persons who surround him are not to be considered a mere promiscuous assemblage of individuals; among them several figures may each be said to personify a class, and the different sects of Grecian philosophy may be easily distinguished. Here the Cynic, revolving deeply, and fabricating objections; there the Stoic, leaning on his staff, giving a steady but scornful attention, and fixed in obstinate incredulity; there the disciples of Plato, not conceding a full belief, but pleased at least with the beauty of the doctrine, and listening with gratified attention. Further on is a promiscuous group of disputants, sophists, and freethinkers, engaged in vehement discussion, but apparently more bent on exhibiting their own ingenuity than anxious to elicit truth or acknowledge conviction. At a considerable distance in the background are seen two doctors of the Jewish law. The varied groups, the fine thinking heads among the auditors, the expression of curiosity, reflection, doubt, conviction, faith, as revealed in the different countenances and attitudes, are all as fine as possible ; particularly the man who has wrapped his robe around him, and appears buried in thought. " This figure also is borrowed from Masaccio. The closed eyes, which in Masaccio might be easily mistaken for sleeping, are not in the least ambiguous in the cartoon ; his eyes, indeed, are closed, but they are closed with such vehemence that the agitation of a mind perplexed in the extreme is seen at the first glance. But what is most extraordinary, and I think particularly to be admired, is that the same idea is continued through the whole figure, even to the drapery, which is so closely muffle about him that even his hands are not seen. By this happy correspondence between the expression of the countenance and the disposition of the parts, the figure appears to think from head to foot." *

* Sir Joshua Reynolds.

7. The Charge to St. Peter.

"Feed my sheep."—JOHN 21: 16.

Christ is standing and pointing with the right hand to a flock of sheep; his left hand is extended towards Peter, who, holding the key, kneels at his feet. The other ten apostles stand behind him, listening with various gestures and expression to the words of the Saviour. In the background a landscape, and on the right the Lake of Gennesareth and a fisher's bark. In the tapestry the white robe of our Saviour is strewed with golden stars, which has a beautiful effect, and doubtless existed in the cartoon, though no trace of this is now visible.

As the transaction here represented took place between Christ and St. Peter only, there was little room for dramatic effect. Richardson praises the introduction of the sheep, as the only means of making the incident intelligible; but I agree with Dr. Waagen that herein Raphael has perhaps, in avoiding one error, fallen into another, and, not able to give us the real meaning of the words, has turned into a palpable object what was merely a figurative expression, and thus produced an ambiguity of another and of a more unpleasant kind.

The figure of Christ is wonderfully noble in conception and treatment; the heads of the apostles finely diversified: in some we see only affectionate acquiescence, duteous submission ; in others wonder, displeasure, and jealous discontent   The figures of the apostles are in the cartoon happily relieved from each other by variety of local tint, which cannot be given in a print, and hence the heavy effect of the composition when studied through the engraving only.

These are the subjects of the famous Cartoons of Raphael. To describe the effect of the light and sketchy treatment, so easy, and yet so large and grand in style, we shall borrow the words of an eloquent writer.

" Compared with these," says Hazlitt, as finely as truly, " all other pictures look like oil and varnish ; we are stopped and attracted by the coloring, the pencilling, the finishing, the instrumentalities of art ; but *here* the painter seems to have flung his mind upon the canvas. His thoughts, his great ideas alone, prevail ; there is nothing between us and the subject ; we look through a frame and see Scripture histories, and are made actual spectators in miraculous events. Not to speak it profanely, they are a sort of a revelation of the subjects of which they treat ; there is an ease and freedom of manner about them which brings preternatural characters and situations home to us with the familiarity of every-day occurrences ; and while the figures fill, raise, and satisfy the mind, they seem to have cost the painter nothing. Everywhere else we see the means ; here we arrive at the end apparently without any means. There

is a spirit at work in the divine creation before us ·
we are unconscious of any steps taken, of any prog
ress made ; we are aware only of comprehensive
results — of whole masses of figures : the sense of
power supersedes the appearance of effort.   It is as
if we had ourselves seen these persons and things
at some former state of our being, and that the
drawing certain lines upon coarse paper by some
unknown spell brought back the entire and living
images, and made them pass before us, palpable to
thought, feeling, sight.   Perhaps not all this is
owing to genius ; something of this effect may be
ascribed to the simplicity of the vehicle employed
in embodying the story, and something to the de-
caying and dilapidated state of the pictures themselves.   They are the more majestic for being in
ruins.   We are struck chiefly with the truth of
proportion, and the range of conception — all made
spiritual.   The corruptible has put on incorrup-
tion ; and, amidst the wreck of color and the mouldering of material beauty, nothing is left but a
universe of thought, or the broad imminent shadows of ' calm contemplation and majestic pains.' "

There exist two sets of copies of the same size
as the originals : one executed by Sir James Thorn-
hill, and presented by the Duke of Bedford to the
Royal Academy ; and another set presented by
the Duke of Marlborough to the University of
Oxford.

It is a matter of regret, but hardly of surprise

that the cartoons have never yet been adequately
engraved. The first complete series which appeared
was by Simon Gribelin, a French engraver, who
came over in 1680, and was published in the reign
of Queen Anne. The prints are small, neat memoranda of the compositions, nothing more.

The second set was executed by Sir Nicholas
Dorigny, who undertook the work under the
patronage of the government, and presented to the
king, George I., in 1719, two sets of the finished
engravings; on which occasion the king bestowed
on him a purse of one hundred guineas, and, at
the request of the Duke of Devonshire, knighted
him. These engravings are large, and tolerably
but coarsely executed, and are preferred by connoisseurs; but on the whole they are poor as works
of art.

There are two small sets in mezzotinto, and
another small set by Filtler.

The set of large engravings by Thomas Holloway
was begun by him in 1800, and was not quite completed at his death, in 1826. These engravings
have been praised for the " finished and elaborate
style in which they have been executed," and they
deserve this praise; but, as transcripts of the cartoons, they are altogether false in point of style.
They are too metallic, too mechanical, too labored:
a set of masterly etchings would better convey an
impression of the slight, free execution, the spiritual
ease, of the originals. These engravings give one

the idea of being done from highly-finished, deeply colored oil-pictures.

Since 1837 a large set has been commenced by John Burnett, in a mixed, rather coarse style, but effective and spirited ; they are sold at a cheap rate.

Lastly, a set has been commenced by Mr. L. Grüner, whose exquisite taste and classical style of engraving, as well as his profound acquaintance with the works and genius of Raphael, render him particularly fit for the task.

Raphael finished these cartoons in 1516. They are all from fourteen to eighteen feet in length, and about twelve feet high ; the figures above life-size, drawn with chalk upon strong paper, and colored in distemper. He received for his designs four hundred and thirty-four gold ducats (about six hundred and fifty pounds), which were paid to him, three hundred on the 15th of June, 1515, and one hundred and thirty-four in December, 1516. The rich tapestries worked from these cartoons, in wool, silk, and gold, were completed at Arras, and sent to Rome, in 1519. For these the pope paid to the manufacturer at Arras fifty thousand gold ducats ; they were exhibited for the first time on St. Stephen's Day, December 26, 1519. Raphael had the satisfaction, before he died, of seeing them hung in their places, and of witnessing the wonder and applause they excited through the whole city. Their subsequent fate was very curious and eventful. In the sack of Rome, in 1527, they were car-

ried away by the French soldiery; but were restored, in 1553, during the reign of Pope Julius
III., by the Duc de Montmorenci, all but the piece
which represented the Coronation of the Virgin,
which is supposed to have been burned for the sake
of the gold thread. Again, in 1798, they made part
of the French spoliations, and were actually sold
to a Jew at Leghorn, who burnt one of them for
the purpose of extracting the precious metal contained in the threads. As it was found, however,
to furnish very little, the proprietor judged it better
to allow the others to retain their original shape,
and they were soon afterwards repurchased from
him by the agents of Pius VII., and reïnstated in
the galleries of the Vatican. Several sets of tapestries were worked from the cartoons: one was sent
as a present to Henry VIII., and after the death
of Charles I. sold into Spain; another of the same
set was exhibited in London about a year ago, and
has since been sold to the King of Prussia.

While all Rome was indulging in ecstasies over
the rich and dearly-paid tapestries, which were not
hen, and are still less *now*, worth one of the cartoons, these precious productions of the artist's own
mind were lying in the warehouse of the weaver at
Arras, neglected and forgotten. Some were torn
into fragments, and parts of them exist in various
collections. Seven still remained in some garret or
cellar, when Rubens, just a century afterwards,
mentioned their existence to Charles I., and advised

him to purchase them for the use of a tapestry manufactory which King James I. had established at Mortlake. The purchase was made. They had been cut into long slips about two feet wide, for the convenience of the workmen, and in this state they arrived in England.* On Charles' death, Cromwell bought them, at the sale of the royal effects, for three hundred pounds. We had very nearly lost them again in the reign of Charles II.; for Louis XIV. having intimated, through his ambassador Barillon, a wish to possess them at any price, the needy, careless Charles was on the point of yielding them, and would have done so but for the representations of the Lord Treasurer Danby, to whom, in fact, we owe it that they were not ceded to France. They remained, however, neglected in one of the lumber-rooms at Whitehall till the reign of William III., and narrowly escaped being destroyed by fire when Whitehall was burned, in 1698. It must have been shortly after that King William ordered them to be repaired, the fragments pasted together, and stretched upon linen;

* There can be no doubt of the purpose for which Charles I acquired them. The entry in the king's catalogue runs thus: 'In a slit wooden case some two cartoons of Raphael Urbino's, *for hangings to be made by;* and the other five are, by the king's appointment, delivered to Mr. Francis Cleyne, at Mortlake, *to make hangings by.*" It appears that Cromwell had some intention of continuing the manufactory of tapestry at Mortlake as a national undertaking, and retained the cartoons for purposes connected with it.

and being just at that time occupied with the alterations and improvements at Hampton Court, Sir Christopher Wren had his commands to plan and erect a room expressly to receive them, — the room in which they now hang.

In the Vatican there is a second set of ten tapestries, for which Raphael gave the original designs; but he did not execute the cartoons, and the style of drawing in those fragments which remain is not his. A very fine fragment of one of these cartoons, *The Massacre of the Innocents*, is in our National Gallery. It is very different in the style of execution from the cartoons at Hampton Court, and has been painted over in oil, when or by whom is not known, but certainly before 1730. The subjects of the second set were all from the life of Christ, and were as follows:

1. The Slaughter of the Innocents.
2. The Adoration of the Shepherds.
3. The Adoration of the Magi.
4. The Presentation in the Temple.
5. The Resurrection.
6. The Noli me Tangere.
7. The Descent into Purgatory.
8. Christ and the Disciples at Emmaus.
9. The Ascension.
10. The Descent of the Holy Ghost

The tapestries of these subjects still hang in the Vatican, and all have been engraved.

The fame of Raphael had by this time spread to

other countries. Horace Walpole, in the " Aneo-
dotes of Painting," assures us that Henry VIII ,
who on coming to the throne was desirous of emu-
lating Francis I. as a patron of art, invited Raphael
to his court ; but he does not say on what authority
he states this as a fact. At all events, the young
king was obliged to content himself with the little
St. George sent to him by the Duke of Urbino, as
a specimen of Raphael's talent ; and with Holbein,
whom he soon after engaged in his service, as his
court painter, — perhaps the best substitute for
Raphael in point of original genius then to be obtained by offers of gold or patronage. Francis I.
was also most anxious to attract Raphael to his
court ; and not succeeding, he desired to have a
picture by his hand, leaving him the choice of subject. As Raphael had chosen St. George as the
fittest subject for the King of England, he now,
with equal propriety and taste, chose St. Michael,
the patron saint of the most celebrated military
order in France, as likely to be the most acceptable
subject for the French king, and represented the
archangel as victorious over the Spirit of Evil. The
figures are as large as life. St. Michael, beaming
with angelic beauty and power, stands with one
foot on the Evil One, and raises his lance to thrust
him down to the deep. Satan is so represented
that very little of his hideous and prostrate form is
visible, the grand victorious spirit filling the whole
canvas and the eye of the spectator. The king ex-

pressed his satisfaction in a right royal and graceful fashion. and rewarded the artist munificently. Raphael, considering himself overpaid, and not to be outdone in generosity, sent to the king his famous Holy Family (called The large Holy Family, because the figures are life-size), in which the infant Christ is seen in act to spring from the cradle into his mother's arms, while angels scatter flowers from above. Engravings and copies without number exist of this famous picture. The original is in the gallery of the Louvre. Raphael sent also his St. Margaret overcoming the Dragon, a compliment apparently to the king's favorite sister, Margaret, Queen of Navarre: this also is in the Louvre. When they were placed before Francis I., he ordered his treasurer to count out twenty-four thousand livres (about three thousand pounds, according to the present value of money), and sent it to the painter with the strongest expressions of his approbation. At a later period he purchased the beautiful portrait of Joanna of Arragon, vice-queen of Naples, which is also in the Louvre.

About the same period (that is, between 1517 and 1520) Raphael painted for the convent of St. Sixtus, at Piacenza, one of the grandest and most celebrated of all his works, called, from its original destination, the Madonna di San Sisto. It represents the Virgin standing in a majestic attitude; the infant Saviour *enthroned* in her arms; and around her head a glory of innumerable cherubs melting into light. Kneeling before her we see on one side St. Sixtus, on the other St Barbara, and beneath her feet two heavenly cherubs gaze up in adoration. In execution, as in design, this is probably the most perfect picture in the world. It is painted throughout by Raphael's own hand; and as no sketch or study of any part of it was ever known to exist, and as the execution must have been, from the thinness and delicacy of the colors, wonderfully rapid, it is supposed that he painted it at once on the canvas — a *creation* rather than a picture. In the beginning of the last century the Elector of Saxony, Augustus III., purchased this picture from the monks of the convent for the sum of sixty thousand florins (about six thousand pounds), and it now forms the chief boast and ornament of the Dresden Gallery. The finest engraving is that of Frederic Müller, good impressions of which are worth twenty or thirty guineas; but there is also a very beautiful and faithful lithograph by Hofstängel, which may be purchased for half as many shillings.

For his patron Agostino Chigi, Raphael painted in fresco the history of Cupid and Psyche. The palace which belonged to the Chigi family is now the Villa Farnesina, on the walls of which these famous frescoes may still be seen in very good preservation. In Grüner's admirable work on the " Decoration of the Palaces and Churches in Italy " there is a perspective view of the corridor of the

Farnesina, snowing how this beautiful series of compositions is arranged on the ceiling and walls In the same palace he painted the Triumph of Galatea. In this fresco he was greatly assisted by Giulio Romano.

During the last ten years of his life the fame of Raphael was very much extended by means of the engraver Marc Antonio Raimondi, who, after studying design in the school of Francia at Bologna, betook himself to Rome, and gained the admiration and good-will of Raphael by the perfect engravings he made from some of his beautiful works. Marc Antonio lived for some time in Raphael's own house, and engraved for him and under his direction most of those precious and exquisite compositions, the most wonderful creations of the mind of Raphael, of which there exist no finished pictures, and in some cases no drawings nor memoranda. Among these may be mentioned a few which are to be found in the Print-room of the British Museum: 1. The Lucretia, a single figure, wonderfully beautiful. 2. The Massacre of the Innocents. 3. Eve presenting to Adam the forbidden fruit. 4. The Last Supper. 5. The Mater Dolorosa, the Virgin lamenting over the dead body of our Saviour. 6. Another of the same subject, containing several figures. These are only a few of the most precious, for within the present limits it is impossible to go into detail. Some time after the death of Raphael, Marc Antonio was very deservedly banished from

Rome by Clement VII. Tempted by gold, he had lent his unrivalled skill to shameful purposes. According to Malvasia, he was afterwards assassinated at Bologna.

The last great picture which Raphael undertook, and which at the time of his death was not quite completed, was the Transfiguration of our Saviour on Mount Tabor. This picture is divided into two parts. The lower part contains a crowd of figures, and is full of passion, energy, action. In the centre is the demoniac boy, convulsed and struggling in the arms of his father. Two women, kneeling, implore assistance; others are seen crying aloud and stretching out their arms for aid. In the disciples of Jesus we see exhibited, in various shades of expression, astonishment, horror, sympathy, profound thought. One among them, with a benign and youthful countenance, looks compassionately on the father, plainly intimating that he can give no help. The upper part of the picture represents Mount Tabor. The three apostles lie prostrate, dazzled, on the earth; above them, transfigured in glory, floats the divine form of the Saviour, with Moses and Elias on either side. " The two-fold action contained in this picture, to which shallow critics have taken exception, is explained historically and satisfactorily merely by the fact that the incident of the possessed boy occurred in the absence of Christ; but it explains itself in a still higher sense, when we consider the deeper universal meaning of the picture. For this purpose it is not even necessary to consult the books of the New Testament for the explanation of the particular incidents : the lower portion represents the calamities and miseries of human life, the rule of demoniac power, the weakness even of the faithful when unassisted, and directs them to look on high for aid and strength in adversity. Above, in the brightness of divine bliss, undisturbed by the sufferings of the lower world, we behold the source of our consolation and of our redemption from evil."

At this time the lovers of painting at Rome were divided in opinion as to the relative merits of Michael Angelo and Raphael, and formed two great parties, that of Raphael being by far the most numerous.

Michael Angelo, with characteristic haughtiness disdained any open rivalry with Raphael, and put forward the Venetian, Sebastian del Piombo, as no unworthy competitor of the great Roman painter. Raphael bowed before Michael Angelo, and, with the modesty and candor which belonged to his character, was heard to thank heaven that he had been born in the same age and enabled to profit by the grand creations of that sublime genius. But he was by no means inclined to yield any supremacy to Sebastian ; he knew his own strength too well. To decide the controversy, the Cardinal

Giulio de' Medici, afterwards Pope Clement VII ,
commissioned Raphael to paint this picture of the
Transfiguration, and at the same time commanded
from Sebastian del Piombo the Raising of Lazarus,
which is now in our National Gallery (No. 1).
Both pictures were intended by the cardinal for
his cathedral at Narbonne, he having lately been
created Archbishop of Narbonne, by Francis I.
Michael Angelo, well aware that Sebastian was a
far better colorist than designer, furnished him
with the cartoon for his picture, and, it is said,
drew some of the figures (that of Lazarus, for
example) with his own hand on the panel ; but
he was so far from doing this secretly, that Raphael heard of it, and exclaimed, joyfully, " Michael Angelo has graciously favored me, in that
he has deemed me worthy to compete with himself, and not with Sebastian ! " But he did not
live to enjoy the triumph of his acknowledged
superiority, dying before he had finished his picture, which was afterwards completed by the hand
of Giulio Romano.

During the last years of his life, and while engaged in painting the Transfiguration, Raphael's
active mind was employed on many other things.
He had been appointed by the pope to superintend the building of St. Peter's, and he prepared
the architectural plans for that vast undertaking.
He was most active and zealous in carrying out the
pope's project for disinterring and preserving the

remains of art which lay buried beneath the ruins
of ancient Rome. A letter is yet extant addressed
by Raphael to Pope Leo X., in which he lays down
a systematic, well-considered plan for excavating
by degrees the whole of the ancient city; and a
writer of that time has left a Latin epigram to
this purpose — that Raphael had sought and found
in Rome "*another Rome.*" — "To seek it," adds
the poet, "was worthy of a great man; to reveal
it, worthy of a god." He also made several drawings and models for sculpture, particularly for a
statue of Jonah, now in the church of Santa
Maria del Popolo. Nor was this all. With a
princely magnificence, he had sent artists at his
own cost to various parts of Italy and into Greece,
to make drawings from those remains of antiquity
which his numerous and important avocations
prevented him from visiting himself. He was in
close intimacy and correspondence with most of
the celebrated men of his time; interested himself in all that was going forward; mingled in
society, lived in splendor, and was always ready
to assist generously his own family, and the pupils
who had gathered round him. The Cardinal Bibbiena offered him his niece in marriage, with a
dowry of three thousand gold crowns; but the
early death of Maria di Bibbiena prevented this
union, for which it appears that Raphael himself
had no great inclination. In possession of all
that ambition could desire, for him the cup of life

was still running over with love, hope, power, glory — when, in the very prime of manhood, and in the midst of vast undertakings, he was seized with a violent fever, — caught, it is said, in superintending some subterranean excavations, — and expired after an illness of fourteen days. His death took place on Good Friday (his birth-day), April 6, 1520, having completed his thirty-seventh year. Great was the grief of all classes ; unspeakable that of his friends and scholars. The pope had sent every day to inquire after his health, adding the most kind and cheering messages ; and when told that the beloved and admired painter was no more, he broke out into lamentations on his own and the world's loss. The body was laid on a bed of state, and above it was suspended the last work of that divine hand, the glorious Transfiguration. From his own house near St. Peter's a multitude of all ranks followed the bier in sad procession ; and his remains were laid in the church of the Pantheon, near those of his betrothed bride, Maria di Bibbiena, in a spot chosen by himself during his lifetime.

Several years ago (in the year 1833) there arose among the antiquarians of Rome a keen dispute concerning a human skull, which, on no evidence whatever, except a long-received tradition, had been preserved and exhibited in the Academy of St. Luke, as the skull of Raphael. Some even expressed a doubt as to the exact place of his sepulchre, though upon this point the contemporary testimony seemed to leave no room for uncertainty To ascertain the fact, permission was obtained from the papal government, and from the canons of the church of the Rotunda (that is, of the Pantheon), to make some researches ; and on the fourteenth of September, in the same year, after five days spent in removing the pavement in several places, the remains of Raphael were discovered in a vault behind the high altar, and certified as his by indisputable proofs. After being examined, and a cast made from the skull and from the right hand, the skeleton was exhibited publicly in a glass case, and multitudes thronged to the church to look upon it. On the 18th of October, 1833, a second funeral ceremony took place. The remains were deposited in a pine-wood coffin, then in a marble sarcophagus, presented by the pope (Gregory XVI.), and reverently consigned to their former resting-place, in presence of more than three thousand spectators, including almost all the artists, the officers of government, and other persons of the highest rank in Rome.

Besides his grand compositions from the Old and New Testament, and his frescoes and arabesques in the Vatican, Raphael has left about one hundred and twenty pictures of the Virgin and Child. all various — only resembling each other in the pecu·

liar type of chaste and maternal loveliness which he has given to the Virgin, and the infantine beauty of the Child. The most celebrated of his Madonnas, in the order in which they were painted, are : 1. The Madonna di Foligno, in the Vatican. 2. The Madonna of the Fish, at Madrid. 3. The Madonna del Cardellino, at Florence. 4. The Madonna di San Sisto, at Dresden. 5. The Madonna called the Pearl, at Madrid. Eight of his Madonna pictures are in England, in private galleries.

There are but few pictures taken from mythology and profane history, the Cupid and Psyche and the Galatea being the most important ; but a vast number of drawings and compositions, some of them of consummate beauty.

He painted about eighty portraits, of which the most famous are Julius II.; Leo X. (the originals of both these are at Florence) ; Cardinal Bibbiena ; Cardinal Bembo ; and Count Castiglione (the last at Paris) ; the Youth with his Violin, at Rome ; Bindo Altoviti, supposed for a long time to be his own portrait, now at Munich ; the beautiful Joanna of Arragon, in the Louvre. The portrait called the Fornarina had long been supposed to represent a young girl to whom Raphael had attached himself soon after his arrival in Rome ; but this appears very doubtful : Passavant supposes it to represent Beatrice Pio, a celebrated improvisatrice of that time. Besides these, we have seventeen architec tural designs for buildings, public and private and several designs for sculpture, ornaments, &c. But it is not any single production of his hand, however rarely beautiful, nor his superiority in any particular department of art; it is the number and the variety of his creations, the union of inexhaustible fertility of imagination with excellence of every kind, — faculties never combined in the same degree in any artist before or since, — which have placed Raphael at the head of his profession, and have rendered him the wonder and delight of all ages.

We shall now proceed to give an account of some of Raphael's most famous scholars.

WE have already had occasion to observe the great number of scholars, some of them older than himself, who had assembled round Raphael, and the unusual harmony in which they lived together. Vasari relates that, when he went to court, a train of fifty painters attended on him from his own house to the Vatican. They came from every part of Italy: from Florence, Milan, Venice, Bologna, Ferrara, Naples, and even from beyond the Alps, to study under the great Roman master. Many of them assisted, with more or less skill, in the execution of his great works in fresco ; some imitated him in one thing, some in another ; but the unrivalled charm of Raphael's productions lies in the impress of the mind which produced them : this he could not impart to others. Those who followed servilely a particular manner of conception and drawing, which they called " Raphael's style," degenerated into insipidity and littleness. Those who had original power deviated into exaggerations and perversities. Not one among them approached *him*. Some caught a faint reflection of his grace some of his power : but they turned it to other pur

(280)

poses; they worked in a different spirit; they followed the fashion of the hour. While he lived his noble aims elevated them, but when he died they fell away, one after another. The lavish and magnificent Pope Leo X. was succeeded in 1521 by Adrian VI., a man conscientious even to severity, sparing even to asceticism, and without any sympathies either for art or artists. During his short pontificate of two years all the works in the Vatican and St. Peter's were suspended, the poor painters were starving, and the dreadful pestilence which raged in 1523 drove many from the city. Under Clement VII., one of the Medici, and nephew of Leo X., the arts for a time revived; but the sack of Rome by the barbarous soldiery of Bourbon in 1527 completed the dispersion of the artists who had flocked to the capital: each returning to his native country or city, became also a teacher; and thus what was called " Raphael's School," or the " Roman School," was spread from one end of Italy to the other.

Raphael had left by his will his two favorite scholars, Gian Francesco Penni and Giulio Romano as executors, and to them he bequeathed the task of completing his unfinished works.

GIAN FRANCESCO PENNI, called Il Fattore, was his beloved and confidential pupil, and had assisted him much, particularly in preparing his cartoons; but everything he executed from his own mind and after Raphael's death has, with much tenderness and *Raffaelesque* grace, a sort of feebleness more of mind than hand. His pictures are very rare. He died in 1528.

His brother Luca Penni was in England for same years in the service of Henry VIII., and employed by Wolsey in decorating his palace at Hampton Court; some remains of his performances there were still to be seen in the middle of the last century; but Horace Walpole's notion that Luca Penni executed those three singular pictures, the Field of the Cloth of Gold, the Battle of the Spurs, and the Embarkation of Henry VIII., appears to be quite unfounded.

Giulio Pippi, surnamed, from the place of his birth, Il Romano, and generally styled Giulio Romano, was also much beloved by Raphael, and of all his scholars the most distinguished for original power. While under the influence of Raphael's mind, he imitated his manner and copied his pictures so successfully, that it is sometimes difficult for the best judges to distinguish the difference of hand. The Julius II. in our National Gallery is an instance. After Raphael's death, he abandoned himself to his own luxuriant genius. He lost the simplicity, the grace, the chaste and elevated feeling, which had characterized his master. He became strongly imbued with the then reigning taste for classical and mythological subjects, which he treated not exactly in a classical spirit, but with great boldness and fire, both in conception and exe sution. He did not excel in religious subjects. If he had to paint the Virgin, he gave her the air and form of a commanding Juno; if a Saviour, he was like a Roman emperor; the apostles in his pictures are like heathen philosophers: but when he had to deal with gods and Titans, he was in his element.

For four years after the death of Raphael he was chiefly occupied in completing his master's unfinished works; at the end of that time he went to Mantua and entered the service of the Duke Gonzaga, as painter and architect. He designed for him a splendid palace called the Palazzo del Te, which he decorated with frescoes in a grand but coarse style. In one saloon he represented Jupiter vanquishing the giants; in another, the history of Psyche. Everywhere we see great luxuriance of fancy, wonderful power of drawing, and a bold, large style of treatment; but great coarseness of imagination, red, heavy coloring, and a pagan rather than a *classical* taste.

In character, Giulio Romano was a man of generous mind; princely in his style of living; an accomplished courtier, yet commanding respect by a lofty sense of his own dignity as an artist. He amassed great riches in the service of the Duke Gonzaga, and spent his life at Mantua. His most important works are to be found in the palaces and churches of that city.

When Charles I. purchased the entire collection of the Dukes of Mantua, in 1629, there were among

them many pictures by Giulio Romano.   One of
these was the admirable copy of Raphael's fresco
of the battle between Constantine and Maxentius.
now in the guard-room at Hampton Court.   In the
same gallery are seven others, all mythological, and
characteristic certainly, but by no means favorable
specimens of his genius; they have besides been
coarsely painted over by some restorer, so as to
retain no trace of the original workmanship.   The
most important picture which came into the possession of King Charles was a Nativity, a large
altar-piece, which, after the king's death, was sold
into France.   It is now in the Louvre (1075).   A
very pretty little picture is the Venus persuading
Vulcan to forge the arrows of Cupid ; also in the
Louvre (1077).   Engravings after Giulio Romano
are very commonly met with.

Giulio Romano was invited by Francis I. to
undertake the decoration of his palace at Fontainebleau ; but, not being able to leave Mantua, he sent
his pupil Primaticcio, who covered the walls with
frescoes and arabesques, much in the manner of
those in the Palazzo del Te ; that is to say, with
gods and goddesses, fauns, satyrs, nymphs, Cupids,
Cyclops, Titans, in a style as remote from that of
Raphael as can well be imagined, and yet not des-
titute of a certain grandeur.

PRIMATICCIO, NICOLÒ DEL ABATE, Rosso, and
others who worked with them, are designated in

the history of art as the " Fontainebleau School,"
of which Primaticcio is considered the chief.*

Giovanni da Udine, who excelled in painting
animals, flowers, and still life, was Raphael's chief
assistant in the famous arabesques of the Vatican.

Perino del Vaga, another of Raphael's scholars,
carried his style to Genoa, where he was chiefly em
ployed ; and Andrea di Salerno, a far more
charming painter, who was at Rome but a short
time, has left many pictures at Naples, nearer to
Raphael in point of feeling than those of other
scholars who had studied under his eye for years.
Andrea seems also to have been allied to his master
in mind and character, for Raphael parted from
him with deep regret.

Polidoro Caldara, called from the place of his
birth Polidoro da Caravaggio, was a poor boy who
had been employed by the fresco painters in the
Vatican to carry the wet mortar, and afterwards to
grind their colors. He learned to admire, then to
emulate what he saw, and Raphael encouraged and
aided him by his instructions. The bent of Polidoro's genius, as it developed itself, was a curious
and interesting compound of his two vocations. He
had been a mason, or what we should call a brick-
layer's boy, for the first twenty years of his life.
From building houses he took to decorating them,

---

* The frescoes executed by these painters in the palace of Fontainebleau have lately been restored, with admirable success, by
M. Alaux, a French painter of eminence.

and from an early familiarity with the remains of antiquity lying around him, the mind of the un·educated mechanic became unconsciously imbued with the very spirit of antiquity; not one of Raphael's scholars was so distinguished for a classical purity of taste as Polidoro. He painted chiefly in chiaro'scuro (that is, in two colors, light and shade) friezes, composed of processions of figures, such as we see in the ancient bas-reliefs, sea and river gods, tritons, bacchantes, fauns, satyrs, Cupids. At Hampton Court there are six pieces of a small narrow frieze, representing boys and animals, which apparently formed the top of a bedstead or some other piece of furniture; these will give some faint idea of the decorative style of Polidoro. This painter was much employed at Naples, and afterwards at Messina, where he was assassinated by one of his servants for the sake of his money.

PELLEGRINO DA MODENA, an excellent painter, and one of Raphael's most valuable assistants in his Scriptural subjects, carried the "Roman School" to Modena.

At this time there was in Ferrara a school of painters very peculiar in style, distinguished chiefly by extreme elegance of execution, a miniature-like neatness in the details, and deep, vigorous, contrasted colors — as intense crimson, viv'd green, brilliant white, approximated; — a little grotesque in point of taste, and rather like the very early German school in feeling and treatment, but with more grace and ideality. There is a picture in our National Gallery by Mazzolino da Ferrara (No. 82), which will give a very good idea of this style, both in its beauties and its singularities.

One of these Ferrarese painters, Benvenuto Garofalo, studied for some time at Rome in the school of Raphael, but it does not appear that he assisted, like most of the other students, in any of his works. He was older than Raphael, and already advanced in his art before he went to Rome; but while there he knew how to profit by the higher principles which were laid down, and studied assiduously; with a larger, freer style of drawing, and a certain elevation in the expression of his heads acquired in the school of Raphael, he combined the glowing color which characterized the first painters of his native city. There is a small picture by Garofalo in our National Gallery (No. 81), which is a very fair example of his style. The subject is a Vision of St. Augustine, rendered still more poetical by the introduction of the Virgin and Child above, and the figure of St. Catherine, who stands behind the saint. Garofalo's small pictures are not uncommon; his large pictures are chiefly confined to Ferrara and the churches around it.

Tibaldi of Bologna, Innocenza da Imola, and Timoteo della Vite, were also painters of the

Roman school, whose works are very seldom met with in England.

Another painter, who must not be omitted, was GIULIO CLOVIO. He was originally a monk, and began by imitating the miniatures in the illuminated missals and psalm-books used in the church. He then studied at Rome, and was particularly indebted to Michael Angelo and Giulio Romano. His works are a proof that greatness and correctness of style do not depend on size and space; for into a few inches square, into the arabesque ornaments round a page of manuscript, he could throw a feeling of the sublime and beautiful worthy of the great masters of art. The vigor and precision of his drawing in the most diminutive figures, the imaginative beauty of some of his tiny compositions (for Giulio was no copyist), is almost inconceivable. His works were enormously paid, and executed only for sovereign princes and rich prelates. Fifteen years of his life were spent in the service of Pope Paul III. (1534–1549), for whom his finest productions were executed. He died in 1578, at the age of eighty.

Besides the Italians, many painters came from beyond the Alps to place themselves under the tuition of Raphael; among these were Bernard von Orlay from Brussels, Michael Coxcis from Mechlin, and George Penz from Nuremberg. But the influence of Raphael's mind and style is not very apparent in any of these painters, of whom we shall

have more to say hereafter. By George Penz, there
is a beautiful portrait of Erasmus in the Royal
Gallery at Windsor.

PEDRO CAMPANA, who was a great favorite of
Charles V., carried the principles of the Roman
school into Spain.

On the whole, we may say that while Michael
Angelo and Raphael displayed in all they did the
inspiration of genius, their scholars and imitators
inundated all Italy with mediocrity :

> " Art with hollow forms was fed,
> But the *soul* of art lay dead."

19

CORREGGIO AND GIORGIONE, AND THEIR SCHOLARS.

WHILE the great painters of the Florentine
school, with Michael Angelo at their head, were
carrying out the principle of *form*, and those of
Rome — the followers and imitators of Raphael —
were carrying out the principle of *expression;* —
and the first school deviating into exaggeration, and
the latter degenerating into mannerism, — there
arose in the north of Italy two extraordinary and
original men, who, guided by their own individual
genius and temperament, took up different principles, and worked them out to perfection. One
revelling in the illusions of *chiaro`scuro*, so that to
him all nature appeared clothed in a soft transparent
veil of lights and shadows; the other delighting in
the luxurious depth of tints, and beholding all
nature steeped in the glow of an Italian sunset.
They chose each their world, and " drew after them
a third part of heaven."

Of the two, Giorgione appears to have been the
most original, — the most of a creator and inventor.
Correggio may possibly have owed his conception
of melting, vanishing out ~s and transparent

shadows, and his peculiar feeling of grace, to Lionardo da Vinci, whose pictures were scattered over
the whole of the north of Italy. Giorgione found
in his own fervid, melancholy character the mystery
of his coloring, — warm, glowing, yet subdued, —
and the noble yet tender sentiment of his heads:
characteristics which, transmitted to Titian, became in coloring more sunshiny and brilliant,
without losing depth and harmony; and in ex
pression more cheerful, still retaining intellect and
dignity.

We will first speak of Correggio, so styled from
his birthplace, a small town not far from Modena,
now called Reggio. His real name was Antonio
Allegri, and he was born towards the end of the
year 1493. Raphael was at this time ten years
old, Michael Angelo twenty, and Lionardo da
Vinci in his fortieth year. The father of Antonio
was Pellegrino Allegri, a tradesman possessed of
moderate property in houses and land. He gave
his son a careful education, and had him instructed
in literature and rhetoric, as well as in the rudiments of art, which he imbibed at a very early age
from an uncle, Lorenzo Allegri, a painter of little
merit. Afterwards he studied for a short time
under Andrea Mantegna ; and although, when this
painter died, in 1506, Antonio was but thirteen, he
had so far profited by his instructions and those of
Francesco Mantegna, who continued his father's
school, that he drew well and caught that taste

and skill in foreshortening which distinguished his
later works.   It was an art which Mantegna may
almost be said to have invented, and which was first
taught in his academy ; but the dry, hard, precise,
meagre style of the Mantegna school, Correggio soon
abandoned for a manner entirely his own, in which
movement, variety, and, above all, the most delicate
gradation of light and shadow, are the principal
elements.   All these qualities are apparent in the
earliest of his authenticated pictures, painted in
1512, when he was about eighteen.   It is one of the
large altar-pieces in the Dresden Gallery, called the
Madonna di San Francesco, because St. Francis is
one of the principal figures.   The influence of the
taste and manner of Lionardo da Vinci is very conspicuous in this picture.

In 1519, having acquired some reputation and
fortune in his profession, Correggio married Giro-
lama Merlini ; and in the following year, being
then six-and-twenty, he was commissioned to paint
in fresco the cupola of the church of San Giovanni
at Parma.   He chose for his subject the Ascension
of Christ, who in the centre appears soaring upwards into heaven, surrounded by the Twelve Apostles, seated around on clouds, and who appear to be
watching his progress to the realms above ; below
are the four Evangelists in the four arches, with
the four Fathers of the Church.   The figures in the
upper part are of course colossal, and foreshortened
with admirable skill, so as to produce a wonderful

effect when viewed from below. In the apsis of the
same church, over the high altar, he painted the
Coronation of the Virgin ; but this was destroyed
when the church was subsequently enlarged, and
is now only known through engravings and the
copies made by Annibal Carracci, which are preserved at Naples. For this work Correggio received
five hundred gold crowns, equal to about fifteen
hundred pounds at the present day.

About the year 1525, Correggio was invited to
Mantua, where he painted for the reigning Duke,
Federigo Gonzaga, the Education of Cupid, which
is now in our National Gallery. For the same
accomplished but profligate prince he painted the
other mythological stories of Io, Leda, Danaë, and
Antiope.*

Passing over, for the present, a variety of works
which Correggio painted in the next four or five
years, we shall only observe that the cupola of San
Giovanni gave so much satisfaction, that he was
called upon to decorate in the same manner the
cathedral of Parma, which is dedicated to the Virgin Mary. In the centre of the dome he represented
the Assumption — the Madonna soaring into heaven,
while Christ descends from his throne in bliss to
meet her. An innumerable host of saints and angels, rejoicing and singing hymns of triumph, sur-

* The Io and the Leda are in the Berlin Gallery ; the Danaë, in
the Borghese Gallery ; and the Antiope, in the Louvre. The latter
once belonged to King Charles.

round these principal personages. Lower down in a circle stand the Apostles, and, lower still, Genii bearing candelabra and swinging censers. In lu-nettes below are the four Evangelists, the figure of St. John being one of the finest. The whole composition is full of glorious life; wonderful for the relief, the bold and perfect foreshortening, the management of the chiaro'scuro; but, from the innumerable figures, and the play of the limbs seen from below, — legs and arms being more conspicuous than bodies, — the great artist was reproached in his lifetime with having painted " un guazzetto di rane " (a fricassée of frogs).* There are several engravings of this magnificent work; but those who would form a just idea of Correggio's sublime conception and power of drawing should see some of the cartoons prepared for the frescoes and drawn in chalk by Correggio's own hand. A few of these, representing chiefly angels and cherubim, were discovered a few years ago at Parma, rolled up in a garret. They were conveyed to Rome, thence brought to England by Dr. Braun, and are now in the British Museum, having been lately purchased by the trustees. These heads and forms are gigantic, nearly twice the size of life; yet such is the excellence of the drawing, and the perfect grace and sweetness of the expression, that they strike the fancy as sublimely beautiful, without giving the

* In cookery only the hind-legs of the frogs are used; the bodies are thrown away.

slightest impression of exaggeration or effort. Our artists who are preparing cartoons for works on a large scale could have no finer studies than these grand fragments, emanations of the mind and creations of the hand of one of the most distinguished masters in art. They show his manner of setting to work, and are in this respect an invaluable lesson to young painters.

Correggio finished the dome of the cathedral of Parma in 1530, and returned to his native town, where he resided for the remainder of his life. We find that in the year 1533 he was one of the witnesses to a marriage which was celebrated in the castle of Correggio, between Ippolito, Lord of Correggio, and son of Veronica Gambara, the illustrious poetess (widow of Ghiberto da Correggio), and Chiara da Correggio, his cousin. Correggio's presence on this occasion, and his signature to the marriage-deed, proved the estimation in which he was held by his sovereigns. In the following year he had engaged to paint for Alberto Panciroli an altarpiece; the subject fixed upon is not known, but it *is* certainly known that he received in advance, and before his work was commenced, twenty-five gold crowns. It was destined never to be begun, for soon after signing this agreement Correggio was seized with a malignant fever, of which he died, after a few days' illness, March 5, 1534, in the forty-first year of his age. He was buried in his family sepulchre in the Franciscan convent at

Correggio, and a few words placed over his tomb merely record the day of his death, and his name and profession — "Maestro Antonio Allegri, de pintore."

There is a tradition that Correggio was a self educated painter, unassisted except by his own transcendent genius ; that he lived in great obscurity and indigence, and that he was ill remunerated for his works. And it is further related, that having been paid in copper coin a sum of sixty crowns for one of his pictures, he carried home this load in a sack on his shoulders, being anxious to relieve the wants of his family ; and stopping, when heated and wearied, to refresh himself with a draught of cold water, he was seized with a fever, of which he died. Though this tradition has been proved to be false, and is completely refuted by the circumstances of the last years of his life related above, yet the impression that Correggio died miserably and in indigence prevailed to a late period.* From whatever cause it arose, it was early current. Annibal Carracci, writing from Parma fifty years after the death of Correggio, says, "I rage and weep to think of the fate of this poor Antonio ; so great a man — if, indeed, he were not rather an angel in the flesh — to be lost here, to live unknown, and to die unhappily ! " Now, he who painted the dome

* The death of Correggio is the subject of a very beautiful tragedy by Œhlenschläger, of which there is a critical account, with translations, in one of the early volumes of *Blackwood's Magazine.*

of the Cathedral of Parma, and who stood by as
one of the chosen witnesses of the marriage of his
sovereign, could not have lived unknown and unre-
garded ; and we have no just reason to suppose that
this gentle, amiable, and unambitious man died
unhappily. With regard to his deficient education,
it appears certain that he studied anatomy under
Lombardi, a famous physician of that time ; and his
works exhibit not only a classical and cultivated
tate, but a knowledge of the sciences—of optics,
mathematics, perspective, and chemistry—as far as
they were then carried. His use and skilful pre-
paration of rare and expensive colors imply neither
poverty nor ignorance. His modest, quiet, amiable
temper and domestic habits may have given rise to
the report that he lived neglected and obscure in his
native city ; he had not, like other great masters
of his time, an academy for teaching, and a retinue of scholars to spread his name and contend for
the supremacy of their master. Whether Correggio
ever visited Rome is a point undecided by any evidence for or against, and it is most probable that
he did not. It is said that he was at Bologna,
where he saw Raphael's St. Cecilia, and, after
contemplating it for some time with admiration,
he turned away, exclaiming, " And I too am a
painter (anch'io sono pittore) ! " — an anecdote
which shows that, if unambitious and unpresum-
ing, he was not without a consciousness of his own
merit.

The father of Correggio, Pellegrino Allegri, **who** survived him, repaid the twenty-five gold crowns which his son had received in advance for work he did not live to complete. The only son of Correggio, Pomponio Quirino Allegri, became a painter, but never attained to any great reputation, and appears to have been of a careless, restless disposition.

We shall now give some account of Correggio's works. His two greatest performances, the dome of the San Giovanni and that of the Cathedral of Parma, have been mentioned. His smaller pictures, though not numerous, are diffused through so many galleries, that they cannot be said to be rare. It is remarkable that they are very seldom met with in the possession of individuals, but, with few exceptions, are to be found in royal and public collections.

In our National Gallery are five pictures by Correggio. Two are studies of angels' heads, which, as they are not found in any of the existing frescoes, are supposed to have formed part of the composition in the San Giovanni, which, as already related, was destroyed. The other three are among his most celebrated works. The first, Mercury teaching Cupid to read in the presence of Venus, is an epitome of all the qualities which characterize the oil-painter; that peculiar smiling grace which is the expression of a kind of Elysian happiness, and that flowing outline, that melting softness of tone which are quite illusive. " Those who may not perfectly understand what artists and critics mean when they dwell with rapture on Correggio's wonderful *chiaro'scuro*, should look well into this picture. They will perceive that in the painting of the limbs they can look through the shadows into the substance, as it might be into the flesh and blood; the shadows seem mutable, accidental, and aërial, as if *between* the eye and the colors, and not incorporated with them. In this lies the inimitable excellence of Correggio." *

This picture was painted for Federigo Gonzaga, Duke of Mantua. It was brought to England in 1629, when the Mantua Gallery was bought by our Charles I., and hung in his apartment at Whitehall; afterwards it passed into the possession of the Duke of Alva; then, during the French invasion of Spain, Murat secured it as his share of the plunder; and his widow sold it to the Marquess of Londonderry, from whom it was purchased by the nation. The Ecce Homo was purchased at the same time. It is chiefly remarkable for the fine head of the Virgin, who faints with anguish on beholding the suffering and degradation of her Son; the dying away of sense and sensation under the influence of mental pain is expressed with admirable and affecting truth. The rest of the picture is perhaps rather feeble, and the head of

* "Public Galleries of Art," Murray, 1841, in which there is a history of the picture, too long to be inserted here.

Christ not to be compared to one crowned with thorns which is in the possession of Lord Cowper, nor with another in the Bridgewater collection. The third picture is a small but most exquisite Madonna, known as the *Vierge au Panier*, from the little basket in front of the picture. The Virgin, seated, holds the infant Christ on her knee, and looks down upon him with the fondest expression of maternal rapture, while he gazes up in her face. Joseph is seen in the background. This, though called a Holy Family, is a simple domestic scene; and Correggio probably in this, as in other instances, made the original study from his wife and child. Another picture in our gallery ascribed to Correggio, the Christ on the Mount of Olives, is a very fine old copy, perhaps a duplicate, of an original picture now in the possession of the Duke of Wellington.

In the gallery of Parma are five of the most important and beautiful pictures of Correggio. The most celebrated is that called the St. Jerome. It represents the saint presenting to the Virgin and Child his translation of the Scriptures, while on the other side the Magdalen bends down and kisses with devotion the feet of the infant Saviour.

The Dresden Gallery is also rich in pictures of Correggio. It contains six pictures, of which four are large altar-pieces, bought out of churches in Modena. Among these is the famous picture of the Nativity, called the Notte, or *Night*, of Correggio because it is illuminated only by the unearthly splendor which beams round the head of the infant Saviour; and the still more famous Magdalen, who lies extended on the ground intently reading the Scriptures. No picture in the world has been more universally admired and multiplied, through copies and engravings, than this little picture.

In the Florence Gallery are three pictures. One of these is the Madonna on her knees, adoring with ecstasy her Infant, who lies before her on a portion of her garment.

In the Louvre are two of his works— the Marriage of St. Catherine, and the Antiope, painted for the Duke of Mantua.

In the Naples Gallery there are three; one of them a most lovely Madonna, called, from the peculiar head-dress, the Zingarella, or Gypsy.

In the Vienna Gallery are two; and at Berlin three — among them the Io and the Leda.

There is in the British Museum a complete collection of engravings after Correggio.

Correggio had no school of painting, and all his authentic works, except his frescoes, were executed solely by his own hand. In the execution of his frescoes he had assistants, but they could hardly be called his *pupils*. He had, however, a host of imitators, who formed what has been called the School of Parma, of which he is considered the head. The most famous of these imitators was Francesco Mazzola, of whom we are now to speak.

PARMIGIANO.

Born 1503, died 1540.

FRANCESCO MAZZOLA, or MAZZUOLI, called PARMI-GIANO, and, by the Italians, IL PARMIGIANINO (to express by this endearing diminutive the love as well as the admiration he inspired even from his boyhood), was a native of Parma, born on the 11th of January, 1503. He had two uncles who were painters, and by them he was early initiated into some knowledge of designing, though he could have owed little else to them, both being very mediocre artists. Endowed with a most precocious genius, ardent in every pursuit, he studied indefatigably, and at the age of fourteen he produced a picture of the Baptism of Christ, wonderful for a boy of his age, exhibiting even thus early much of that easy grace which he is supposed to have learned from Correggio ; but Correggio had not then visited Parma. When he arrived there, four years after-wards, for the purpose of painting the cupola of San Giovanni, Francesco, then only eighteen, was selected as one of his assistants, and he took this opportunity of imbuing his mind with a style which certainly had much analogy with his own taste and character. Parmigiano, however, had too much genius, too much ambition, to follow in the foot-steps of another, however great. Though not great

enough himself to be first in that age of greatness,
yet, had his rivals and contemporaries been less than
giants, he must have overtopped them all. As it
was, feeling the impossibility of rising above such
men as Michael Angelo, Raphael, Correggio, yet
feeling also the consciousness of his own power, he
endeavored to be original by combining what has
not yet been harmonized in nature, therefore could
hardly succeed in' art — the grand drawing of Michael Angelo, the antique grace of Raphael, and
the melting tones and sweetness of Correggio. Perhaps, had he been satisfied to look at nature through
his own soul and eyes, he would have done better ;
had he trusted himself more, he would have escaped
some of those faults which have rendered many of
his works unpleasing, by giving the impression of
effort, and of what in art is called *mannerism*. Ambitious, versatile, accomplished, generally admired
for his handsome person and graceful manners, Parmigiano would have been spoiled by vanity, if he
had not been a man of strong sensibility and of
almost fastidious sentiment and refinement. When
these are added to genius, the result is generally a
tinge of that melancholy, of that dissatisfaction with
all that is achieved or acquired, which seem to have
entered largely into the temperament of this painter,
rendering his character and life extremely interesting, while it strongly distinguishes him from the
serenely mild and equal-tempered Raphael, to whom
he was afterwards compared.

When Parmigiano was in his twentieth year, he set off for Rome. The recent accession of Clement VII., a declared patron of art, and the death of Raphael, had opened a splendid vista of glory and success to his imagination. He carried with him to Rome three pictures. One of these was an example of his graceful genius. It represented the Infant Christ seated on his mother's knee, and taking some fruit from the lap of an angel. The second was a proof of his wonderful dexterity of hand. It was a portrait of himself seated in his atelier amid his books and musical instruments; but the whole scene represented on the panel as if viewed in a convex mirror. The third picture was an instance of the success with which he had studied the magical effects of chiaro'scuro in . Correggio,— torchlight, daylight, and a celestial light, being all introduced without disturbing the harmony of the coloring. This last he presented to the pope, who received both the young painter and his offering most graciously. He became a favorite at Rome, and, as he studiously imitated while there the works of Raphael, and resembled him in the elegance of his person and manners, and the generosity of his disposition, the poets complimented him by saying, or singing, that the late-lost and lamented Raphael had revived in the likeness of Parmigiano. We can now measure more justly the distance which separated them.

While at Rome, Francesco was greatly patron

ized by the Cardinal Ippolito de Medici, and
painted for him several beautiful pictures; for the
pope also several others, and the portrait of a
young captain of his guard, Lorenzo Cibo, which
is supposed to be the fine portrait now at Windsor.
For a noble lady, a certain Donna Maria Buffalini,
he painted a grand altar-piece to adorn the chapel
of her family at Città di Castello. This is the celebrated Vision of St. Jerome, now in our National Gallery. It represents the Virgin holding a book, with
the Infant Christ leaning on her knee, as seen above
in a glory, while St. John the Baptist points to the
celestial vision, and St. Jerome is seen asleep in the
background. This picture is an eminent example
of all the beauties and faults of Parmigiano. The
Madonna and the Child are models of dignity and
grace; the drawing is correct and elegant; the
play of the lights and shadows in delicate management, worthy of Correggio. On the other hand, the
attitude of St. John the Baptist is an attempt at
singularity in drawing, which is altogether forced
and theatrical; while the foreshortened figure of
St. Jerome in the background is most *uncomfort-
ably* distorted. Notwithstanding these faults, the
picture has always been much celebrated. When
the church in which it stood was destroyed by an
earthquake, the picture was purchased from among
the ruins, and afterwards sold to the Marquis of
Abercorn for fifteen hundred guineas; subsequently
it passed through the hands of two great collectors,
20)

Mr. Hart Davis and Mr. Watson Taylor, and was at length purchased by the members of the British Institution, and by them generously presented to the nation.

It is related that Rome was taken by assault, and pillaged by the barbarous soldiery of the Constable de Bourbon, at the very time that Parmigiano was painting on this picture ; and that he was so absorbed by his work, that he heard nothing of the tumult around him, till some soldiers, with an officer at their head, broke into his atelier. As he turned round in quiet surprise from his easel, they were so struck by the beauty of his work, as well as by the composure of the artist, that they retired without doing him any injury. But another party afterwards seized him, insisted on ransom, and robbed him of all he possessed. Thus reduced to poverty, he fled from Rome, now a scene of indescribable horrors, and reached Bologna barefoot and penniless.

But the man of genius has at least this high privilege, that he carries with him everywhere two things of which no earthly power can rob him — his talent and his fame. On arriving at Bologna, he drew and etched some beautiful compositions. He is said by some to have himself invented the art of *etching*, — that is, of·corroding, or, as it is technically termed, *biting* the lines on the copper-plate by means of nitrous acid, instead of cutting them with the graver. By this new-found art he was

relieved from the immediate pressure of poverty, and
very soon found himself, as a painter, in full employment. He executed at Bologna some of his
most celebrated works: the Madonna della Rosa
of the Dresden Gallery, and the Madonna *dell' collo
lungo* (or *long-necked* Madonna) in the Pitti Palace
at Florence ; also, a famous altar-piece called the
St. Margaret. Of all these there are numerous
engravings.

After residing nearly four years at Bologna, Parmigiano returned, rich and celebrated, to his native
city. He reached Parma in 1531, and was immediately engaged to paint in fresco a new church
which had recently been erected to the honor of
the Virgin Mary, and called the *Steccata*. There
were, however, some delays on the side of his em-
ployers, and more on his own, and four years
passed before he set to work. Much indignation
was excited by his dilatory conduct ; but it was
appeased by the interference of his friend Francesco
Boiardo, who offered himself as his surety for the
completion of his undertaking within a given time.
A new contract was signed, and Parmigiano there-
upon presented to his friend his picture of Cupid
framing his Bow, a lovely composition, so beautiful that it has been again and again attributed to
Correggio, and engraved under his name, but it is
undoubtedly by Parmigiano. Several repetitions
of it were executed at the time, so much did it delight all who saw it. Engravings and copies like-

wise abound ; a very good copy is in the Bridge-water Gallery. The picture which is regarded as the original is in the gallery of the Belvedere at Vienna.

At last he began his works in the Steccata, and there he executed his figure of Moses in act to break the Tables of the Law, and his Eve in act to pluck the forbidden fruit. The former is a proof of the height he could aspire to in sublime conception ; we have few examples in art of equal grandeur of character and drawing. The poet Gray acknowledged that, when he pictured his Bard,

> " Loose his beard and hoary hair
>   Streamed like a meteor on the troubled air,"

he had this magnificent figure full in his mind. The Eve, on the other hand, is a perfect example of that peculiar grace in which Parmigiano excelled.

After he had painted these and a few other figures in the church, more delays ensued. It is said by some that Parmigiano had wasted his money in gambling and dissipation, and now gave himself up to the pursuit of the philosopher's stone, with a hope of repairing his losses. One of his biographers has taken pains to disprove these imputations ; but that he was improvident, restless, and fond of pleasure, is admitted. Whatever might have been the cause, he broke his contract, and was thrown into prison. To obtain his freedom, he entered into a new engagement, but was no sooner at liberty than ne escaped to the territory of Cremona. Here his constitutional melancholy seized him ; and though he lived, or rather languished, long enough to paint some beautiful pictures, he died in a few months afterwards, and was, at his own request, laid in the earth without any coffin or covering, only a cross of cypress-wood was placed on his breast. He died just twenty years after Raphael, and at the same age, having only completed his thirty-seventh year.

Parmigiano, in his best pictures, is one of the most fascinating of painters, — dignified, graceful, harmonious. His children, cupids, and angels, are in general exquisite; his portraits are noble, and are perhaps his finest and most faultless productions, — the Moses and the Eve excepted. It was the error of Parmigiano that in studying grace he was apt to deviate into affectation, and become what the French call *manière;* all *studied* grace is disagreeable. In his female figures he lengthened the limbs, the necks, the fingers, till the effect was not grace, but a kind of stately feebleness ; and as he imitated at the same time the grand drawing and large manner of Michael Angelo, the result conveys an impression of something quite incongruous in nature and in art. Then his Madonnas have in general a mannered grandeur and elegance, something between goddesses and duchesses ; and his female saints are something between nymphs and maids of honor. For instance, none of his compositions, not even the Cupid shaping his Bow, has been more popular than his Marriage of St Catherine, of which there are so many repetitions: a famous one in the collection of Lord Normanton; another, smaller and most exquisite, in the Grosvenor Gallery, — not to speak of an infinitude of copies and engravings; but is not the Madonna, with her long, slender neck, and her half-averted head, far more aristocratic than divine? and does not St. Catherine hold out her pretty finger for the ring with the air of a lady-bride? — and most of the sacred pictures of Parmigiano are liable to the same censure.   Annibal Carracci, in a famous sonnet, in which he pointed out what was most worthy of imitation in the elder painters, recommends, significantly, "a little" of the grace of Parmigiano; thereby indicating, what we feel to be the truth, that he had *too much*.

GIORGIONE.

Born 1478, died 1511.

This painter was another great *inventor* — one of those who stamped his own individuality on his art. He was essentially a poet, and a *subjective* poet, who fused his own being with all he performed and created.   If Raphael be the Shakspeare, then Giorgione may be styled the Byron, of painting.

He was born at Castel Franco, a small town in

the territory of Treviso, and his proper name was Giorgio Barbarelli. Nothing is known of his family or of his younger years, except that, having shown a strong disposition to art, he was brought, when a boy, to Venice, and placed under the tuition of Gian Bellini. As he grew up he was distinguished by his tall, noble figure, and the dignity of his deportment; and his companions called him Giorgione, or George the Great, by which nickname he has, after the Italian fashion, descended to posterity.

Giorgione appears to have been endowed by nature with an intense love of beauty, and a sense of harmony which pervaded his whole being. He was famous as a player and composer on the lute, to which he sung his own verses. In his works two characteristics prevail — sentiment and color, both tinged by the peculiar temperament of the man. The sentiment is noble, but melancholy; and the color decided, intense, and glowing. His execution had a freedom, a careless mastery of hand, or, to borrow the untranslatable Italian word, a *sprezzatura*, unknown before his time. The idea that he founded his style on that of Lionardo da Vinci cannot be entertained by those who have studied the works of both. Nothing can be more distinct in character and feeling.

It is to be regretted that of one so interesting in his character and his works we know so little; yet more to be regretted that a being gifted with the passionate sensibility of a poet should have been employed chiefly in decorative painting, and that too confined to the outsides of the Venetian palaces. These creations have been destroyed by fire, ruined by time, or effaced by the damps of the Lagune. He appears to have early acquired fame in his art, and we find him in 1504 employed, together with Titian, in painting with frescoes the exterior of the Fondaco dei Tedeschi (the hall of Exchange belonging to the German merchants). That part intrusted to Giorgione he covered with the most beautiful and poetical figures; but the significance of the whole was soon after the artist's death forgotten, and Vasari tells us that in his time no one could interpret it. It appears to have been a sort of arabesque on a colossal scale.

Giorgione delighted in fresco as a vehicle, because it gave him ample scope for that largeness and freedom of outline which characterized his manner. Unhappily, of his numerous works, only the merest fragments remain. We have no evidence that he exercised his art elsewhere than at Venice, or that he ever resided out of the Venetian territory. In his pictures, the heads, features, costumes, are all stamped with the Venetian character. He had no school, though, induced by his social and affectionate nature, he freely imparted what he knew, and often worked in conjunction with others. His love of music and his love of pleasure sometimes led him astray from his art

but were oftener his inspirers. Both are embodied
in his pictures, particularly his exquisite pastorals
and concerts, over which, however, he has breathed
that cast of thoughtfulness and profound feeling
which, in the midst of harmony and beauty, is like
a revelation or a prophecy of sorrow. All the rest
of what is recorded concerning the life and death of
Giorgione may be told in a few words. Among the
painters who worked with him was Pietro Luzzo, of
Feltri, near Venice, known in the history of art as
Morta da Feltri, and mentioned by Vasari as the inventor, or rather reviver, of arabesque painting in
the antique style, which he had studied amid the
dark vaults of the Roman ruins. This Morto, as
Ridolfi relates, was the friend of Giorgione, and lived
under the same roof with him. He took advantage
of Giorgione's confidence to seduce and carry off
from his house a girl whom he passionately loved.
Wounded doubly by the falsehood of his mistress
and the treachery of his friend, Giorgione sank into
despair, and soon afterwards died, at the early age of
thirty-three. Morto da Feltri afterwards fled from
Venice, entered the army, and was killed at the battle of Zara, in 1519. Such is the Venetian tradition.

Giorgione's genuine pictures are very rarely to
be met with ; of those ascribed to him the greater
number were painted by Pietro della Vecchia, a
Venetian, who had a peculiar talent for imitating
Giorgione's manner of execution and style of color.
These imitations deceive picture-dealers and collect

ors : they could not for one moment deceive those who had looked into the *feeling* impressed on Giorgione's works. The only picture which could have imposed on the true lover of Giorgione is that in the possession of Lord Francis Egerton, the Four Ages, by Titian, in which the tone of sentiment as well as the manner of Giorgione are so happily imitated that for many years it was attributed to him. It was painted by Titian when he was the friend and daily companion of Giorgione, and under the immediate influence of his feelings and genius.

We may divide the undoubted and existing pictures of Giorgione into three classes.

I. The historical subjects, which are very uncommon ; such seem to have been principally confined to his frescoes, and have mostly perished. Of the few which remain to us, the most famous is a picture in the Brera at Milan, the Finding of Moses. It may be called rather a *romantic* and poetical version than an historical representation of the scene. It would shock Sir Gardner Wilkinson. In the centre sits the princess under a tree ; she looks with surprise and tenderness on the child, which is brought to her by one of her attendants. The squire or seneschal of the princess, with knights and ladies, stand around ; on one side two lovers are seated on the grass ; on the other are musicians and singers, pages with dogs. All the figures are in the Venetian costume ; the coloring is splendid, and the grace and harmony of the whole composi tion is even the more enchanting from the *naïveté* of the conception. This picture, like many others of the same age and style, reminds us of those poems and tales of the middle ages, in which David and Jonathan figure as "*preux chevaliers*," and Sir Alexander of Macedon and Sir Paris of Troy fight tournaments in honor of ladies' eyes and the "blessed Virgin." They must be tried by their own aim and standard, not by the severity of antiquarian criticism.

In the Academy of Venice is preserved another historical picture, yet more wildly poetical in conception. It commemorates a fact—a dreadful tempest which occurred in 1340, and threatened to overwhelm the whole city of Venice. In Giorgione's picture the demons are represented in an infernal bark exciting the tempest, while St. Mark, St. Nicholas, and St. George, the patron saints of Venice, seated in a small vessel tossed amid the waves, oppose with spiritual arms the powers of hell, and prevail against them.

In our National Gallery there is a small historical picture, the death of Peter, the Dominican friar and inquisitor, called St. Peter the Martyr, who was assassinated. This picture is not of much value, and a very inferior work of the master.

Sacred subjects of the usual kind were so seldom painted by Giorgione, that there are not perhaps half a dozen in existence.

II. There is a class of subjects which Giorgione

represented with peculiar grace and felicity. They are in painting what idyls and lyrics are in poetry, and seem like direct inventions of the artist's own mind, though some are supposed to be scenes from Venetian tales and novels now lost. These generally represent groups of cavaliers and ladies seated in beautiful landscapes under the shade of trees, conversing or playing on musical instruments. Such pictures are not unfrequent, and have a particular charm, arising from the union of melancholy feeling with luxurious and festive enjoyment, and a mysterious allegorical significance now only to be surmised. In the collection of Lord North-wick, at Cheltenham, there is a most charming picture in this style, and in the possession of Mr. Cunningham there is another. To this class may also be referred the exquisite pastoral group of Jacob and Rachel, in the Dresden Gallery.

III. His portraits are magnificent. They have all, with the strongest resemblance to general nature, a grand ideal cast; for it was in the character of the man to idealize everything he touched. Very few of his portraits are now to be identified. Among the finest and most interesting may be mentioned his own portrait in the Munich Gallery, which has an expression of the profoundest melancholy. In the Imperial Gallery at Vienna — rich in his works — there is a picture representing a young man crowned with a garland of vine-leaves; another comes behind him with a concealed dagger, and appears to watch the moment to strike. The expression in the two heads can never be forgotten by those who have looked on them. The fine portrait of a cavalier, with a page riveting his armor, is well known. It is in the possession of the Earl of Carlisle, and styled, without much probability, Gaston de Foix. A beautiful little full-length figure in armor, now in the collection of Mr. Rogers, bears the same name, and is probably a study for a St. Michael or a St. George. Lord Byron has celebrated in some beautiful lines the impression made on his mind by a picture in the Manfrini Palace, at Venice; but the poet errs in styling it the "portraits of his son, and wife, and self." • Giorgione never had either son or wife. The picture alluded to represents a Venetian lady, a cavalier, and a page, — portraits evidently, but the names are unknown.

The striking characteristic of all Giorgione's pic tures, whether portraits, ideal heads, or composi tions, is the ineffaceable impression they leave on the memory — the impression of *reality*. In the ap parent simplicity of the means through which this effect is produced, the few yet splendid colors, the vigorous decision of touch, the depth and tenderness of the sentiment, they remind us of the old religious music to which we have listened in the Italian churches — a few simple notes, long sustained, deli- ciously blended, swelling into a rich, full, and per- fect harmony, and melting into the soul.

Though Giorgione left no scholars, properly so

called, he had many imitators, and no artist of his time exercised a more extensive and long-felt influence. He diffused that taste for vivid and warm color which we see in contemporary and succeeding artist-, and he tinged with his manner and feeling the whole Venetian school. Among those who were inspired by this powerful and ardent mind, may be mentioned Sebastian del Piombo, of whom some account has already been given (see p. 220) ; Jacopo Palma, called *Old* Palma, b. 1518, d. 1548 ; Paris Bordone, b. 1500, d. 1570 ; Pordenone, b. 1486, d. 1540 ; and, lastly, TITIAN, the great representative of the Venetian school. The difference between Giorgione and Titian, as colorists, seems to be this, that the colors of Giorgione appear as if lighted up from within, and those of Titian as if lighted from without. The epithet *fiery* or *glowing* would apply to Giorgione ; the epithet *golden* would express the predominant hues of Titian.

TITIAN.

Born 1477, died 1576.

TIZIANO VECELLI was born at Cadore in the Friuli, a district to the north of Venice, where the ancient family of the Vecelli had been long settled. There is something very amusing and characteristic in the first indication of his love of art; for while it is recorded of other young artists that they took a piece of charcoal or a piece of slate to trace the images in their fancy, we are told that the infant Titian, with an instinctive feeling prophetic of his future excellence as a colorist, used the expressed juice of certain flowers to paint a figure of a Madonna. When he was a boy of nine years old his father, Gregorio, carried him to Venice and placed him under the tuition of Sebastian Zuccato, a painter and worker in mosaic. He left this school for that of the Bellini, where the friendship and fellowship of Giorgione seems early to have awakened his mind to new ideas of art and color. Albert Durer, who was at Venice in 1494, and again in 1507, also influenced him. At this time, when Titian and Giorgione were youths of eighteen and nineteen, they lived and worked together. It has been already related that they were employed in

painting the frescoes of the Fondaco dei Tedeschi.
The preference being given to Titian's performance,
which represented the story of Judith, caused such
a jealousy between the two friends, that they ceased
to reside together; but at this time, and for some
years afterwards, the influence of Giorgione on the
mind and the style of Titian was such that it became difficult to distinguish their works; and on
the death of Giorgione, Titian was required to
complete his unfinished pictures. This great loss
to Venice and the world left him in the prime of
youth without a rival. We find him for a few
years chiefly employed in decorating the palaces of
the Venetian nobles, both in the city and on the
mainland. The first of his historical compositions
which is celebrated by his biographers is the Presentation of the Virgin in the Temple, a large picture, now in the Academy of Arts at Venice; and
the first portrait recorded is that of Catherine,
Queen of Cyprus, of which numerous repetitions
and copies were scattered over all Italy. There is
a fine original in the Dresden Gallery. This unhappy Catherine Cornaro, the "daughter of St.
Mark," having been forced to abdicate her crown
in favor of the Venetian state, was at this time
living in a sort of honorable captivity at Venice.
She had been a widow for forty years, and he has
represented her in deep mourning, holding a rosary
in her hand — the face still bearing traces of that
beauty for which she was celebrated.

It appears that Titian was married about 1512, but of his wife we do not hear anything more. It is said that her name was Lucia, and we know that she bore him three children — two sons, and a daughter called Lavinia. It seems probable, on a comparison of dates, that she died about the year 1530.

One of the earliest works on which Titian was engaged was the decoration of the convent of St. Antony, at Padua, in which he executed a series of frescoes from the life of St. Antony. He was next summoned to Ferrara by the Duke Alphonso I., and was employed in his service for at least two years. He painted for this prince the beautiful picture of Bacchus and Ariadne, which is now in our National Gallery, and which represents on a small scale an epitome of all the beauties which characterize Titian, in the rich, picturesque, animated composition, in the ardor of Bacchus, who flings himself from his car to pursue Ariadne; the dancing bacchanals, the frantic grace of the bacchante, and the little joyous satyr in front, trailing the head of the sacrifice. He painted for the same prince two other festive subjects: one in which a nymph and two men are dancing, while another nymph lies asleep; and a third, in which a number of children and cupids are sporting round a statue of Venus. There are here upwards of sixty figures in every variety of attitude, some fluttering in the air, some climbing the fruit-trees, some shooting arrows or embracing each other. This picture is known as the Sacrifice to the Goddess of Fertility. While it remained in Italy it was a study for the first painters, — for Poussin, the Carracci, Albano, and Fiamingo the sculptor, so famous for his models of children.* At Ferrara, Titian also painted the portrait of the first wife of Alphonso, the famous and infamous Lucrezia Borgia ; and here also he formed a friendship with the poet Ariosto, whose portrait he painted.

At this time he was invited to Rome by Leo X., for whom Raphael, then in the zenith of his powers, was executing some of his finest works. It is curious to speculate what influence these two distinguished men might have exercised on each other had they met ; but it was not so decreed. Titian was strongly attached to his home and his friends at Venice ; and to his birthplace, the little town of Cadore, he paid an annual summer visit. His long absence at Ferrara had wearied him of courts and princes ; and, instead of going to Rome to swell the luxurious state of Leo X., he returned to Venice and remained there stationary for the next few years, enriching its palaces and churches with his magnificent works. These were so numerous that it would be in vain to attempt to give an account even of those considered as the finest among

* These two pictures are now at Madrid. A good copy of the last used to hang in the dark at Hampton Court, and has been lately removed to Windsor.

them. Two, however, must be pointed out as pre-
eminent in beauty and celebrity. First, the Assumption of the Virgin, painted for the church of
Santa Maria de' Frari, and now in the Academy of
the Fine Arts at Venice, and well known from the
magnificent engraving of Schiavone — the Virgin is
soaring to heaven amid groups of angels, while the
apostles gaze upwards; and, secondly, the Death
of St. Peter Martyr when attacked by assassins at
the entrance of a wood; the resignation of the
prostrate victim and the ferocity of the murderer,
the attendant flying " in the agonies of cowardice,"
with the trees waving their distracted boughs amid
the violence of the tempest, have rendered this picture famous as a piece of scenic poetry as well as
of dramatic expression.

The next event of Titian's life was his journey to
Bologna in 1530. In that year the Emperor
Charles V. and Pope Clement VII. met at Bologna,
each surrounded by a brilliant retinue of the most
distinguished soldiers, statesmen, and scholars, of
Germany and Italy. Through the influence of his
friend Aretino, Titian was recommended to the
Cardinal Ippolito de' Medici, the pope's nephew,
through whose patronage he was introduced to the
two potentates who sat to him. One of the portraits of Clement VII., painted at this time, is now
in the Bridgewater Gallery. Charles V. was so
satisfied with his portrait, that he became the zeal
ous friend and patron of the painter. It is not pre

cisely known which of several portraits of the
emperor painted by Titian was the one executed at
Bologna on this memorable occasion, but it is supposed to be that which represents him on horseback
charging with his lance, now in the Royal Gallery
at Madrid, and of which Mr. Rogers possesses the
original study. The two portraits of Ippolito de'
Medici in the Pitti Palace and the Louvre were also
painted at this period.

After a sojourn of some months at Bologna,
Titian returned to Venice loaded with honors and
rewards. There was no potentate, prince, or poet,
or reigning beauty, who did not covet the honor
of being immortalized by his pencil. He had, up to
this time, managed his worldly affairs with great
economy; but now he purchased for himself a house
opposite to Murano, and lived splendidly, combining with the most indefatigable industry the liveli-
est enjoyment of existence; his favorite companions
were the architect Sansovino and the witty profligate Pietro Aretino. Titian has often been reproached with his friendship for Aretino, and
nothing can be said in his excuse, except that the
proudest princes in Europe condescended to flatter
and caress this unprincipled literary ruffian, who
was pleased to designate himself as the " friend of
Titian, and the scourge of princes." One of the
finest of Titian's portraits is that of Aretino, in the
Munich Gallery.

Thus in the practice of his art, in the society of

his friends, and in the enjoyment of the pleasures of life, did Titian pass several years. The only painter of his time who was deemed worthy of competing with him was Licinio Regillo, better known as Pordenone. Between Titian and Pordenone there existed not merely rivalry, but a personal hatred, so bitter that Pordenone affected to think his life in danger, and when at Venice painted with his shield and poniard lying beside him. As long as Pordenone lived, Titian had a spur to exertion, to emulation. All the other good painters of the time, Palma, Bonifazio, Tintoretto, were his pupils or his creatures; Pordenone would never owe anything to him; and the picture called the St. Justina, at Vienna, shows that he could equal Titian on his own ground.

After the death of Pordenone at Ferrara, in 1539, Titian was left without a rival. Everywhere in Italy art was on the decline: Lionardo, Raphael, Correggio, had all passed away. Titian himself, at the age of sixty, was no longer young, but he still retained all the vigor and the freshness of youth; neither eye nor hand, nor creative energy of mind, had failed him yet. He was again invited to Ferrara, and painted there the portrait of the old pope Paul III. He then visited Urbino, where he painted for the duke the famous Venus which hangs in the Tribune of the Florence Gallery, and many other pictures. He again, by order of Charles V. repaired to Bologna, and painted the emperor standing and by his side a favorite Irish wolf-dog. This picture was given by Philip IV. to our Charles I., but after his death was sold into Spain, and is now at Madrid.

Pope Paul III. invited him to Rome, whither he repaired in 1548. There he painted that wonderful picture of the old pope with his two nephews, the Duke Ottavio and Cardinal Farnese, which is now at Vienna. The head of the pope is a miracle of character and expression. A keen-visaged, thin little man, with meagre fingers like birds'-claws, and an eager cunning look, riveting the gazer like the eye of a snake — nature itself! — and the pope had either so little or so much vanity as to be perfectly satisfied. He rewarded the painter munificently; he even offered to make his son Pomponio Bishop of Ceneda, which Titian had the good sense to refuse. While at Rome he painted several pictures for the Farnese family, among them the Venus and Adonis, of which a repetition is in our National Gallery, and a Danaë which excited the admiration of Michael Angelo. At this time Titian was seventy-two.

He next, by command of Charles V., repaired to Augsburgh, where the emperor held his court: eighteen years had elapsed since he first sat to Titian, and he was now broken by the cares of government, — far older at fifty than the painter at seventy-two. It was at Augsburgh that the incident occurred which has been so often related

Titian dropped his pencil, and Charles, taking it up
and presenting it, replied to the artist's excuses
that " Titian was worthy of being served by Cæsar."
This pretty anecdote is not without its parallel in
modern times. When Sir Thomas Lawrence was
painting at Aix-la-Chapelle, as he stooped to place
a picture on his easel, the Emperor of Russia anticipated him, and, taking it up, adjusted it himself;
but we do not hear that he made any speech on the
occasion. When at Augsburgh, Titian was en-
nobled and created a count of the empire, with a
pension of two hundred gold ducats, and his son
Pomponio was appointed canon of the cathedral of
Milan. After the abdication and death of Charles
V., Titian continued in great favor with his successor Philip II., for whom he painted several pictures. It is not true, however, that Titian visited
Spain. The assertion that he did so rests on the
sole authority of Palomino, a Spanish writer on
art, and, though wholly unsupported by evidence,
has been copied from one book into another. Later
researches have proved that Titian returned from
Augsburgh to Venice; and an uninterrupted series
of letters and documents, with dates of time and
place, remain to show that, with the exception of
this visit to Augsburgh and another to Vienna, he
resided constantly in Italy, and principally at
Venice. from 1530 to his death. Notwithstanding
the compliments and patronage and nominal rewards he received from the Spanish court, Titian

was worse off under Philip II. than he had been under Charles V. : his pension was constantly in arrears ; the payments for his pictures evaded by the officials ; and we find the great painter constantly presenting petitions and complaints in moving terms, which always obtained gracious but illusive answers. Philip II., who commanded the riches of the Indies, was for many years a debtor to Titian for at least two thousand gold crowns ; and his accounts were not settled at the time of his death. For our Queen Mary of England, who wished to patronize one favored by her husband, Titian painted several pictures, some of which were in the possession of Charles I. ; others had been carried to Spain after the death of Mary, and are now in the Royal Gallery at Madrid.

Besides the pictures painted by command for royal and noble patrons, Titian, who was unceasingly occupied, had always a great number of pictures in his house which he presented to his friends, or to the officers and attendants of the court, as a means of procuring their favor. There is extant a letter of Aretino, in which he describes the scene which took place when the emperor summoned his favorite painter to attend the court at Augsburgh. "It was," he says, "the most flattering testimony to his excellence to behold. As soon as it was known that the divine painter was sent for, the crowds of people running to obtain, if possible, the productions of his art ; and how they endeavored to pur

chase the pictures, great and small, and everything
that was in the house, at any price; for everybody
seems assured that his august majesty will so treat
his Apelles that he will no longer condescend to
exercise his pencil except to oblige him.''

Years passed on, and seemed to have no power
to quench the ardor of this wonderful old man.
He was eighty-one when he painted the Martyrdom
of St. Laurence, one of his largest and grandest
compositions. The Magdalen, the half-length
figure with uplifted streaming eyes, which he sent
to Philip II., was executed even later; and it was
not till he was approaching his ninetieth year
that he showed in his works symptoms of enfeebled
powers; and then it seemed as if sorrow rather
than time had reached him and conquered him at
last. The death of many friends, the companions
of his convivial hours, left him "alone in his
glory." He found in his beloved art the only
refuge from grief. His son Pomponio was still the
same worthless profligate in age that he had been
in youth. His son Orazio attended upon him with
truly filial duty and affection, and under his
father's tuition had become an accomplished artist;
but as they always worked together, and on the
same canvas, his works are not to be distinguished
from his father's. Titian was likewise surrounded
by painters who, without being precisely his scholars, had assembled from every part of Europe to

profit by his instructions.* The early morning **and** the evening hour found him at his easel ; or lingering in his little garden (where he had feasted with Aretino and Sansovino, and Bembo and Ariosto, and " the most gracious Virginia," and " the most beautiful Violante "), and gazing on the setting sun, with a thought perhaps of his own long and bright career fast hastening to its close ; — not that such anticipations clouded his cheerful spirit, — buoyant to the last ! In 1574, when he was in his ninety-seventh year, Henry III. of France landed at Venice on his way from Poland, and was magnificently entertained by the Republic. On this occasion the king visited Titian at his own house, attended by a numerous suite of princes and nobles. Titian entertained them with splendid hospitality ; and when the king asked the price of some pictures which pleased him, he presented them as a gift to his majesty, and every one praised his easy and noble manners and his generous bearing.

Two years more passed away, and the hand did not yet tremble nor was the eye dim. When the plague broke out in Venice, in 1576, the nature of the distemper was at first mistaken, and the most common precautions neglected ; the contagion spread, and Titian and his son were among those who perished. Every one had fled, and before life

* It seems, however, generally admitted that Titian, either from impatience or jealousy, or both, was a very bad instructor in his art.

was extinct some ruffians entered his chamber and carried off, before his eyes, his money, jewels, and some of his pictures. His death took place on the 9th of September, 1575. A law had been made during the plague that none should be buried in the churches, but that all the dead bodies should be carried beyond the precincts of the city ; an exception, however, even in that hour of terror and anguish, was made in favor of Titian. His remains were borne with honor to the tomb, and deposited in the church of Santa Maria de' Frari, for which he had painted his famous Assumption. There he lies beneath a plain black marble slab, on which is simply inscribed

" TIZIANO VECELLIO."

In the year 1794 the citizens of Venice resolved to erect a noble and befitting monument to his memory. Canova made the design ; — but the troubles which intervened, and the extinction of the Republic, prevented the execution of this project. Canova's magnificent model was appropriated to another purpose, and now forms the cenotaph of the Archduchess Christina, in the church of the Augustines at Vienna.

This was the life and death of the famous Titian. He was preëminently the painter of nature ; but to him nature was clothed in a perpetual garb of beauty, or rather to him nature and beauty were one In historical compositions and sacred subjects

he has been rivalled and surpassed, but as a portrait painter never; and his portraits of celebrated
persons have at once the truth and the dignity of
history. It would be in vain to attempt to give
any account of his works; numerous as they are,
not all that are attributed to him in various galleries are his. Many are by Palma, Bonifazio, and
others his contemporaries, who imitated his manner
with more or less success. As almost every gallery
in Europe, public and private, contains pictures
attributed to him, we shall not attempt to enu-
merate even the acknowledged *chefs d'œuvre*. It
will be interesting, however, to give some account
of those of his works contained in our national and
royal galleries. In our National Gallery there are
five, of which the Bacchus and Ariadne, the Venus
and Adonis, and the Ganymede, are fair examples
of his power in the poetical department of his art.
But we want one of his inestimable portraits. In
the gallery at Hampton Court there are seven or
eight pictures attributed to him, most of them in
a miserably ruined condition. The finest of these
is a portrait of a man in black, with a white shirt
seen above his vest up to his throat; in his right
hand a red book, his fore-finger between the leaves.
It is called in the old catalogues Alessandro de'
Medici, and has been engraved under the name
of Boccaccio; * but it has no pretensions to either

* The engraving, which is most admirable, was executed by Cor-
nelius Vischer when the picture was in Holland, in the possession

name. It is a wonderful piece of life. There is also a lovely figure of a standing Lucretia, about half life-size, with very little drapery — not at all characteristic of the modest Lucretia, who arranged her robes that she might fall with decorum. She holds with her left hand a red veil over her face, and in the right a dagger with which she is about to stab herself. This picture belonged to Charles I., and came to England with the Mantua Gallery, in 1629; it was sold in 1650, after the king's death, for two hundred pounds (a large price for the time), and afterwards restored. In the collection at Windsor there are the portraits of Titian and Andrea Franceschini, half-length, in the same picture. Franceschini was Chancellor of the Republic, and distinguished for his literary attainments; he is seen in front in a robe of crimson (the habit of a cavaliero of St. Mark), and holds a paper in his hand. The acute and refined features have that expression of mental power which Titian, without any apparent effort, could throw into a head. The fine old face and flowing beard of Titian appear behind. This picture belonged to Charles I., and was sold after his death for one hundred and twelve pounds; it has been called in various catalogues Titian and Aretino, which is an obvious mistake. The well-known portraits of Aretino

of a great collector of that time, named Van Keynst; from whom the states of Holland purchased it with several others, and presented them to Charles I.

have all a full beard and thick lips, a physiognomy quite distinct from that of the Venetian senator in this picture, which is identical with the engraved portraits of Franceschini.

In the Louvre there are twenty-two pictures by Titian; in the Vienna Gallery, fifty-two. The Madrid Gallery contains most of the fine pictures painted for Charles V. and Philip II.

Before we quit the subject of Titian, we may remark that a collection of his engraved portraits would form a complete historical gallery, illustrative of the times in which he lived. Not only was his art at the service of princes and their favorite beauties, but it was ever ready to immortalize the features of those who were the objects of his own affection and admiration. Unfortunately, it was not his custom to inscribe on the canvas the names of those who sat to him. Many of the most glorious heads he ever painted remain to this hour unknown. Amid all their *reality* (and nothing in painting ever so conveyed the idea of a presence), they have a particular dignity which strikes us with respect; we would fain interrogate them, but they look at us life-like, grandly, calmly, like beings of another world; they seem to recognize us and we can never recognize them. Only we feel the certainty that just as they now look, so they lived and looked in long past times. Such a portrait is that in the Hampton Court gallery; that

grave, dark man, — in figure and attitude so tran·
quil, so contemplative, but in his eyes and on his
lips a revelation of feeling and eloquence. And
such a picture is that of the lady in the Sciarra
Palace at Rome, called expressively "Titian's Bella
Donna." It has no other name, but no one ever
looked at it without the wish to carry it away; and
no anonymous portrait has ever been so multiplied
by copies. But, leaving these, we will subjoin here
a short list of those great and celebrated personages who are known to have sat to Titian, and
whose portraits remain to us, a precious legacy,
and forming the truest commentary on their lives,
deeds, and works.

Charles V.: Titian painted this Emperor several
times, with and without his armor. He has always
a grave, even melancholy expression; very short
hair and beard; a large, square brow; and the full
lips and projecting under-jaw, which became a de-
formity in his descendants.

His wife, the Empress Isabella, holding flowers in
her hand.

Philip II.: like his father, but uglier, more melancholy, less intellectual. The Duke of Devonshire
has a fine full-length, in rich armor. There is a very
good one at Florence in the Pitti Palace; and another
at Madrid. In the Fitzwilliam Museum, at Cambridge, is the picture called "Philip II. and the Princess Eboli," of which there are several repetitions.

Francis I.: half-length, in profile; now in th.. Louvre. Titian did not paint this king from nature, but from a medal which was sent to him to copy.

The Emperor Ferdinand I.

The Emperor Rudolph II.

The Sultan Solyman II. His wife Roxana. These are engraved after Titian, but from what originals we know not. They cannot be from nature.

The Popes Julius II. (doubtful), Clement VII., Paul III., and Paul IV.

All the Doges of Venice of his time.

Francesco, Duke of Urbino, and his Duchess Eleonora; two wonderful portraits, now in the Florence Gallery.

The Cardinal Ippolito de' Medici; in the Louvre, and in the Pitti Palace.

The Constable de Bourbon.

The famous and cruel Duke of Alva

Andrea Doria, Doge of Genoa.

Ferdinand Leyva, who commanded at the battle of Pavia.

Alphonso d'Avalos, in the Louvre.

Isabella d'Este, Marchioness of Mantua.

Alphonso, Duke of Ferrara, and his first wife, Lucrezia Borgia. In the Dresden Gallery there is a picture by Titian, in which Alphonso is presenting his wife Lucrezia to the Madonna.

Cæsar Borgia.

Catherine Cornaro, Queen of Cyprus.

The Poet Ariosto : in the Manfrini Palace, at Venice.

Bernardo Tasso.

Cardinal Bembo.   Cardinal Sforza.   Cardinal Farnese.

Count Castiglione.

Pietro Aretino : several times ; the finest is at Florence ; another at Munich. The engravings, by Bonasone, of Aretino and Cardinal Bembo, rank among the most exquisite works of art.   There are impressions of both in the British Museum.

Sansovino, the famous Venetian architect.

The Cornaro family : in the possession of the **Duke** of Northumberland.

Fracastaro, a famous Latin poet.

Irene da Spilemborgo, a young girl who had distinguished herself as a musician, a poetess, and **to** whom Titian himself had given lessons in painting. She died at the age of eighteen.

Andrea Vesalio, who has been called the father of anatomical science — the particular friend of Titian, and his instructor in anatomy.   He was accused falsely of having put a man to death for anatomical purposes, and condemned.   Philip II., unwilling to sacrifice so accomplished a man to mere popular prejudice, commuted his punishment to a forced pilgrimage to the Holy Land.   He obeyed the sentence ; but on his return he was wrecked on the island of Zante, and died there of hunger in 1564.   This magnificent portrait, which

Titian seems to have painted with enthusiasm, is in the Pitti Palace at Florence.

Titian painted several portraits of himself, but none which represent him young. In the fine portrait at Florence he is about fifty; and in the other known representations he is an old man, with an aquiline nose, and long, flowing beard. Of his daughter Lavinia there are many portraits. She was her father's favorite model, being very beautiful in face and form. In a famous picture, now at Berlin, she is represented lifting with both hands a dish filled with fruits. There are four repetitions of this subject: in one the fruits are changed into a casket of jewels; in another she becomes the daughter of Herodias, and the dish bears the head of John the Baptist. All are striking, graceful, full of animation.

The only exalted personage of his time and country whom Titian did not paint was Cosmo I., Grand Duke of Florence. In passing through Florence, in 1548, Titian requested the honor of painting the Grand Duke. The offer was declined. It is worthy of remark that Titian had painted, many years before, the father of Cosmo, Giovanni de' Medici, the famous captain of the *Bande Neri*.

THE VENETIAN PAINTERS OF THE SIXTEENTH CENTURY.

TINTORETTO — PAUL VERONESE — JACOPO BASSANO.

Titian was the last great name of the earlier schools of Italy — the last really *great* painter which she produced. After him came many who were good artists, excellent artificers ; but, compared with the heaven-endowed creators in art, the poet-painters who had gone before them, they were mere mechanics, the best of them. No more Raphaels, no more Titians. no more Michael Angelos, before whom princes stood uncovered ! but very good painters, bearing the same relation to their wondrous predecessors that the poets, wits, and playwrights, of Queen Anne's time, bore to Shakspeare. There was, however, an intervening period between the death of Titian and the foundation of the Caracci school, a sort of interregnum, during which the art of painting sank to the lowest depths of labored inanity and inflated mannerism. In the middle of the sixteenth century Italy swarmed with painters. These go under the general name of the *mannerists*, because they all imitated the *manner* of

(339)

some one of the great masters who had gone before them. There were imitators of Michael Angelo, of Raphael, of Correggio :—Vasari and Bronzino, at Florence ; the two brothers Taddeo and Federigo Zuccaro, and the Cavalier d'Arpino, at Rome ; Federigo Barroccio, of Urbino ; Luca Cambiasi, of Genoa ; and hundreds of others, who covered with frescoes the walls of villas, palaces, churches, and produced some fine and valuable pictures, and many pleasing and graceful ones, and many more that were mere vapid or exaggerated repetitions of worn-out subjects. And patrons were not wanting, nor industry, nor science ; nothing but original and elevated feeling, — " the inspiration and the poet's dream."

But in the Venetian school still survived this in·spiration, this vital and creative power, when it seemed extinct everywhere besides. From 1540 to 1590 the Venetians were the only *painters* worthy the name in Italy. This arose from the elementary principle early infused into the Venetian artists,— the principle of looking to Nature, and imitating her, instead of imitating others and one another. Thus, as every man who looks to Nature looks at her through his own eyes, a certain degree of indi·viduality was retained even in the decline of the art. There were some who tried to look at Nature in the same point of view as Titian, and these are generally included under the general denomination

of the School of Titian, though in fact he had **no**
school properly so called.

Morone was a portrait painter who in some of
his heads equalled Titian. We have in England
only one known picture by him, but it is a masterpiece, — the portrait of a Jesuit, in the gallery of
the Duke of Sutherland, which for a long time
went by the name of Titian's Schoolmaster. It
represents a grave, acute-looking man, holding a
book in his hand, which he has just closed ; his
finger is between the leaves, and, leaning from his
chair, he seems about to address you.

> The very life is warm upon that lip,
> The fixture of the eye has motion in 't,
> And we are mocked by art !

Bonifazio, who had studied under Palma and
Titian, painted many pictures which are frequently attributed to both these masters. Superior
to Bonifazio was Alessandro Bonvicino, by whom
there are several exquisite pictures in the Milan
Gallery.

Andrea Schiavone, whose elegant pictures are
often met with in collections, was a poor boy, who
began the world as an assistant mason and house-
painter, and who became an artist from the love of
art ; but by some fatality, or some quality of mind
which we are wont to call a *fatality*, he remained
always poor. He painted numerous pictures

which others obtained, and sold again for high prices, enriching themselves at the expense of his toil of hand and head. At length he died, and in such wretched circumstances that he was buried by the charity of a few friends. In general the Venetian painters were joyous beings; Schiavone was a rare and melancholy exception. Very different was the temper and the fate of Paris Bordone. of Treviso, a man without much genius, weak in drawing, capricious or commonplace in invention, without fire or expression, but a divine colorist, and stamping on his pictures his own buoyant, life-enjoying nature; in this he was like Titian, but utterly inferior in all other respects. Some of his portraits are very beautiful, particularly those of his women, which have been often mistaken for Titian's.

The elder Palma is also considered as a scholar of Titian, though deriving as little from his personal instruction as did Tintoretto, Bordone, and others of the school. The date of his birth has been rendered uncertain by the mistakes of various authors, who confounded the elder and the younger Palma; but it appears that he was born between 1500 and 1515. He resembled in his manner both Titian and Giorgione. In some pictures he has shown the dignity of Titian, in others a touch of the melancholy sentiment of Giorgione. But not half the pictures attributed to Palma Vecchio are by him We have not one in our National Gallery

and those at Hampton Court which are attributed
to him are not genuine — mere third-rate pictures
of the Venetian school. This painter had three
daughters of remarkable beauty. Violante, the
eldest and most beautiful, is said to have been
loved by Titian, and to be the original of some of
his most exquisite female portraits. One called
Flora, because she has flowers in her hand; and
another in the Pitti Palace, in a rich dress. We
have the three daughters of Palma, painted by himself, in the Vienna Gallery; one, a most lovely
creature, with long light brown hair, and a violet
in her bosom, is without doubt Titian's Violante.
In the Dresden Gallery are the same three beautiful
girls in one picture, the head in the centre being
the Violante.

It remains to give some account of two really
great men, who were contemporaries of Titian, but
could hardly be called his rivals, his equals, or his
imitators. They were both inferior to him, but
original men in their different styles.

The first was TINTORETTO, born in 1512; his real
name was Jacopo Robusti. His father was a dyer
(in Italian, *Tintore*); hence he received in childhood
the diminutive nickname *Il Tintoretto*, by which he
is best known to us. He began, like many other
painters whose genius we have recorded, by drawing all kinds of objects and figures on the walls of
his father's house. The dyer, being a man of sense,

did not attempt to oppose his son's predilection for art, but procured for him the best instruction his means would allow, and even sent him to study under Titian. This did not avail him much, for that most excellent painter was by no means a good instructor, and it is said that he became jealous of the progress of Tintoretto, or perhaps required more docility. Whatever might be the cause, he expelled him from his academy, saying, somewhat rashly, that "he would never be anything but a dauber." Tintoretto did not lose courage; he pursued his studies, and after a few years set up an academy of his own, and on the wall of his paint-ing-room he placed the following inscription, as being expressive of the principles he intended to follow: "*Il disegno di Michael Agnolo: il colorito di Tiziano*" (the drawing of Michael Angelo, and the coloring of Titian). Tintoretto was a man of extraordinary talent, unequalled for the quickness of his invention and the facility and rapidity of his execution. It frequently happened that he would not give himself the trouble to make any design or sketch for his picture, but composed as he went along, throwing his figures on the canvas and paint-ing them in at once, with wonderful power and truth, considering the little time and pains they cost him. But this want of study was fatal to his real greatness. He is the most unequal of painters. In his compositions we find often the grossest faults in close proximity with the highest beauty

Now he would paint a picture almost equal to
Titian ; then produce one so coarse and careless
that it seemed to justify Titian's expression of a
" dauber." He abused his mechanical power by
the utmost recklessness of pencil ; but then, again,
his wonderful talent redeemed him, and he would
enchant his fellow-citizens by the grandeur, the
dramatic vivacity, the gorgeous colors, and the
luxuriant invention, displayed in some of his vast
compositions. Tho larger the space he had to fill,
the more he seemed at home ; his small pictures are
seldom good. His portraits in general are mag
nificent ; less refined and dignified than those of
Titian, less intellectual, but quite as full of life.

Tintoretto painted an amazing number of pictures, and of an amazing size, — one of them is
seventy-four feet in length and thirty feet in
height. One edifice of his native city, the school
of St. Roch, contains fifty-seven large compositions,
each containing many figures tho size of life.
The two most famous of his pictures are, a Crucifixion, in which the Passion of our Saviour is
represented like a vast theatrical scene, crowded
with groups of figures on foot, on horseback, exhibiting the greatest variety of movement and ex
pression ; and a large picture, called the Miracle
of St. Mark, in the Academy of Venice, of which
Mr. Rogers possesses the first sketch : a certain
slave having become a Christian, and having per-
severed in paying his devotions at the shrine of St

Mark, is condemned to the torture by his heathen
lord ; but just as he is bound and prostrate, St.
Mark descends from above to aid his votary ; the
executioner is seen raising the broken instruments
of torture, and a crowd of people look on in various attitudes of wonder, pity, interest. The whole
picture glows with color and movement.

In our National Gallery we have only one small,
unimportant work by Tintoretto, but there are ten
or eleven in the Royal Galleries. He was a favorite painter of Charles I., who purchased many of
his works from Venice. Two pictures, once really
fine, which belonged to this king, are now at
Hampton Court, — Esther fainting before Ahasu-
erus, and the Nine Muses. They have suffered ter-
ribly from audacious restorers ; but in this last
picture the figure of the Muse on the right, turning
her back, is in a grand style, not unworthy, in its
large, bold, yet graceful drawing, of the hand of
Michael Angelo himself. In the same collection
are three very fine portraits.

Tintoretto died in 1588. His daughter, Marietta
Robusti, whose talent for painting was sedulously
cultivated by her father, has left some excellent
portraits ; and in her own time obtained such celebrity that the Kings of France and Spain invited
her to their courts with the most tempting offers of
patronage, but she would never leave her father
and her native Venice. She died at the age of
thirty.

PAUL CAGLIARI of Verona, better known as Paul Veronese, was born in that city in 1530, the son of a sculptor, who taught him early to draw and to model; but the genius of the pupil was so diametrically opposed to this style of art, that he soon quitted the studio of his father for that of his uncle Antonio Badile, a very good painter, from whom he learned that florid grace in composition which he afterwards carried out in a manner so consummate and so characteristic. At that time Verona, like all the other cities of Italy, could boast of a crowd of painters; and Paul Cagliari, finding that he could not stand against so many competitors, repaired to Venice, where he remained for some time, studying the works of Titian and Tintoretti, but without attracting much attention himself, till he had painted, in the church of St. Sebastian, the history of Esther. This was a subject well calculated to call forth his particular talent in depicting the gay; the sumptuous accessories of courtly pomp, banquet scenes, processions, &c.; and from this time he was continually employed by the splendor-loving citizens of Venice, who delighted in his luxuriant magnificence, and overlooked, or perhaps did not perceive, his thousand sins against fact, probability, costume, time, and place. We are obliged to do the same thing in these days, if we would duly appreciate the works of this astonishing painter. We must shut our eyes to the violation of all proprieties of chronology and costume.

and see only the abounding life, the wondrous
variety of dignified and expressive figures crowded
into his scenes, — we may a little marvel how they
got there, — and the prodigality of light and colors,
all harmonized by a mellowness of tone which renders them most attractive to the eye. To give an
idea of Paul Veronese's manner of treating a subject,
we will take one of his finest and most characteristic pictures, the Marriage of Cana, which was
painted for the Refectory of the Convent of San
Giorgio at Venice, and is now in the Louvre. It is
not less than thirty feet long and twenty feet high,
and contains about one hundred and thirty figures,
life-size. The Marriage Feast of the Galilean citizen is represented with a pomp worthy of " Ormuz
er of Ind : " a sumptuous hall of the richest architecture ; lofty columns, long lines of marble balus-
trades rising against the sky ; a crowd of guests
splendidly attired, some wearing orders of knighthood, are seated at tables covered with gorgeous
vases of gold and silver, attended by slaves, jesters,
pages, and musicians. In the midst of all this
dazzling pomp, this display of festive enjoyment,
these moving figures, these lavish colors in glowing
approximation, we begin after a while to distinguish the principal personages, — our Saviour, the
Virgin Mary, the Twelve Apostles, mingled with
Venetian senators, and ladies clothed in the rich
costume of the sixteenth century, — monks, friars,
poets artists, all portraits of personages existing

in his own time ; while in a group of musicians he
has introduced himself and Tintoretto playing the
violoncello, while Titian plays the bass.   The bride
in this picture is said to be the portrait of Eleanor
of Austria, the sister of Charles V., and second wife
of Francis I., of whom there is a most beautiful
portrait at Hampton Court.   There is a series of
these Scriptural banquet-scenes, painted by Paul
Veronese, all in the same extraordinary style, but
varied with the utmost richness of fancy, invention,
and coloring.   Christ entertained by Levi, now in
the Academy of Venice ; the Supper in the house
of Simon the Pharisee, with Mary Magdalen at the
feet of our Saviour, now in the Durazzo Palace at
Genoa, of which the first sketch, a magnificent piece
of color, is in the possession of Mr. Rogers ; and the
Supper at Emmaus, in which he has introduced his
wife and others of his family as spectators.

Paul Veronese died in 1588.   He was a man of
amiable manners, of a liberal, generous spirit, and
extremely pious.   When he painted for churches
and convents, he frequently accepted very small
prices, sometimes merely the value of his canvas
and colors.   For that stupendous picture in the
Louvre, the Marriage of Cana, he received not
more than forty pounds of our money.

He painted all subjects, even the most solemn, in
the same gorgeous style.   He had sons and relations who were educated in his atelier and assisted
in painting his great pictures, and who after his

death continued to carry on a sort of manufactory of pictures in the same magnificent ornamental style ; but they were far inferior painters, and had not, like him, the power of redeeming gross faults of judgment and taste by a vivid imagination and strong feeling of character.

Almost all galleries and collections contain specimens of the works of this splendid and popular painter ; but the finest are in the churches at Venice, in the Louvre, and in the Dresden Gallery, where there are fifteen of his pictures.

In our National Gallery there is a fine picture of the Consecration of St. Nicholas, Bishop of Myra, in 1391. The principal personages are very nobly conceived, and the foreshortened figure of the angel descending above the kneeling saint, and holding the mitre and crosier, explains the subject in a manner at once very poetical and very intelligible. The little sketch of Europa is a study for the splendid picture now at Vienna.

Before we close the list of the elder painters of Italy, we must mention as flourishing at this time the Da Ponte family of Bassano. Giacomo da Ponte, called Old Bassano, was the head of it. His father had been a painter before him, and he, with his four sons, Leandro, Francesco, Gian Battista, and Girolamo, set up in their native town of Bassano a kind of manufactory of pictures, which were sold in the fairs and markets of the neighboring cities, and became popular all over the north of Italy. The Bassani were among the earliest painters of the *genre* style ; they treated sacred and solemn subjects in a homely, familiar manner, which was pleasing and intelligible to the people, and, at the same time, with a power of imitation, a light and spirited execution, and in particular a gem-like radiance of color which fascinates even judges of art. There are pictures of the elder Bassano which at the first glance remind one of a handful of rubies and emeralds. His best and largest works are at Bassano; his small pictures are numerous, and scattered through most galleries. He painted sheep, cattle, and poultry well, and was fond of introducing them in the pastoral scenes of the Old Testament, where they are appropriate. Sometimes, unhappily, where they are least appropriate they are the principal objects. His scenery and grouping have a rural character ; and his personages, even sacred and heroic, look like peasants. They are not vulgar, but rustic. The same kind of spirit informed the Bassani that afterwards informed the Dutch school — the imitation of familiar objects without elevation and without selection ; but the nature of Italy was as different from that of Holland as Bassano is different from Jan Steen. Like all the Venetians, the Bassani were good portrait painters. We have a fine portrait by Jacopo Bassano in our National Gallery, and at Hampton Court several very fine and characteristic pictures, which will give an excellent idea of his general manner. The best are Jacob's Journey and the Deluge. Mr. Rogers possesses the two best pictures of this artist now in England; they are small, but most beautiful, vivid as gems in point of color, with more dignity and feeling than is usual. The subjects are, the Good Samaritan, and Lazarus at the door of the Rich Man. Nothing could tempt Bassano from the little native town where he flourished, grew rich, and brought up a numerous family. He died in 1592.

All these men had original genius and that individuality of character which lends a vital interest to all productions of art, whether the style be elevated and ideal or confined to the imitation of common nature; but to them succeeded a race of *mannerists* and imitators, so that about the close of the sixteenth century all originality seemed extinguished at Venice, as well as everywhere else. And here we close the history of the earlier painters of Italy.